The Arts of the Japanese Sword

THE ARTS OF THE EAST
edited by Basil Gray

THE ARTS OF THE JAPANESE SWORD
by B. W. Robinson

ANCIENT CHINESE BRONZES
by William Watson

CHINESE CARVED JADES
by S. Howard Hansford

CHINESE AND JAPANESE CLOISONNÉ ENAMELS
by Sir Harry Garner

THE ARTS
OF
THE JAPANESE SWORD

by

B. W. ROBINSON

M.A., B.LITT.

Keeper of the Department of Metalwork,
Victoria and Albert Museum

FABER AND FABER

London . Boston

First published in 1961
by Faber and Faber Limited
3 Queen Square London WC1
Second edition 1970
Reprinted 1978 and 1981
Printed in Great Britain by
Robert MacLehose and Company Limited
Printers to the University of Glasgow

ISBN 0 571 04723 8

Preface

It is not, perhaps, surprising that little or nothing original has been, or is likely to be, written on the Japanese sword by anybody who is not a Japanese. At best, a non-Japanese writer can only hope to serve up a cold collation of ingredients culled from Japanese authorities, with an occasional seasoning from his own necessarily limited observation. The reason for this is that although there are many thousands of Japanese swords in Europe, the vast majority of them are comparatively late blades of no more than middling quality; one may search European museums and private collections in vain for authenticated works of many of the greatest swordsmiths and schools, especially of the earlier periods — they simply do not exist outside Japan. European amateurs of the subject are thus unable, through no fault of their own, to spend the necessary years in patient study and comparison of the finest representative blades of all schools and periods, and so can never acquire that deep knowledge and wide experience that are the marks of the Japanese *kanteisha*. In writing the section on blades, therefore, I have leaned heavily on the Japanese authorities, especially Honami Kōson, Fujishiro Yoshio, and Homma Junji, and have followed to some extent the arrangement of my little handbook *A Primer of Japanese Sword-blades* (1955), now out of print, from which the illustrations of *hamon* and the table of characters used in swordsmiths' names have been incorporated.

With the mounts the case is a little better, and their great popularity as collector's pieces for more than sixty years has produced a considerable body of European literature, much of it in the form of catalogues of collections — Hawkshaw, Naunton, Seymour Trower, Behrens — the best of which were written by Henri L. Joly just before the Great War. But the foremost name among European authorities on Japanese sword-furniture is that of Albert J. Koop, formerly Keeper of the Department of Metalwork in the Victoria and Albert Museum, whose death in 1945 after a long and crippling illness was such a sad loss to Japanese studies in this country. For more than thirty years he had worked and planned to make the Museum's collection truly full and representative, and his efforts were crowned with a large measure of success. Unfortunately, however, though he left copious notes, he never published the results of his labours in book form. These notes have accordingly been freely used in the second part of the book, though naturally I take full responsibility for the arrangement and manner of presentation. Koop always gave freely of his time and knowledge to anyone who called on him and displayed a genuine interest in the arts of Japan, and I can well remember his kindness and help to me as a

PREFACE

schoolboy when I showed him various trifles I had acquired and asked for an interpretation of the signatures and inscriptions. I therefore welcome this opportunity of making public some of the fruits of his work.

It is worth mentioning here that for all who wish to read for themselves the signatures, dates, and other inscriptions that occur on Japanese blades and their mounts, *Japanese Names and how to read them* (London, 1923, but still obtainable) which he wrote in collaboration with Hogitarō Inada, is an almost indispensable companion. In a book such as the present the ideal is to have every Japanese name and term followed by the characters with which it is written. But the prohibitive cost of incorporating Japanese characters in the text has forced a compromise. I have therefore drawn up several tables of characters used in signatures and dates, in the names of provinces, and in the names of swordsmiths and makers of sword-furniture mentioned in the text, to which reference is made by numbers in square brackets.

The subject of the Japanese sword, with its continuous history of some 1,500 years, is a vast one; the names of over 12,000 swordsmiths and 3,000 makers of sword-furniture are known and recorded, and the different styles and schools they represent are legion. The most comprehensive Japanese treatise on the whole subject (*Nippon-tō Kōza*, 1935) runs to 25 volumes of 5,000 pages, and is the work of more than seven different authorities. In the rather more limited space at my disposal, therefore, my main problem has been to compress and to prune, but at the same time to avoid omitting anything essential. On the question of what to put in and what to leave out personal opinions are bound to vary; I can only hope that I have struck a reasonable balance between the technical, the historical, and the aesthetic, and that the result may prove to be of some practical use to the aspiring amateur and the seasoned collector alike. My thanks are due to several friends, especially Field Marshal Sir Francis Festing, G.C.B., K.B.E., D.S.O., Chief of the Imperial General Staff, the late Captain A. D. E. Craig, Engineer Commander A. R. Newman, R.N. (retired), and Mr Clement Milward, for a number of helpful suggestions, and to the first two also for permission to illustrate swords from their collections; and to my wife for her encouragement and for much valuable work on the typewriter.

London, 1961   B. W. R.

NOTES

VAM = Victoria and Albert Museum.

Measurements of blades include the tang.

Numbers in square brackets after Japanese names throughout the book refer to the tables of characters in Appendix E unless otherwise stated.

Only the basic metal is given in the descriptions of sword-furniture.

Contents

Illustrations

ILLUSTRATIONS

PART ONE

The Blade

Introductory

That the sword has been described as 'the living soul of the *samurai*', and as 'the pride of warriors and the theme of poets', that next to his honour the warrior looked upon his swords as his most precious possession and paid them a veneration almost superstitious, and that for more than five centuries whole schools of metalworkers have devoted their best work to nothing else but the making and decoration of sword-furniture — all this is so well known that it need not be enlarged upon here. A glance at the numberless references to the sword in Japanese legends and at the particulars of the minute etiquette ruling its use and wear, will suffice to show how immense an influence this weapon wielded in the life of the *samurai* or 'soldier and gentleman' of Old Japan. Apart from its extraordinary effectiveness as a weapon, probably surpassing that of any other nation, the Japanese sword was regarded as the truest emblem of the warrior's virtue, valour and strength, having the power to stiffen his resolution and to guard him from any temptations to deeds unworthy of his own or his ancestors' name and fame. It is worth noting that the Five Elements, earth, metal, fire, water, and wood, all had a part in its making, the blade especially combining the icy purity and self-restraint of the metal with the energy and zest of the fire that helped to forge it.

Evolution and History of the Japanese Sword

A. The Kotō ('Old Sword') Period

The earliest swords found in Japan are of bronze, the art of casting having been imported by the first Japanese immigrants into the country. The swords of these early colonists, as found in their tumuli, resemble both in shape and method of manufacture those of the European Bronze Age, being straight, two-edged, of lanceolate shape, and cast whole in stone moulds.

About the second century B.C. came the last wave of immigrants, who introduced the practice of burial in dolmens instead of tumuli, and the art of iron-working as an improvement on bronze-casting. The weapon of the Dolmen Period was a slung sword with a straight, pointed, single-edged blade, the hilt having an obliquely-set ovoid pommel (usually of wood overlaid with plain or gilt copper), a copper guard in the form of a thick oval plate lightened by a ring of trapezoidal openings, and a scabbard of wood with metal decorations and strengthening bands (Pl. 6).

We are not here concerned, however, with the excavated swords from the tumuli and dolmens; they belong to the realm of archaeology. The Japanese themselves used to trace the craft of the swordsmith back to the 'Age of the Gods', and there are several episodes in the *Kojiki*, the *Nihongi*, and other ancient chronicles in which swords play a part. Even the primeval divinity Izanagi-no-mikoto, we read, possessed a sword (called *Totsuka-no-tsurugi* — 'Ten hand's breadths sword'), as did Susa-no-o-no-mikoto, the unruly brother of the Sun Goddess Amaterasu. This latter weapon was called *Orochi-no-aramasa*, and with it Susa-no-o beheaded a monstrous serpent or dragon, in whose tail he discovered a sacred sword which he presented to his sister. This latter sword, called at first *Ame-no-murakumo-no-hōken* ('Heavenly precious sword of the gathering clouds'), and later *Kusanagi-no-tsurugi* ('Grass-mowing sword') in memory of its miraculous saving of Prince Yamato-dake from death on a burning grass-moor, is one of the Three Regalia (the other two being a Mirror and a Jewel). These stories and many others like them, are, of course, almost pure legend, but they do serve to show how much the Japanese mind was taken up with swords even in the remotest ages. The naming of famous blades, too, is significant, and the practice has persisted almost down to the present day (Pl. 23a). Even the names of swordsmiths are preserved in some of the old stories, and such shadowy figures as Ama-tsu-ma-ura, Yasote, and Kawakami-moto are found listed side-by-side with historical craftsmen in the earlier Japanese books on the subject.

The Dolmen Period ended with the seventh century of our era, but meanwhile the introduction of Chinese civilization in the train of Buddhism (about A.D. 550) brought with it the type of sword known as *ken* or (in pure Japanese) *tsurugi* (Pl. 7b). This has a straight two-edged blade which may or may not widen slightly near the obtuse point; in section it is commonly of plain lozenge form more or less flattened; the central ridge, however, on each side may be replaced by a narrow plane or even by a groove. This type does not seem to have been in use for long, and was soon ousted by the 'modern' type of Japanese sword with a curved single-edged blade which was a direct development of the Dolmen Period sword. *Ken* blades of comparatively recent manufacture are, however, frequently found. They were either made for dedication in a temple, or else, of small size and mounted as daggers, were no doubt due to an archaistic fancy on the part of the original owner (Pl. 22b). The *Ama-goi no tsurugi* ('Praying for rain sword') at Kōya-san Monastery, used by Kōbō Daishi (774–835), and the *Kusanagi no tsurugi* ('Grass-cutting sword' — see above) preserved at Atsuta as part of the Imperial Regalia, are the two most famous examples of the *ken* type. With the reign of the Empress Suiko (593–629) we are on rather firmer

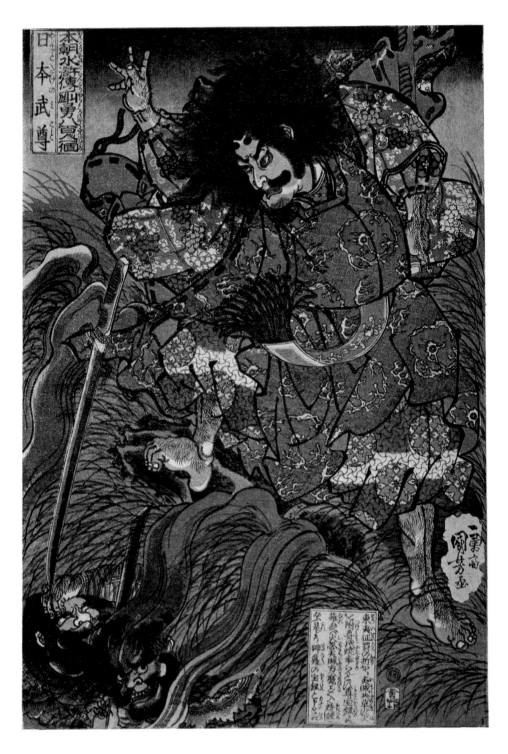

A. PRINCE YAMATO-DAKE AND THE
'GRASS-MOWING SWORD'

Colour-print by KUNIYOSHI, *c.* 1835. *Author's Collection.* (See page 16.)

historical ground, and it is recorded that a number of Chinamen were employed in making swords for her troops. A poem of hers is preserved, addressed to her Prime Minister, Soga no Umako, in which she says: 'Ye sons of Soga! As for horses, the colts of Hyūga province (are best); as for swords, the good blades of Kure (are best)!' Kure, or Go, was what the Japanese called the ancient kingdom of Wu in China, and so was used for China itself. This, then, was the period in which the foreign-style *ken* or *tsurugi* was preferred by the Japanese.

However, the single-edged blade of the Dolmen Period was, within a very short time after the close of that age, developed into the highly specialized form which has persisted with practically no alteration right down to the present day, the successive generations of smiths having apparently found it inexpedient or even impossible to improve upon it. This development undoubtedly began by the imparting of a curve to the blade, a characteristic feature of the modern sword, and one which may even have been introduced towards the end of the Dolmen Period. It has been pointed out that the act of forging automatically curves the bar which is to become a blade, and that this curvature must be corrected if the blade is required to be straight.

About A.D. 700, according to tradition, lived Amakuni [17, 154] of Yamato, the first smith to engrave his signature on his blades. But modern writers place him somewhat later — perhaps about the end of the ninth or beginning of the tenth century. Several of the older Japanese books on swords illustrate blades bearing his signature or attributed to him, notably one called *Kogarasu-maru* ('little crow') which was an heirloom in the Taira family; this latter is the only one that has survived. However the sword of the Emperor Shōmu (724–49) is preserved in excellent condition in the Imperial Repository of Shōsō-in, Nara, and admirably illustrates the transitional type between the swords found in the dolmen burials and the normal curved type that evolved soon after (Pl. 7a).

The credit for this development is impossible to assign to any individual swordsmith, but it seems probable that Yasutsuna [50, 185] of Hōki did much to establish it (Pl. 7c). His traditional dates are 749–811, but they may well be a century too early. A number of his blades have survived, the most famous being *Dōji-giri* ('Monster-cutter'), so called because it was used by the hero Raikō (Minamoto no Yorimitsu, 944–1021) to kill the monstrous brigand chief Shuten-dōji; it was originally made, according to the older Japanese writers, for the General Tamura-maro (758–811) to use in his campaign against the northern aborigines. Sanemori [140, 49], son of Yasutsuna, gained a reputation as a swordsmith almost equal to that of his father. The only other swordsmith of this earliest period of the craft who can be regarded as historical is Shinsoku [127, 135], a Shintō priest in the province of Buzen, who is said to have made a sword for a son of the Emperor Heijō (806–9).

With the reign of the Emperor Ichijō (989–1021) we arrive at the first 'peak' period in the history of the Japanese sword. During the previous generation swordsmiths had been active in the provinces of Buzen, Hōki,

Bizen, and probably Mutsu (Yasufusa [50, 93] and the Maikusa school), and now fresh schools sprang up in Yamashiro and Satsuma. Of these centres the most important were Bizen and Yamashiro (Kyōto). The former province preserved its character as the swordsmith's home *par excellence* until at least the middle of the last century, and even at this remote period at the end of the tenth century, could boast of five smiths of the first rank: Tomonari [23, 73], Masatsune [31, 102], and the three brothers Kanehira [39, 32], Takahira [137, 32], and Sukehira [63, 32]. Sanjō Munechika [87, 96] of Kyōto was an even more outstanding figure, and his pupils Yoshiiye [51, 138] and Kanenaga [131, 25] ably maintained the Yamashiro tradition. Chōyen [83, 184] of Buzen was another eminent swordsmith who was active at this time.

In the reign of the Emperor Go-Reizei (1046–68) Chinese traders came to Japan to buy swords, which soon enjoyed a high reputation in China. A contemporary Sung poet, Ou-yang Yung-shuh, wrote a poem in their praise, and since his time eulogies of the kind are frequently met with in Chinese works. The poem runs:

> *Treasure-swords of Japan are got from the East by merchants of Yueh. Their scabbards are of fragrant wood covered with fish-skin; gold and silver and copper and other metals adorn them. They are worth hundreds of gold pieces. Who wears such a sword can slay the barbarians.*

By this time, indeed, the Japanese had left the Chinese far behind in the swordsmith's craft.

During the eleventh and twelfth centuries there were several civil wars to maintain the demand for good blades. Miike Tenta Motozane [15, 140] or Mitsuyo [55, 38], of Chikugo (*c.* 1075) and Yasutsugu [50, 42] of Aoye, Bitchū (*c.* 1125) were the most outstanding swordsmiths, and the latter founded the Aoye school (Pl. 13*a*) which produced many notable craftsmen in that and the following centuries, especially his son Moritsugu [49, 42]. Two other famous schools were also founded at this time: the Senju-in of Yamato, by Yukinobu [43, 99] (*c.* 1150), and the Gwassan school in the northern province of Dewa (Pl. 13*c*), founded by Oniō-maru [134, 16, 12]. The latter school was famous for the beautiful regular graining of its blades, known as *ayasugi-hada* (Pl. 24*d*). Gwassan Sadayoshi [114, 51] (working in 1865) traced his descent in unbroken line from Oniō-maru, and worked in the traditional Gwassan style (Pl. 23*a*).

This was a period during which the great military clans of the Taira and Minamoto played a more and more prominent part in the affairs of the country, with a corresponding decline in the effective power of the central government. Revolts were crushed in 1062 by Minamoto no Yoriyoshi and in 1091 by Minamoto no Yoshiiye, and in 1113 the warrior-monks of Kōfukuji were in open rebellion. By the middle of the twelfth century the Taira had begun to eclipse the Minamoto, and after the civil wars of the periods Hōgen and Heiji (1156–60), during which the Minamoto espoused the cause of the deposed Emperor Sutoku, the Taira emerged supreme under their ruthless leader Kiyomori. After his death, however, the Minamoto reasserted themselves, and after a bloody struggle the Taira were finally annihilated at the battle of Dan-no-ura (1185). Yoritomo, the victorious Minamoto leader, then initiated the Shōgunate, or military sovereignty, and from this time until the Imperial Restoration of 1868 the successive Shōguns were the *de facto* rulers of the country, the Emperor at Kyōto exercising no more than a titular authority.

This brings us to the second great 'peak' in the history of the Japanese sword. It so happened that the Emperor Go-Toba, who succeeded his brother Antoku (drowned at Dan-no-ura), grew up to be an enthusiastic connoisseur of sword-blades, and after his abdication and later during his exile, he was able to devote himself to the art of forging. His motive, it is said, was a desire for a fine blade with which to kill the regent, Hōjō Yoshitoki, who had exiled him to Sanuki. The recent civil wars of the Taira and Minamoto had called forth a multitude of swordsmiths of great skill, and the best of these were summoned to Go-Toba to discuss with him the problems of their craft, to experiment with new ideas, and to give him instruction. It may be of interest here to give the yearly rosters of swordsmiths as they were detailed to attend on the retired Emperor:

(a) 1st month. *Norimune* [106, 87] of Bizen (1152–1214). Founder of the Ichimonji school of Fukuoka, Bizen, so called from their practice of engraving the character *ichi* [1] on the tangs of their blades, signifying 'the one and only'.

2nd month. *Sadatsugu* [114, 42] of Bitchū (b. 1126). Third in line of the Aoye school, most members of which used -*tsugu* [42] as the second character of their names.

3rd month. *Nobufusa* [72, 93] of Bizen (b. 1125). Of the Fukuoka Ichimonji school.

4th month. *Kuniyasu* [154, 50] of Awataguchi. Son of Kuniiye [154, 138], founder of the Awataguchi school of Kyōto, who came originally from Yamato (Pl. 8c).

5th month. *Tsunetsugu* [102, 42] of Bitchū (b. 1135). Of the Aoye school; brother of Sadatsugu (Pl. 13a).

6th month. *Kunitomo* [154, 23] of Awataguchi (1146–1216). Son of Kuniiye.

7th month. *Muneyoshi* [87, 51] of Bizen. Of the Fukuoka Ichimonji school; son-in-law of Norimune.

8th month. *Tsugiiye* [42, 138] of Bitchū. Of the Aoye school; son of Sadatsugu.

9th month. *Sukemune* [63, 87] of Bizen. Of the Fukuoka Ichimonji school; son of Norimune.

10th month. *Yukikuni* [43, 154] of Bizen. Of the Fukuoka Ichimonji school; son of Norimune's cousin Sukeyuki.

11th month. *Sukenari* [63, 73] of Bizen. Of the Fukuoka Ichimonji school.

12th month. *Sukenobu* [63, 72] of Bizen. Of the Fukuoka Ichimonji
school.

Instructors to the Emperor: *Hisakuni* [9, 154] of Awataguchi (1149–
1216) (Pl. 8*a*), perhaps the greatest of the Awataguchi smiths, and
Nobufusa [99, 93] of Bizen, son of the other Nobufusa (see above).

(*b*) 1st month. *Kanemichi* [131, 183] of Bizen (Fukuoka Ichimonji).
               Kunitomo [154, 23] of Awataguchi (see above).
2nd month. *Morozane* [129, 186] of Bizen (Old Bizen school).
               Nagasuke [83, 63] of Bizen (Old Bizen school).
3rd month. *Shigehiro* [110, 29] of Yamato (Senju-in school).
               Yukikuni [43, 154] of Bizen (see above).
4th month. *Chikafusa* [96, 93] of Bizen (Early Osafune school).
               Yukihira [43, 32] of Bungo (1145–1222). Called Kishin-
               dayu.
5th month. *Kanechika* [39, 96] of Bizen (Early Osafune school).
               Sanefusa [140, 93] of Bizen (Fukuoka Ichimonji).
6th month. *Noritsugu* [106, 42] of Bizen (Old Bizen school).
               Yoshifusa [51, 93] of Bizen (Fukuoka Ichimonji).
7th month. *Tomosuke* [161, 63] of Bizen (Fukuoka Ichimonji).
               Munetaka [87, 156] of Hōki (Fukuoka Ichimonji).
8th month. *Akizane* [149, 186] of Bizen (Old Bizen school).
               Sanetsune [186, 175] of Bizen (Old Bizen school).
9th month. *Kanesuye* [39, 36] of Bizen (Early Osafune school).
               Nobufusa [99, 93] of Bizen (see above).
10th month. *Tomotada* [161, 92] of Mimasaka (Old Bizen school).
               Sanetsune [186, 175] of Mimasaka (Old Bizen school).
               Son of Sanetsune of Bizen.
11th month. *Kanesuke* [39, 63] of Bizen (Fukuoka Ichimonji).
               Norimune [106, 87] of Bizen (see above).
12th month. *Norizane* [106, 140] of Bitchū (Aoye school).
               Koresuke [109, 21] of Bizen (Early Osafune school).

(*c*) The following attended the Emperor for two months at a time during
his exile in Oki (1226):

1st and 2nd months. *Norikuni* [106, 154] of Awataguchi (1174–1238).
               Son of Kunitomo.
3rd and 4th months. *Kagekuni* [164, 154] of Awataguchi (1174–1233).
               Pupil of Hisakuni.
5th and 6th months. *Kunitsuna* [154, 185] of Awataguchi (1163–
               1255). Lived also in Sagami.
7th and 8th months. *Muneyoshi* [87, 51] of Bizen (see above).
9th and 10th months. *Nobumasa* [99, 31] of Bizen (Fukuoka Ichi-
               monji).
11th and 12th months. *Sukenori* [63, 106] of Bizen (Fukuoka Ichimonji).
               Son of Sukemune.

A conspectus of these swordsmiths will give a good idea of the proportionate distribution of the craft throughout the provinces at this period:

Bizen	-	-	- 25	Mimasaka	-	-	- 2
Yamashiro (Awataguchi)	-	6	Bungo	-	-	-	- 1
Bitchū	-	-	-	- 3	Hōki	-	-	-	- 1
				Yamato (Senju-in)	-	- 1

The period 1250–1350 constitutes the third and perhaps the highest 'peak' in our historical survey. It covers the careers of the three swordsmiths who are often spoken of as the greatest of all time: Tōshirō Yoshimitsu [51, 55] of Awataguchi (Pl. 8b), Gorō Masamune [31, 87] of Sagami (Pl. 11a, 14a), and Gō Yoshihiro [179, 29] of Etchū. Yoshimitsu was a pupil of Awataguchi Kuniyoshi [154, 51], grandson of Awataguchi Kunitomo who, as we have seen, worked for the Emperor Go-Toba. He seems to have made few long swords, but a number of his *tantō*, or dirk-blades, are scheduled as 'National Treasures'; seventeen of them were listed in the early eighteenth-century *Meibutsu-shū*, or 'Register of Famous Blades'. They were considered particularly lucky to the Tokugawa family, and there is a story that after an early reverse Tokugawa Iyeyasu used one in an attempt to commit *seppuku*; the blade would not pierce him, though it had easily passed the severest tests. He took this as an omen, changed his mind, and went on, after his great victory at Sekigahara (1600), to found the Tokugawa line of Shōguns.

Masamune is generally regarded as the greatest swordsmith of all. He learnt his craft mainly from his father Yukimitsu [43, 55] (Pl. 14b), from Shintōgo Kunimitsu [154, 55], and from Daishimbō Yūkei [11, 173, 93, 128, 197], but he made a comprehensive study of the methods of all the best masters of the time. Pupils resorted to him from all over Japan, and the most outstanding of them are known as *Masamune no jūtetsu*, or 'Masamune's ten brilliant pupils'. These were:

Rai Kunitsugu [154, 42] of Yamashiro (1247–1325), grandson of Rai Kuniyuki.

Hasebe Kunishige [154, 110] of Yamashiro (1270–1347) (Pl. 15b).

Kinjū (Kaneshige) [215, 110] of Mino (1232–1322).

Kanemitsu [131, 55] of Bizen (1280–1358), son of Kagemitsu of Osafune.

Shidzu Kaneuji [131, 20] of Mino (1284–1344), originally of Yamato (Pl. 11c).

Gō Yoshihiro [179, 29] of Etchū (1299–1325).

Sayeki Norishige [106, 110] of Etchū (1290–1366).

Naotsuna [106, 185] of Iwami (1280–1348).

Chōgi (Nagayoshi) [83, 179] of Bizen (1288–1370).

Sa [37] of Chikuzen (1277–1356), son of Jitsua [186, 78] and grandson of Sairen [45, 195]. Of these, Gō Yoshihiro, as already mentioned, is considered almost the equal of Yoshimitsu and Masamune, and, if he had lived longer, might even have surpassed them.

Of Masamune's other pupils, his adopted son Sadamune [114, 87] (1298–1349) (Pl. 11b, 15c) was by far the most outstanding, and had three 'brilliant pupils' of his own (*Sadamune no santetsu*):

Motoshige [15, 110] (II) of Bizen.

Hōjōji Kunimitsu [154, 55] of Tajima.

Nobukuni [99, 154] of Yamashiro.

Other well-known pupils of Masamune were Akihiro [104, 198] (Pl. 15a), Hiromitsu [198, 55], Hiromasa [198, 31], and Masahiro [31, 198], all of whom were followed in their turn by pupils or sons bearing the same names.

This brilliant period was so prolific, that we must content ourselves with a bare mention of some of the most notable schools that sprang up in the various provinces. Bizen still led the field in numbers and volume of production; the Osafune school took on a new lease of life with Mitsutada [55, 92], his son Nagamitsu [83, 55] (Pl. 10c), and his grandson Kagemitsu [164, 55]: the Yoshioka Ichimonji, an offshoot of the Fukuoka Ichimonji school, was founded by Sukeyoshi [63, 51]; Moriiye [49, 138] was the first of the Hatakeda smiths; and the Ukai school produced the famous brothers Unshō [162, 33] and Unji [162, 42]. In Yamato the Tayema and Tegai schools were founded by Kuniyuki [154, 43] and Kanenaga [39, 25] respectively, both at about the end of the thirteenth century. In Yamashiro at the Imperial capital the Rai school arose right at the beginning of our period, and to it belonged Rai Kuniyuki [154, 43], Rai Kunitoshi [154, 101] the centenarian, and Rai Kunimitsu [154, 55], all smiths of the first importance, as well as Masamune's pupil Rai Kunitsugu [154, 42]. The Yenju or Kikuchi school of Higo was an early offshoot of the Rai, its founder, Kunimura [154, 60], having married a daughter of Rai Kuniyuki; another offshoot of the same school in the province of Bungo derived from Ryōkai [2, 74], the priest-son of Rai Kunitoshi. Other schools of this period that are worthy of note are the Naminohira of Satsuma (Pl. 13b), of which Yasuyuki [50, 43] was the most prominent member; the Mihara school of Bingo, founded by Masaiye [31, 138] towards the end of the period; and the Sengo school of Ise (Pl. 16), dominated by the sinister figure of Muramasa [60, 31], whose blades have always had a reputation for bloodthirstiness and ill-luck. The classical example of this was the *samurai*-turned-robber Shirai Gompachi, who roamed the streets of Yedo at night with his Muramasa blade, watching for likely victims whom he would cut down and rob, in order to obtain money to spend on his mistress, the beautiful Komurasaki of the 'Three Sea-shores' in the Yoshiwara. The whole tragic story is admirably told in Mitford's *Tales of Old Japan*.

The fifteenth century is remarkable for the number of gifts of swords sent by successive Ashikaga Shōguns to the Ming Emperors of China. The practice was begun by Yoshimitsu in 1401 and continued at intervals until the last gift of this kind was made in 1483 by the ex-Shōgun Yoshimasa to the Emperor Ch'êng Hua. It has been calculated that 619 swords (*tachi*), 500 glaives (*naginata*), and 100 lances (*yari*) in all were sent as presents to China during this period. It was a time of fierce rivalry between the great territorial lords, which broke out into open warfare in the first year of the period Ōnin (1467) and again at the beginning of the period Taiyei (1521), the whole era being called *Sengoku*, or 'the country at war'. From this turmoil first Oda Nobunaga (d. 1582) emerged supreme, followed by

Toyotomi Hideyoshi (d. 1598); and finally Tokugawa Iyeyasu in 1600 defeated a coalition of his rivals at the bloody battle of Sekigahara, and inaugurated the Tokugawa Shōgunate, which lasted until the restoration of the Emperor's power in 1868. The swordsmith's craft, as might be expected, flourished exceedingly throughout this disturbed period, but no great figures emerged comparable with those of the century 1250–1350 (Pl. 17).

B. The Shintō ('New Sword') Period

The beginning of the Tokugawa regime proved to be another 'peak' with Umetada Myōju [80, 187] and Horikawa Kunihiro [154, 198] at Kyōto (the former descended in the twenty-fifth generation from Sanjō Munechika, who, as we have seen, flourished under the Emperor Ichijō at the end of the tenth century) (Pl. 18a, c), and Noda Hankei [204, 197] at Yedo (Pl. 19b). Both Myōju and Kunihiro had begun their careers in the Kotō period. Eminent among Myōju's many pupils was Tadayoshi [92, 51] of Hizen, and his contemporary Mishina Yoshimichi [51, 183] (Pl. 18b), who had migrated from Mino to Kyōto, was also a top-ranking swordsmith. Shimosaka Yasutsugu [152, 209] (Pl. 19a) of Echizen was the swordsmith particularly attached to the Shōgun Iyeyasu, and was given the privilege of engraving the Tokugawa badge of three hollyhock leaves (aoi) on the tangs of his blades; he was also a pioneer in the use of foreign iron (namban-tetsu).

Two generations later, during the third quarter of the seventeenth century, the swordsmiths of Ōsaka had come very much to the fore (Pl. 20), the most notable being Tsuta Sukehiro [63, 198], Inouye Shinkai [140, 59] ('the Masamune of Ōsaka'), Kobayashi Kunisuke [154, 63], Kobayashi Kuniteru [154, 193], and Awataguchi Tadatsuna [92, 185], whilst at Yedo Nagasone Kotetsu Okisato [94, 190, 202, 64] achieved a reputation perhaps higher than any of his contemporaries (Pl. 19c). Two swordsmiths of Satsuma province, Mondo no Shō Masakiyo [31, 144] (1670–1730) and Ippei Yasuyo [50, 26] (1680–1728) reached the first rank during the period Genroku (1688–1704).

C. The Shinshintō ('Recent Sword') Period

From about the period Kyōho (1716–36) the swordsmith's craft was in something of a decline until near the end of the eighteenth century, when a vigorous revival was launched by Kawabe Suishinshi Masahide [31, 65], ably seconded by his pupils Shōji Naotane [91, 98] and Hosokawa Masayoshi [31, 179], and by the Satsuma swordsmiths Motohira [15, 32] and Masayoshi [31, 67 or 89] (Hōki no Kami, Pl. 22a). These men abandoned the rather meretricious elaboration of the previous generation and went back to the golden age of the fourteenth century for their models, most of which were blades of Bizen or Sagami make, though Masahide himself sometimes modelled his work on that of Sukehiro of Ōsaka. Towards the end of his career (he died in 1825) Masahide was running what almost amounted to a factory for sword-blades, which was scathingly alluded to by his contemporaries as 'unlimited partnership — the Kawabe workshop', with Suishinshi himself as 'manager of the forging department' and his pupils running a 'ghost forging branch'. Nevertheless, he turned out some blades of superb quality, and exercised an enormous influence on his contemporaries and successors, not only by training a hundred-odd pupils, but by writing several books embodying his professional principles and ideals.

The result was that during the first half of the nineteenth century, and indeed right up to the Meiji restoration of 1868, a considerable number of first-rate swordsmiths were at work. Masahide's best pupils, Naotane and Masayoshi, together with Motohira and Masayoshi of Satsuma, have already been mentioned; but they were equalled, and sometimes even excelled by Yamaura Kiyomaro [144, 207] ('the Masamune of Yotsuya', 1813–54, Pl. 22c), Jirotarō Naokatsu [91, 158] (pupil of Naotane, c. 1804–1857), and Tegarayama Masashige [31, 204] (1754–1824), whilst an only slightly inferior reputation was enjoyed by such men as Ishidō Korekazu VII [109, 1] (1815–89), Kurihara Nobuhide [99, 65] (pupil of Kiyomaro, Pl. 23c), and Sa Yukihide [43, 65] (1816–85). Several swordsmiths of the same period are interesting as carrying on the tradition of some of the earlier masters, from whom they traced their descent in unbroken line. Such were Tadayoshi VIII [92, 31] of Hizen (from Tadayoshi I, 1572–1632), Tsunahiro X [185, 198] of Sagami (from Tsunahiro I, early sixteenth century, and so from Masamune), Naminohira Yukiyasu [43, 50] (sixty-third of the Naminohira line in Satsuma, from Masakuni [31, 154] who worked under the Emperor Ichijō), Iga no Kami Kinmichi VIII [215, 183] (from Kinmichi I, and so from Shidzu Kaneuji, pupil of Masamune), Yokoyama Sukenaga [128, 25] (fifty-sixth in the Bizen line from Tomonari, one of the Emperor Ichijō's swordsmiths) and his pupil Sukehira [128, 32], and Idzumi no Kami Kanesada IX [131, 88] (from Kanesada I, mid fifteenth century).

With the edict of 1876 prohibiting the wearing of swords, the history of the craft virtually came to an end. A few blades were still made from time to time for presentations and other special occasions, and swordsmiths such as Miyamoto Kanenori [39, 106] (1829–1914, Pl. 23b), Jōunsai Yenshin [184, 140] (1846–1920), and Gwassan Sadakazu [114, 1] (1836–1918) maintained the best traditions of their craft. Apart from the mass-produced 'Shōwa-tō' carried by the majority of Japanese officers during the last war, a number of fine blades, forged in the old style, were made in those years, and may be found in the regulation military mounts; these are known as *gendai-tō* ('modern swords'). Since the war successful efforts have been made by means of periodical competitions in sword-forging and the foundation of the Society for the Preservation of Art Swords (*Nippon Bijutsu Tōken Hōson Kyōkwai*), with its lively periodical *Tōken Bijutsu*, under the able directorship of Professor Homma of the National Museum, Tōkyō, to promote and maintain interest in the subject both in Japan and in Europe and America. Of the swordsmiths now practising in Japan, Miyaguchi Tsunetoshi [102, 187] of Tōkyō is probably the best.

The Smith and His Work

T he swordsmith and the maker of sword-furniture stood socially among the highest in the artisan or artist class, a class legally ranking next below that to which the agricultural labourer belonged. The swordsmith's occupation, in particular, earned him a very high degree of respect, as is strikingly illustrated by the fact that even *samurai* and court-nobles, not to mention some of the Emperors themselves, did not disdain to undertake the forging of a blade. The Emperor Go-Toba (1183–98), for example, declared the making of swords to be an occupation worthy of princes, and a few blades of his forging are still preserved in Japan.

The swordsmith (*kaji*) led in general a semi-religious and abstemious life. Almost every operation in the making of a blade was regarded in the light of a religious ceremony, Shintoistic in its principles and free from all alien influences. In logical consequence we shall find that, with a mere half-dozen exceptions, the nomenclature of the Japanese sword and all that pertains to it is in the vernacular Yamato tongue, as opposed to the Sinico-Japanese vocabulary that was introduced with Buddhism.

For the final and most critical operations of the process the smith donned the court-noble's ceremonial costume (*kariginu* and *yeboshi*). The smithy (*kajiya*) became for the time being a sanctuary, and the approach to it was hung with the Shintō straw-rope (*shime-nawa*) to ward off evil influences. At the outset of each day's task the smith purified himself with cold ablutions, and prayed to the *Kami* for aid in his work. No members of his family were allowed to enter the smithy, excepting his assistant. His food was cooked with the sacred fire; sexual intercourse, animal food, and intoxicating drink were taboo to him during the time of forging. The production of a perfect blade (the self-respecting smith broke up his failures) often involved the labour of several months (Pl. 5).

THE MAKING OF A BLADE

A comprehensive description of the materials and methods employed in forging a Japanese blade would by itself occupy a sizable volume. It is enough to say here that the steel, or combination of iron and steel, which composes the blade was obtained from the native magnetic ore and ferruginous sand, although occasional use was made, from the seventeenth century onwards, of imported foreign or *namban* (literally, 'southern barbarian') iron and steel, as is attested by inscriptions on the tangs of numerous blades.

A bar of iron, serving as a handle, having been welded to a short strip formed of two superimposed and welded pieces of different grades of steel, the billet thus formed was folded on itself, again welded, and then hammered out to its original length. The fire was made of a special kind of pine-charcoal, and before every firing the metal was coated with clay sprinkled with straw-ash, care being taken not to touch it with the hand. This process was repeated some fifteen to twenty times (though authorities differ on these figures), the billet being cooled between the processes, until it consisted of many thousands of layers of steel. Sometimes three or four such billets were separately made and then welded together; the folding process was then repeated five times, finally producing more than four million layers. In either case the resulting bar was then hammered carefully into the required length and shape, a wooden template (*hina-gata*) being sometimes used as a model. The foregoing describes the *muku-gitai* or *muku-tsukuri* ('pure forging' or 'unalloyed make') where the material is steel only, but various methods of combining iron and steel were employed.

Most of these were based on the idea of a core of comparatively soft metal enclosed in, or sandwiched between, one or more pieces of hard steel. The core metal (*shintetsu*) was folded and welded upon itself and again drawn out to its original length about a dozen times. For the surface metal (*uwagane*) high carbon steel or white cast iron was used, previously quenched in water and broken into small pieces to remove slag. These pieces were forged into a bar which was notched and folded upon itself in various ways, welded, and reforged to its original length about fifteen or twenty times. If the process were repeated more than twenty-one times, however, the metal gradually became soft again. A mixture of clay and charcoal was poured over it before each heating. The *shintetsu* and *uwagane* were then combined in different ways, the commonest being the formation of the latter into a bar of V-shaped section, into the hollow of which the former was welded. The resulting bar was formed into the rough shape of the blade as already described.

The beautiful *mokume* or wood-grain effect, so well brought out on the polished surface (*hada*, 'skin') of many old blades, was produced by one of two main methods. In the first, known as *hada-gitai*, the surface of the finished billet was gouged or hammer-dented here and there on both faces, and then the whole hammered or ground flat so as to display a stratification at various angles of the different qualities of component metal. In the second, *masame-tsukuri*, the flat bar was hammered on its edge until this became the new face, or else a square bar was hammered on the angle, until the finished blade displayed the curious and beautiful effect of a well-grained piece of wood. The full effect of the graining is only seen on the unburnished and untempered portion of the blade, being brought up by the special Japanese polishing processes. It is not to be seen on the burnished back-plane (*shinogi-ji*) or the tempered edge (*yakiba*).

When the forging had been completed the scraping-knife (*sen*) and file (*yasuri*) came into play to shape the blade and tang. Rough grinding of the edge, the chasing of the signature and other inscriptions on the tang, and the addition of any grooves (*hi*) or carving (*horimono*) that might be required, could then be performed, though these processes were more often held over until the last.

The blade was then ready for what was regarded as the most critical and important operation of all, the tempering of the edge. For this the whole blade was covered with a mixture of iron-clay (*sabi-doro*), river-sand, and charcoal-powder to the depth of about one eighth of an inch. In this was drawn, close to the edge, using a pointed bamboo stick, a straight or irregular line. While still wet, the clay between this line and the edge was thinned or removed, and the rest was then allowed to dry. The smith then gripped the tang with his pincers, and passed the blade edge downwards over the fire of pine-charcoal until with the aid of the bellows the required temperature was reached. This was ascertained by watching the colour of the glowing blade where the uncovered metal could be seen near the tang, the smithy being specially darkened for the purpose. At this point the blade was plunged into a tank of warm water; the temperature of the water and the time the blade was held in it varied, like so many details of the whole process, with different periods and schools of swordsmiths. This dousing resulted in a soft-tempered back with a hard-tempered fore-part (*yakiba*) which would take an edge like a razor. Such a blade, while being (like all oriental blades) practically inflexible, was at the same time less liable to snap with hard usage.

The smith then minutely examined the blade for flaws (*kizu*) and other imperfections. If it successfully passed his scrutiny, it was handed over to the sharpener (*katana-togi*) who ground and sharpened the edge, burnished the back (*mune*) and ridge-plane (*shinogi-ji*) with a round steel rod (*migaki-hari* or 'polishing-needle') and imparted a dull polish to the remainder by the successive use of as many as nine grades of polishing-stone from the coarse *arato* and *iyoto* to the finest *uchi-gomori* and *kōto*. This whole process might entail a labour of some fifty days, the surface being gone over a score of times, and was performed by holding the blade with cloths and rubbing it backwards and forwards over the stone which was fastened to a board over a low tub of water. In the final stages of polishing, however, the fine powdered stone was rubbed on the blade (not the blade on the stone).

Nomenclature and Expertise

In the period with which we are concerned the *samurai* always carried a pair of swords, one long and one short, known as *daishō* ('large-small', Pl. 26). Lesser mortals might occasionally wear a single sword or dirk, but the *daishō* was the *samurai*'s exclusive privilege. With armour and certain kinds of court dress the long sword was slung from the girdle edge downwards; this type was called *tachi* (Pl. 30, 31). The pair to the *tachi* was the *tantō*, a guardless dirk with a flat blade about ten inches long, which was thrust through the girdle and usually secured there with a cord (*sageo*) (Pl. 27*g*). When wearing ordinary civilian dress, the *samurai* carried both his swords thrust through the girdle, the edges upwards. In this case the long sword was not supplied with suspension-rings, and was called *katana* (Pl. 28). Its companion, the *wakizashi* (Pl. 29), was generally longer than the *tantō*, and was a smaller edition of the *katana* with ridged blade and mounts *en suite*. The *katana* was normally the fighting sword, but some fencing masters practised a style in which *katana* and *wakizashi* were used simultaneously. In an unmounted blade, the only difference between *tachi* and *katana* is in the position of the signature, which is engraved on the side of the blade that would face outwards when the sword was being worn.

Other types of sword are encountered, but not frequently enough to merit more than a bare mention. The *tsurugi* or *ken* has already been noticed. The *nodachi* was an outsize *tachi* sometimes reaching a length of over seven feet, carried by certain stalwarts during the civil wars of the fourteenth century. There were also a number of short daggers for which the Japanese, with their passion for technical terms, have invented a variety of names, such as *kwaiken* (a short dagger sometimes carried by ladies), *aikuchi* (a guardless dirk, the usual manner of mounting *tantō*), *metezashi* (a dagger worn on the right side), *hamidashi* (general term for a dagger), and *yoroi-tōshi* ('armour-piercer' — a dirk with a very thick strong blade). For all practical purposes, however, we can confine ourselves to the *tachi-tantō* and *katana-wakizashi* combinations.

The blade of the Japanese long sword is in general curved, ridged, and single-edged. It was almost entirely a cutting weapon (Japanese fencing, or *kendō*, admits only one thrust — at the throat), and was generally used with two hands. The tang is usually rather less than a quarter of the total length of the blade, being pierced with a hole for the retaining-peg, and often engraved with the maker's name, the date, and other particulars. *Tantō* blades are normally flat, broader in proportion, and straight, or nearly so. The average blade-lengths of the different types of Japanese sword from the point to the beginning of the tang are as follows:

Tachi and *katana:* over 2 *shaku* (1 *shaku* equals 11·93 in.)
Wakizashi: between 1 and 2 *shaku*
Tantō: under 1 *shaku*

The accompanying drawing shows a typical *katana* blade and its various parts:

(*a*) *shiri* — tang-butt
(*b*) *nakago* — tang
(*c*) *mekugi-ana* — peg-hole
(*d*) *hitoye* — back of tang
(*e*) *ha-machi* — notch on edge side
(*f*) *mune-machi* — notch on back side
(*g*) *yakiba* — tempered edge

(*h*) *hamon* — outline of *yakiba*
(*i*) *shinogi* — ridge
(*k*) *jigane* — metal surface between *hamon* and *shinogi*
(*l*) *mune* — back of blade
(*m*) *yokote* — short transverse ridge
(*n*) *ko-shinogi* — continuation of *shinogi* beyond *yokote*

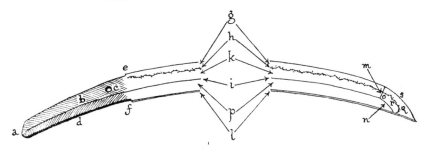

(o) *mitsukado* — point of junction of *shinogi*, *ko-shinogi* and *yokote*

(p) *shinogi-ji* — flat burnished surface between *shinogi* and *mune*

(q) *bōshi* — tempered part above *yokote*

(r) *kissaki* — the point-plane bounded by *yokote* and *ko-shinogi*

(s) *fukura* — edge of *kissaki*

JUDGING A BLADE

The following are a few of the points to examine when judging a Japanese blade, given in the traditional order of inspection. This order can be easily remembered by the mnemonic word SEPT (Shape, Edge, Pattern, Tang).

1. SHAPE (*sugata*, *tsukuri-komi*)

Type: whether *tachi*, *katana*, *wakizashi*, *tantō*, or some other, a few of which are shown at the end of the illustrations of *hamon*: H. *Ken* or *tsurugi*. I. *Kodzuka*-blade (see p. 69). J. *Naginata* or glaive, to be mounted on a long shaft, but sometimes used as a *wakizashi*. K. *Yari* or spear-head, sometimes found mounted as a dagger.

Form: presence or absence of *shinogi*, *yokote*, etc. Those shown at the end of the *hamon* illustrations are: A. *Ryō-ha* (double-edged). B. *Kiri-ha*, where the ridge closely follows the line of the edge. C. *U-no-kubi-dzukuri* ('cormorant's head'); with a *yokote* this form is called *kammuri-otoshi*. D. *Shinogi-dzukuri*, the normal form.

Degree and type of curvature: regular curve (*torii-zori*) or with a strong curve towards the hilt end (*koshi-zori*).

Comparative thickness at *shinogi* and *mune*.

Degree of tapering from *hamachi-munemachi* to *yokote*.

Relative distance of edge and back from *shinogi*.

Length of *kissaki*.

Grooves and engraved designs (*horimono*).

2. (a) TEMPERED EDGE (*yakiba*, *hamon*)

The *hamon* is the outline of the *yakiba*, and various types are illustrated herewith. In each case the Japanese name is followed by an English translation or equivalent term, and by the name of the school or swordsmith with whose work the *hamon* in question is particularly associated.

(1) *Sugu-hotsure-ha:* straight with slight irregularities. Awataguchi.

(2) *Hoso-sugu ha:* narrow straight. Shintōgo Kunimitsu.

(3) *Sugu ko-midare:* straight with small irregularities. Shikkake. *Yakidzume bōshi* (no 'follow-through' down the back of the blade).

(4) *Sugu ha:* straight. Rai. *Bōshi kayeri* (continued down the back of the blade).

(5) *Sugu ha:* straight. Aoye. *Bōshi kayeri.*

(6) *Sugu ha:* straight. Hōshō.

(7) *Sugu-kudzure ha:* 'crumbling' straight. Later Osafune.

(8) *Sugu ha:* straight. Later Seki.

(9) *Sugu-kuichigai ha:* 'nibbled' straight. Horikawa.

(10) *Naka-sugu ha:* straight of medium width. Tadayoshi.

(11) *Naka-sugu ha:* straight of medium width. Nanki Shigekuni.

(12) *Sugu-sunagashi ha:* straight with 'drifting sand'. Kunikane of Sendai. *Hakikake bōshi* (resembling foot-marks swept up with a broom).

(13) *Naka-sugu ha:* straight of medium width. Tadayoshi. *Bōshi ko-maru* (small curve).

(14) *Asaki-notare ha:* shallow undulating. Aoi Shimosaka.

(15) *Naka-sugu ha:* straight of medium width. Tsuta. *Bōshi ko-maru sagari* (small curve set low).

(16) *Sugu ha:* straight. Suishinshi.

(17) *Sugu-sunagashi ha:* straight with 'drifting sand'. Suishinshi.

(18) *Chōji ha:* 'cloves'. Ichimonji.

(19) *Sugu-chōji ha:* straight 'cloves'. Early Osafune. *Bōshi ō-maru* (wide curve).

(20) *Chōji ha:* 'cloves'. Rai. *Bōshi midare-komi* (irregular).

(21) *Gunome-ko-chōji ha:* invected with small 'cloves'. Nagato Sa. *Jizō bōshi* (resembling the head of the divinity Jizō).

(22) *Gunome-chōji ha:* invected with 'cloves'. Osafune.

(23) *Gunome-chōji ha:* invected with 'cloves'. Later Osafune.

(24) *Chōji-ha:* 'cloves'. Ikkanshi.

(25) *Chōji-ha:* 'cloves'. Ishidō.

(26) *Chōji-midare ha:* irregular 'cloves'. Kunisuke of Ōsaka.

(27) *Ko-chōji ha:* small 'cloves'. Toshinori.

(28) *Chōji-ha:* 'cloves'. Gwassan Sadakazu.

(29) *Ko-midare ha:* small irregular. Old Bizen.

(30) *Midare-ha:* irregular. School of Masamune.

(31) *Gunome-midare ha:* irregular invected. Shidzu Kaneuji. *Kwayen bōshi* (flame-like).

(32) *Gunome-ha:* invected. Kanemitsu of Osafune.

(33) *Hitatsura-ha:* mottled all over. Hasebe of Kyōto.

(34) *Hako-midare ha:* irregular 'box' formations. Sengo.

(35) *Ō-midare ha:* large irregular. Later Sagami.

(36) *Sambon-sugi ha:* 'three cedars'. Seki.

(37) *Notare-ha:* undulating. Seki. *Bōshi kayeri.*

(38) *Notare-ha:* undulating. Aoi Shimosaka.

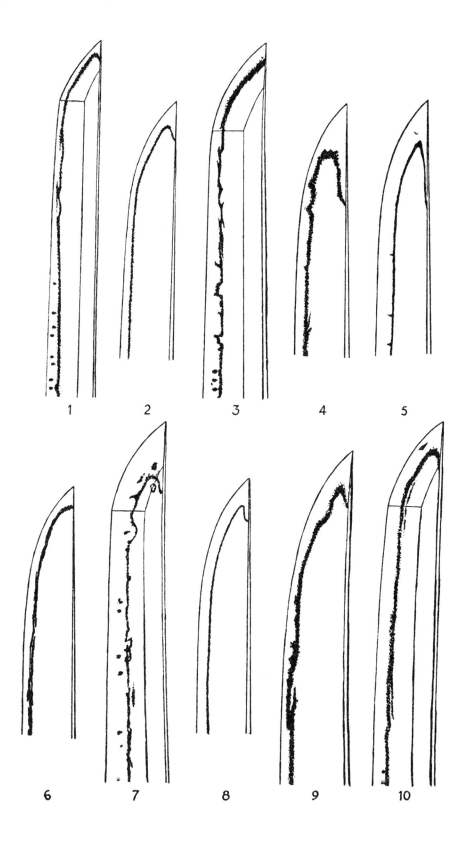

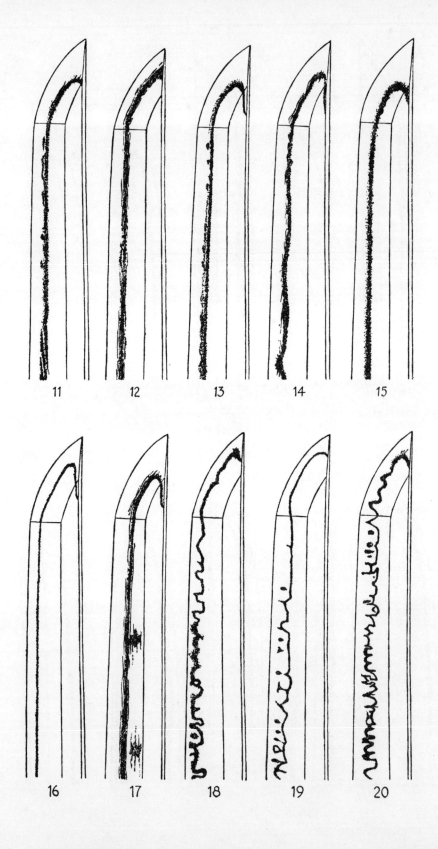

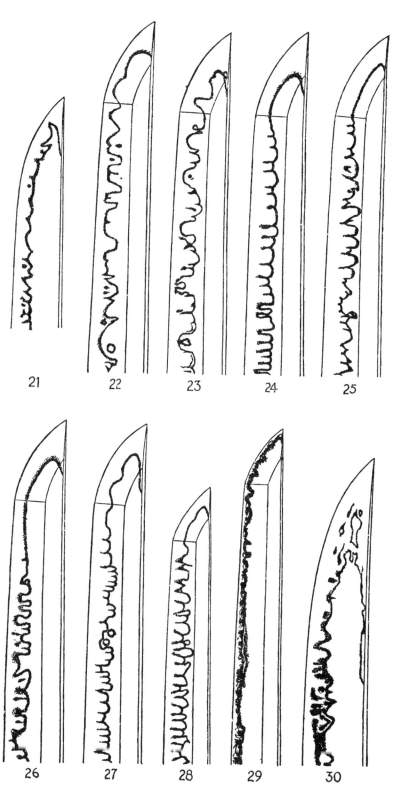

21 22 23 24 25

26 27 28 29 30

c

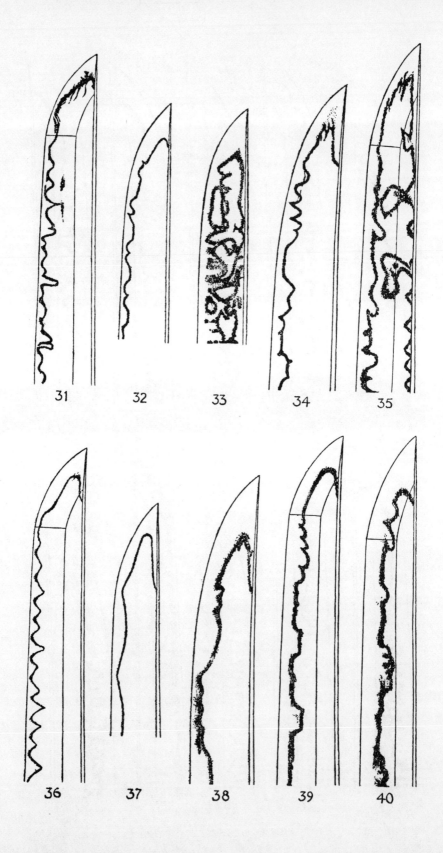

31 32 33 34 35

36 37 38 39 40

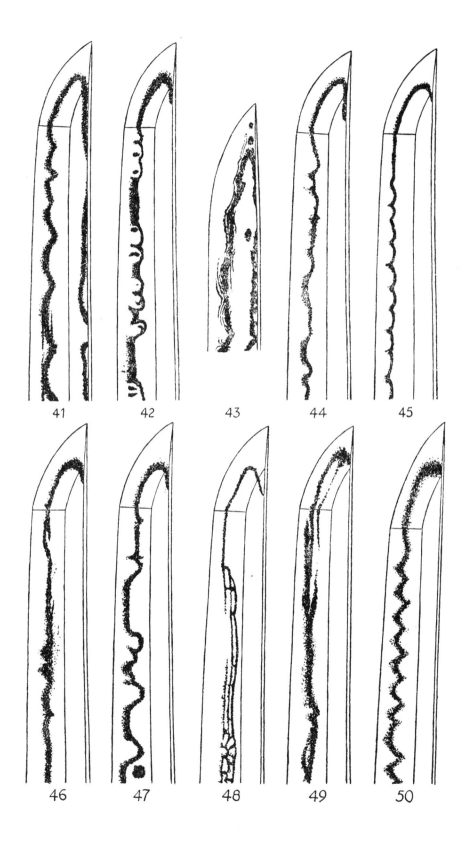

41   42   43   44   45

46   47   48   49   50

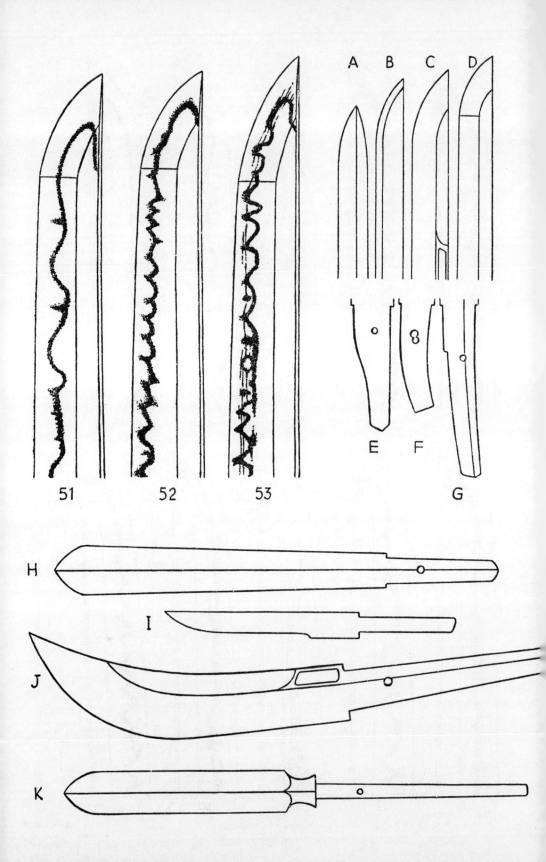

51 52 53 A B C D E F G H I J K

(39) *Hako-midare ha:* irregular 'box' formations. Kanewaka of Kaga.

(40) *Gunome-midare ha:* irregular invected. Horikawa.

(41) *Ō-gunome-midare ha:* large irregular invected. Midzuta.

(42) *Gunome-midare ha:* irregular invected. Tadayoshi.

(43) *Gunome-midare ha:* irregular invected. Noda Hankei.

(44) *Ko-gunome-midare ha:* small irregular invected. Nagasone.

(45) *Sugu-gunome ha:* straight invected. Tsuta.

(46) *Sugu-midare ha:* straight irregular. Inouye Shinkai.

(47) *Tōran-ha:* 'high breaking waves'. Sakakura Terukane.

(48) *Kiku-sui ha:* chrysanthemum and water. Mishina.

(49) *Sugu-ō-midare ha:* straight with large irregularities. Satsuma.

(50) *Gunome-ha:* invected. Satsuma.

(51) *Tōran-ha:* 'high breaking waves'. Owari Seki.

(52) *Saka-gunome ha:* oblique invected. Suishinshi.

(53) *Gunome-midare ha:* irregular invected. Yamaura.

The presence of *niye* (small mirror-like particles of tempered metal) and *nioi* (a misty white line) along the *hamon* should be noted (Pl. 25); larger detached patches of tempered metal appearing in the *jihada* are called *tobi-yaki*. Sometimes the *yakiba* narrows and its outline straightens towards the hilt end; this is known as *yakidashi*, and is characteristic of many Shintō blades (Pl. 20*b*, *c*; 22*a*).

(*b*) TEMPERED EDGE AT THE POINT (*bōshi*)

Type of outline: some variations can be seen in the drawings of *hamon*, and their names are noted in the preceding list.

3. PATTERN OF METAL (*jihada*) (Pl. 24)

Type. and degree, i.e. *mokume* (wood-grain), *masame* (straight grain), *itame* (mixed grain), or *ayasugi* (regular wavy grain).

Colour of metal: old blades are usually darker.

4. TANG (*nakago*)

Form of tang and tang-butt. Three special forms are shown at the end of the *hamon* illustrations: E. *Tanago-bara* ('fish's belly'). F. *Furisode* ('long sleeve'). G. *Kiji-momo* ('pheasant's thigh').

File-marks (*yasuri-me*).

Number and position of *mekugi-ana*.

Signature and other inscriptions.

The signature is usually the first thing the European collector looks at when a Japanese sword comes into his possession (though many blades of the finest quality bear no signature). It is also the first thing looked at by the inexperienced Japanese collector, and his countrymen, always ready with a supply where there is a demand, have been turning out blades bearing the signatures of illustrious ancient swordsmiths for well over three hundred years. As in other branches of collecting, minor names were not really worth the trouble of counterfeiting, and with these one is usually safe; but anybody who acquires a blade purporting to be by Masamune, Kunihiro, or Kiyomaro, would do well to submit it to a panel of Japanese experts and secure an *origami,* or certificate of authenticity. The professional judge of blades (*kanteisha*) has been a respected figure in Japan since the beginning of the Tokugawa regime (though the scientific appraisal of blades dates back to the early Middle Ages), and his opinion is the best available, being the product of generations of study and familiarity with swords and all that has to do with them.

The foundations of this art of expertise were laid by the great sword-smith Masamune (1264–1343). He transmitted his knowledge to his pupil Sadamune, from whom it descended in order to Akihiro, to Saitō Danjō, and finally to Utsunomiya Mikawa. This latter was commissioned by the Shōgun Yoshimasa, in the first year of the period Ōnin (1467), to fix values on various swords which he presented as rewards to his supporters. Another skilful sword-expert at this date was Myōhon Amidabutsu, a name which his successors formed into the family name of Honami. He was also employed by the Shōgun Yoshimasa, and his posterity succeeded to his position of court expert, which they held throughout the Tokugawa period. Honami Kōson, late head of the family and author of the authoritative treatise *Nippon-tō (The Japanese Sword),* died in 1955.

But to return to signatures. The core of the signature is, of course, the name of the swordsmith, written almost invariably with two characters. Many signatures, especially in the early period, consist simply of these two characters, followed sometimes by *saku* or *tsukuru* [x. 18, 34] ('made' sc. this blade). This was the smith's professional name — Yasutsuna, Sukesada, Masahide, and pure Japanese names of this kind, known as *nanori.* The smith sometimes added his family name, but rarely; thus some of the later Bizen smiths constantly began their signatures with the family name of Yokoyama. The personal name, or *zokumyō,* corresponding to our Christian name, and of which Saburō, Dembei, and Shōyemon are typical examples, is of even rarer occurrence.

From about the middle of the sixteenth century the practice arose of awarding swordsmiths (and other artists and craftsmen) the right to use one of the old aristocratic clan-names like Fujiwara, Minamoto and Taira, as well as honorary provincial titles, such as Kaga no Kami, Ōmi no Daijō, and Bizen no Suke. Occasionally also, court titles such as Mondo no Shō and Shuri no Suke were conferred on swordsmiths. Furthermore, a practice arose in the late eighteenth century (though it is occasionally encountered earlier) of adopting in addition a fanciful art-name, which may be found incorporated in the signature. These are almost always written with three characters, of which the third will be *-shi* [x. 2], *-sai* [x. 45], *-ken* [x. 31], or *-tei* [x. 27]. And lastly it must be added that some swordsmiths were, or became, Buddhist priests or 'retired laymen' (*nyūdō*), and either appended a Buddhist name to their normal professional one, or else substituted the former for the latter. Such Buddhist names are written with two characters and are often accompanied by a Buddhist title like *nyūdō* [x. 1, 39], *hokkyō* [x. 21, 43], *hōshi* [x. 21, 30], or *bō* [x. 20].

So much for the names and titles. But frequently the swordsmith included in his signature his place of residence in the order: province, town

TABLE X

1 入	11 以	21 法	31 軒	41 壇
2 子	12 平	22 於	32 原	42 橘
3 土	13 州	23 所	33 彫	43 橋
4 大	14 江	24 持	34 造	44 鍛
5 戶	15 好	25 紀	35 國	45 齋
6 介	16 年	26 重	36 掾	46 應
7 之	17 守	27 亭	37 菅	47 謹
8 月	18 作	28 南	38 源	48 藤
9 日	19 住	29 胴	39 道	49 鐵
10 代	20 坊	30 師	40 需	50 蠻

or village, *no jū* (x. 19, 'living at') or *jū-nin* ('inhabitant of'). The *kōri* or department was very rarely added between the province and town. Names of provinces are written either in full, *Bizen no kuni* ('Province of Bizen'), or in the shortened form consisting normally of the first character of the full name of the province followed by -*shū* [x. 13], as *Bishū* for *Bizen no kuni*. This corresponds to our own usage of writing Hants for Hampshire (see Appendix C). If, however, he was working somewhere outside his native province, he might record this fact, in which case the place in question would be preceded by the character x. 22 *ni oite*, 'at', which, though *written* at the beginning of the place-name, is *read* after it; thus x. 22, 14, 5 is read *Yedo ni oite*, 'at Yedo'.

From the above it should be clear that certain characters in a signature act as 'signposts' to help us find our way about it. These are the following, which should be committed to memory by anybody who aspires to read Japanese signatures for himself — an accomplishment, by the way, not nearly so hard as it may at first appear, given a little patience, and infinitely more satisfying than a state of abject dependence on some so-called 'expert':

x. 35 (*no*) *kuni* — 'province'. The two characters immediately preceding it will be the name of the province in question. But it must be remembered that this character, and several of those that follow, are often used as elements in swordsmiths' professional names.

x. 13 -*shū* — 'province'. As already noted, this character is used in the abbreviated forms of the names of provinces; the character immediately preceding it will identify the province concerned. It is sometimes written with three repetitions of character 4 in Appendix E, arranged in a triangle.

x. 19 (*no*) *jū* — 'living at', 'inhabitant of'. This character always follows a place-name, which may be that of either a province or town.

x. 17 (*no*) *Kami*, following the name of a province (always in its full form) indicates an honorary title, 'Lord of such-and-such a province'. x. 6 (*no*) *Suke*, and x. 4, 36 (*no*) *Daijō*, indicating provincial lords of second and third rank respectively, are used in exactly the same way. x. 36 (*no jō*) is occasionally found without x. 4.

x. 22 *ni oite* — 'at', as already mentioned, is written *before* the place-name it qualifies, but read *after* it.

x. 48, 32 *Fujiwara* (*no*). This is the most frequently used of the old clan-names. There are only five others in use among swordsmiths, and it is a great help to be able to recognize them; they always immediately precede the swordsmith's professional name, or *nanori*. They are (in order of frequency): *Minamoto* [x. 38], *Taira* [x. 12], *Ki* [x. 25], *Tachibana* [x. 42], *Sugawara* [x. 37, 32].

x. 18 *saku* — 'made'. This is the commonest of several characters denoting manufacture; others are x. 34 *tsukuru* — 'made', and x. 44 *kitau* — 'forged'. These are sometimes prefixed by x. 47, *kin* — 'respectfully'.

x. 7 *kore* (*wo*) — 'this' (*wo*, denoting the accusative, like *no*, denoting the genitive, is understood). This character is written *after* any of the 'manufacturing' characters, but is read *before* it.

NOMENCLATURE AND EXPERTISE

If then we take an entirely fictitious swordsmith, Tadatsune, and imagine him using in his signature all the above names, titles, residences, etc., to which he is entitled, we might get something of this kind:

MUSASHI NO KUNI YEDO NI OITE HISHŪ SAGA NO JŪ-NIN YAMAMOTO SABURŌ KOKURYŪSHI TAJIMA NO KAMI FUJIWARA NO TADATSUNE NYŪDŌ DŌKWAN KORE WO SAKU — a total of thirty-two characters — which might be rendered: 'Yamamoto Saburō (with the art-name of) Kokuryūshi (and the honorary provincial title of) Tajima no Kami (and the honorary clan-name of) Fujiwara (his professional name being) Tadatsune (known also as) the retired layman Dōkwan, a native of Saga in the province of Hizen, made this at Yedo in the province of Musashi.' Mercifully for the amateur, however, very few signatures exceed ten characters in length, and the great majority consist of five or less.

When the date is inscribed on the tang of a blade, it nearly always appears on the opposite face from the signature proper. Japanese dates are written in two different ways:

(i) The year-period (nengō) followed by the number of the year [x. 16], month [x. 8], and sometimes day [x. 9] within it. Tables of the year-periods and numerals will be found in Appendices A and B.

(ii) Less frequently, and sometimes in combination with (i), the date is shown by a pair of characters, the first being one of the 'Ten Stems' and the second one of the 'Twelve Signs'. These two sets of characters are used in sixty different combinations, one for each year in the sixty year cycle, which was the alternative method of reckoning time. Such cycles began in 1144, 1204, 1264, and so on up to 1924, the present year (1961) being the 37th of the current cycle, designated by the two characters tsuchinoto-i (see Appendix B). Used by itself, this method is useless in dating a blade unless one can determine the cycle in question by some other consideration, such as the known period of a swordsmith's activity, but it is found fairly frequently in combination with the year-period, in which case, of course, there is no ambiguity.

Other inscriptions found on the tangs of sword-blades are:

(i) Particulars of the metal from which the blade has been forged, and even, sometimes, of the water and clay used in tempering it. These inscriptions begin with the character x. 11 (wo) motte — 'using' — another of the characters which is written first but read last. Thus x. 11, 28, 50, 49 is read namban-tetsu wo motte — 'using southern barbarian iron'. Man-tetsu, which sometimes occurs in inscriptions of this kind on modern swords, means iron, or rather steel, from the railway-lines of the Man-churian Railway, which the Japanese during their occupation of that country found to be very well suited to their purpose.

(ii) Particulars of tests to which the blade may have been submitted. Professional sword-testers, like professional sword-appraisers, were highly respectable personages, many of whom belonged to the families of Yamada and Yamano. These inscriptions vary considerably, but the usual arrange-ment is: (a) date; (b) test applied; (c) name of tester. Key-characters are x. 29, dō ('body' on which the test was carried out), and x. 3, 41, 'dodan'

41

(the block on which the *corpus vile* was laid and which was often cut through at the same stroke). Tests were formerly carried out on the bodies of condemned criminals, or on corpses from the execution-yard. Some twenty different cuts are prescribed; the easiest was reckoned to be the severing of the hand at the wrist, and the most difficult was that across the hips, known as *ryō-kuruma* ('pair of wheels') from the two curved hip-bones through which, as well as the spine at its thickest point, the blade had to pass. In more recent times bundles of straw and bamboo of equivalent 'resistance' to the human body have been used. An expert sword-tester armed with a first-class blade could cut through three and even four bodies at a stroke. Tests were sometimes carried out on an iron plate set edgewise, and some of the stories of the Japanese sword's performance, though circumstantially attested, seem to us quite incredible. In the early seventeenth century a certain Shigetaka was a well-known maker of gun-barrels at Yedo. He became fascinated with sword-forging, however, and finally attained such proficiency that he was able to cut through one of his own gun-barrels with one of his own blades. As a swordsmith he was known as Hankei, and his end, though unpleasant, is distinctly apropos; he was found in the street one morning in 1646, his body cut completely in two from the right hip to the left shoulder. The enquiry established that this had been done by a technique known as *iai*, in which a tremendous stroke is delivered upwards in the same movement as drawing the sword. There was a training film shown to Japanese troops in the last war in the course of which an expert swordsman cut through the barrel of a machine-gun.

(iii) The name of the owner, or patron who commissioned the blade, is occasionally found inscribed on the tang, preceded by the characters x. 23, 24 (*shoji*). When a blade was made as a family heirloom, it was inscribed with the family name followed by x. 26, 10 (*jūdai* — 'heirloom'). The expression x. 46 . . . 40 (*motome . . . ni ojite* — 'to the special order of . . .') is also sometimes used.

(iv) Inscriptions may very occasionally be found inlaid in gold or silver on the tang. These are usually attributions to a particular swordsmith when there is no signature, and may be accompanied by the name and *kakihan* (hand-seal, or personal device) of the member of the Honami family or other expert who made the attribution (Pl. 14*a*). Attributions may also be written in lacquer on the tang (Pl. 9*a*, *c*, 15*b*). Certificates of testing (*tameshi-giri* — see above (ii)) are also occasionally inlaid, and in a few cases where a particularly fine blade has been given a fanciful name such as *Sasa no tsuyu*, 'Dew on the Grass' (Pl. 11*c*), that is inlaid in gold on the tang. One swordsmith, Tsugihira III (of Yedo, mid eighteenth century) actually inlaid his signature in gold.

The Five Traditions (Gokaden)

Plates 8–12

Blades of the Kotō period fall into five main styles, called after the provinces where they originated Yamashiro-den, Yamato-den, Bizen-den, Sōshū-den (Sagami), and Mino-den (later, Seki-den). Their main characteristics are as follows:

	Yamashiro-den	*Yamato-den*	*Bizen-den*	*Sōshū-den*	*Mino-den* *(Seki-den)*
SHAPE	Slim, graceful; regular curve	Slim, graceful; regular curve; high *shinogi*	Medium width, graceful; *koshi-zori*	Wide, long, heavy; curve regular	Wide, long; slight regular curve
EDGE	Narrow and straight with small *niye*	Straight with very slight irregularities; small *niye*	*Chōji*; medium-sized *niye*	Wide *chōji* *midare*; *tobi-yaki* and profuse *niye*	*Sambon-sugi* and other jagged patterns; medium-sized *niye*
PATTERN	Small *mokume*	*Masame*	Medium-sized *mokume*	*Itame*	Small *mokume*
TANG	Long and tapering	Long and tapering	Short with almost parallel sides	*Tanago-bara*	Medium length; tapering

The above is only intended as a very rough guide, but although there were slight variations within the different Traditions at different periods, it gives a fair general idea of the essential characteristics of the blades they produced. The following table shows how the various schools followed these Five Traditions at different stages of the Kotō period. It will be noticed that in the Muromachi period the Yamashiro-den and Yamato-den became virtually indistinguishable, and that in the last (Sengoku) stage the same school was in several instances turning out blades in more than one Tradition; this tendency increased during the sixteenth century, so that in the Shintō period the various styles were thoroughly mixed up, and it is no longer possible to apply the Five Traditions system. Nevertheless there was a good deal of conscious imitation of early styles, particularly under the inspiration of Suishinshi Masahide at the beginning of the nineteenth century.

THE BLADE

CLASSIFICATION ACCORDING TO THE FIVE TRADITIONS

Yamashiro-den	Yamato-den	Bizen-den	Sōshū-den	Mino-den (Seki-den)
HEIAN PERIOD 806–1184				
Sanjō School Yasutsuna Old Bizen School Old Aoye School	Senju-in School Miike Tenta			
KAMAKURA PERIOD I 1184–1219				
Awataguchi Sch. Yukihira of Bungo	Senju-in School	Ichimonji School Awataguchi Sch.		
KAMAKURA PERIOD II 1219–78				
Ayanokōji School Rai School Early Osafune Niō School of Suō	Tegai School Shikkake School Hōshō School Niō School Naminohira Sch.	Early Osafune Hatakeda School Katayama School Ayanokōji School Rai School		
KAMAKURA PERIOD III 1278–1334				
Shintōgo School Ukai School Mihara School Yenju School	Tayema School Sairen-Jitsua Tegai School Hōshō School	Yoshioka School Osafune School Ukai School	Masamune Sch. Tayema School	
YOSHINO PERIOD 1334–94				
Nobukuni School Aoye School	Hōshō School	Osafune School Ōmiya School Yoshii School	Chōgi School School of Sa Early Seki Sch.	Shidzu School Kinjū School
MUROMACHI PERIOD 1394–1467				
	Tegai School Shikkake School Nobukuni School Aoye School Niō School of Suō Mihara School	Osafune School Ōmiya School Yoshii School	Sōshū School Nobukuni Sch. Tegai School	Seki School
SENGOKU PERIOD 1467–1596				
		Osafune School Kanabō School Shimada School Fujishima School Uda School Mihara School Takada School Niō School of Suō	Sōshū School Shimada School Shitahara School Fuyuhiro Seki (a few) Hiroyoshi (Hōki)	Seki School Kanabō School Muramasa Shimada School Shitahara School Fujishima School Takada School Uda School Mihara School Kongōbei School

The Chief Schools of Japanese Swordsmiths

KOTŌ PERIOD

YAMASHIRO PROVINCE

The Sanjō School (at Kyōto) c. 980–1400

The founder was Kokaji Munechika [87, 96] (938–1014) who is said to have been aided in his work by the fox-spirit Inari (Pl. 5). His most celebrated blade was accordingly named *Kogitsune Maru* ('Little Fox'). Yoshiiye [51, 138] and Arikuni [53, 154] were his best pupils, and the latter's son Kanenaga [131, 25] broke away to found the Gojō School. Another school at Kyōto, the Ayanokōji, founded by Sadatoshi [88, 62] about the middle of the thirteenth century, also followed the Sanjō style, producing long swords with rather narrow blades of pronounced curve, *mokume* grain, and *hamon* 1, 18, or 29.

The Awataguchi School (at Kyōto) c. 1200–1300 (Pl. 8)

The first generation of this famous school consisted of Kunitomo [154, 23], Hisakuni [9, 154], Kuniyasu [154, 50], and Kunitsuna [154, 185] (who later lived in Sagami); all these worked for the Emperor Go-Toba (p. 19f.). The greatest master of the school was, however, Tōshirō Yoshimitsu [51, 55], grandson of Kunitomo. They made both long swords and dirks with rather narrow blades, *mokume* grain, and *hamon* 1, 2, or 18.

The Rai School (at Kyōto) c. 1250–1350

Besides producing such celebrated masters as Rai Kuniyuki [154, 43], Rai Kunitoshi [154, 101] and his son Ryōkai [2, 74], Rai Kunitsugu [154, 42], and Rai Kunimitsu [154, 55], this school spread its influence into the provinces of Higo, Ōmi, Tamba, Bungo, Echizen, and Settsu. Their blades are mostly long, with small *mokume* grain and *hamon* 4 or 20.

YAMATO PROVINCE

The Senju-in School (at Nara) c. 1150–1300

Shigehiro [110, 29], co-founder of the school with Yukinobu [43, 99], worked for the Emperor Go-Toba (p. 20). Many members of the school signed simply *Senju-in* [8, 18, 124]. Their blades were mostly long, of pronounced curve, with *itame* or *masame* grain, and *hamon* 3 or 18. An offshoot

45

of the school is found at Akasaka in Mino province in the fourteenth and fifteenth centuries.

The Tegai School (at Nara) c. 1225–1440

A succession of smiths of this school (including the founder) bore the name of Kanenaga [39, 25], and the character *Kane* [39] was a sort of trade-mark of the whole group. They made both long swords and dirks with *itame* or *masame* grain, and *hamon* 3, 5, 6, or 8.

The Shikkake School (at Nara) c. 1250–1440 (Pl. 9c)

The leading Shikkake smiths used the name Norinaga [106, 83]. Their blades resembled those of the Tegai school, except that the *hamon* was usually 3 or 19.

The Tayema School (at Nara) c. 1280–1430

This school was founded by Kuniyuki [154, 43]; most of their blades, both long swords and dirks, conformed to the Yamato style of the two preceding schools, but with *hamon* 3 or 6. The signature on the long blades was usually *tachi* style (p. 28), and sometimes consisted simply of the school name *Tayema*.

The Hōshō School (at Takechi) c. 1260–1360 (Pl. 9a)

The foremost Hōshō smith was Sadamune [114, 87] (to be distinguished from his namesake and contemporary of Sagami province). Most of the blades produced were dirks with *masame* or *itame* grain and *hamon* 6.

ISE PROVINCE

The Sengo School (at Sengo and Kuwana) c. 1360–1500 (Pl. 16)

The first Muramasa [60, 31], who founded this school, was a pupil of Heianjō Nagayoshi [83, 51] of Kyōto; though of excellent quality, his blades had an evil reputation (p. 22). The school produced mostly dirks with *itame* or *masame* grain and *hamon* 34 or 37.

SAGAMI PROVINCE

The School of Masamune (at Kamakura) c. 1250–1600 (Pls. 11, 14, 15)

Kunitsuna [154, 185] of Awataguchi and the two Bizen smiths Ichimonji Sukezane [63, 140] and Bizen Saburō Kunimune [154, 87] worked and trained pupils in Sagami in the early thirteenth century, and the two foremost traditions of the craft from the golden age of the Emperor Go-Toba were thus blended in Masamune's [31, 87] province before his birth. He owed most of his early training to his father Yukimitsu [43, 55] and to Shintōgo Kunimitsu [154, 55], son of Kunitsuna. The 'brilliant pupils' of both Masamune and his son-in-law Sadamune [114, 87] (from whom also derived the Takagi school of Ōmi) have already been listed (p. 21f.), and nearly all of them founded their own schools on returning to their native

46

provinces. Masamune and his pupils produced a preponderance of dirks with *itame* grain; the *hamon* varied greatly, especially among later representatives of the school, and examples occur of 7, 21, 22, 23, 30, 33, 34, and 35. The blades may also carry the engraved design of the dragon and sword.

MINO PROVINCE

The Seki School (at Seki) c. 1450–1600 (Pl. 12, 17*b*)

Kanemoto [131, 15] and Kanesada [131, 88] are the two great names in this school, both being borne by a number of successive swordsmiths. Kanemoto II, often called Seki Magoroku, in particular did much to establish the essentially practical Seki type of blade for both long swords and dirks. The grain is *mokume*, and the *hamon* may be 8, 33, 34, 36, or 57.

DEWA PROVINCE

The Gwassan School, twelfth–sixteenth century (Pl. 13*c*)

The founder, Oniō Maru [134, 16, 12] ('Demon King'), traced his descent from the ancient Maikusa smiths of the neighbouring province of Mutsu (p. 18); all his successors used the name Gwassan [24, 13] ('Moon Mountain'). Gwassan blades, both long swords and dirks, are strongly characterized by the beautiful regular wavy grain known as *ayasugi*; *hamon* is 2.

ETCHŪ PROVINCE

The Uda School, c. 1320–1550

Uda in Yamato province gives its name to this school, because it was the original home of the founder, Kunimune [154, 87] (as also, incidentally, of Amakuni, the traditional father of all Japanese swordsmiths). The names of all the Uda smiths begin with *Kuni* [154]. Both long swords and dirks were produced, with *itame* graining and *hamon* 3 or 6.

KAGA PROVINCE

The Fujishima School, c. 1330–1600

Tomoshige [23, 110], the founder, came originally from Fujishima in Echizen province, and was a pupil of Rai Kunitoshi. Fujishima blades are both long and short with *itame* grain and *hamon* 7, 23, or 36.

HŌKI PROVINCE

The Ōhara School (at Ōhara) c. 850(?)–1025 (Pl. 7*c*)

Yasutsuna [50, 185], as we have seen (p. 17), did more than anyone else to develop the Japanese sword as we know it, and his son Sanemori [140, 49] was almost his equal in renown. Their blades are among the finest and

47

most typical examples of the earliest period, having a pronounced curve and taper, large *itame* grain, and *hamon* 1.

BIZEN PROVINCE

The Old Bizen School, c. 950–1200

It is perhaps curious that Bizen, the sword-making province *par excellence*, does not figure in the earliest traditions of the craft. The first Bizen swordsmith whose name has come down to us is Sanenari [186, 73], whose son Tomonari [23, 73] together with several contemporaries (p. 18) worked for the Emperor Ichijō. Among these was Masatsune [31, 102], son of Arimasa [53, 31], one of the Maikusa smiths of Mutsu. They made mostly long swords with narrow blades of pronounced curve, large *mokume* grain, and *hamon* 18 or 29.

The Ichimonji School (at Fukuoka and Yoshioka) c. 1180–1350

This prolific school, founded by Norimune [106, 87], derived from Masatsune's branch of the Old Bizen group; many members of it worked for the Emperor Go-Toba (p. 19f.). The Yoshioka branch was founded by Sukeyoshi [63, 51] at the end of the thirteenth century, and very similar work was turned out by the Hatakeda smiths of Osafune (c. 1200–1420). Ichimonji branch schools were also established at Katayama (Bitchū) and Kamakura (Sagami) towards the middle of the thirteenth century. Ichimonji blades are mostly long, with pronounced curve, *mokume* and *itame* grain, and *hamon* 1 (Fukuoka only), 18, or 19.

The Osafune School (at Osafune) c. 1230–1600 (Pls. 10, 17a)

If Bizen was the greatest sword-making province, Osafune was the most prolific centre of the craft within its boundaries. From an early period this small village was populated almost entirely by swordsmiths and their families, and in its heyday during the fourteenth century over a hundred swordsmiths were living there simultaneously. Up to 1350 the great names were Mitsutada [55, 92], Nagamitsu [83, 55], Kagemitsu [164, 55], and Chikakage [96, 164], and it was at this time that the teachings of Masamune were brought back from Kamakura by Kanemitsu [131, 55], Chōgi [83, 179], and Motoshige [15, 110]. To the later period (c. 1350 onwards) belong innumerable smiths using -*mitsu* [55] as the second element of their names, and more than thirty who used the name of Sukesada [128, 88]. Osafune blades had a pronounced *Koshi-zori* curve and *mokume* grain (growing smaller towards the end of the period). *Hamon* of early examples is 18, 19, or 32; 20 and 21 among the ex-pupils of Masamune; and in the later period 5, 7, 22, and 23.

The Ukai School (at Ukai) c. 1275–1400

The names of all the smiths of this school begin with *Un-* [162] ('cloud'), the most celebrated being Unshō [162, 33], Unji [162, 42], and Unjū [162, 110]. They made mostly long swords with *mokume* grain and *hamon* 5 or 19.

B. THE EMPEROR GO-TOBA FORGING A BLADE

Colour-print by KUNIYOSHI, *c.*1840, from the 'Hundred Poets Series'
in which Go-Toba is no. 99. *Author's Collection.* (See page 19.)

THE CHIEF SCHOOLS OF JAPANESE SWORDSMITHS

The Yoshii School (at Yoshii) c. 1310–1460

The most outstanding smith of this school was Kagenori [164, 106], and nearly all the others used *-nori* [106] as the second character of their names. They made long swords and dirks with *mokume* grain and *hamon* 32.

BITCHŪ PROVINCE

The Aoye School (at Aoye) c. 1120–1300 (Pl. 13a)

The school was founded by Yasutsugu [50, 42], and the pupils of his brilliant son Moritsugu [49, 42] brought it into great prominence under the Emperor Go-Toba; the most important of these were Sadatsugu [114, 42], Tsunetsugu [102, 42], and Tsunezane [102, 140]. A collateral school, also at Aoye, was founded about 1170 by Noritaka [106, 137], an immigrant from Bizen, and produced Masatsune [31, 102] as its most notable smith. Aoye blades are mostly long, with pronounced curve, *mokume* grain, and *hamon* 5 or 18.

BINGO PROVINCE

The Mihara School (at Mihara) c. 1325–1450

The names of all the Mihara smiths begin with *Masa-* [31]. At first they made mostly long swords, but later dirks and *wakizashi* are in the majority. The grain is *mokume* or *itame* (small *mokume* in later examples), with *hamon* 5, 1, or (later) 7. The Niō School of Suō province produced very similar work.

CHIKUZEN PROVINCE

The Old Chikuzen School, c. 1220–1370

Takatsuna [137, 185] of Bizen migrated to Chikuzen, and his sons Sairen [45, 195] and Nyūsai [3, 45] gained a high reputation as swordsmiths. The son of Sairen was Jitsua [186, 78], who became in his turn father of Sa [37], one of Masamune's 'brilliant pupils'. Yasuyoshi [50, 51] founded a branch of the school of Sa in Nagato province about 1350, and other branches sprang up in Chikugo and Hizen. The early Chikuzen smiths produced mostly wide-bladed long swords with large *itame* grain and *hamon* 1; from the time of Sa, dirks were made in quantity, with *hamon* 21.

The Kongōbei School, c. 1250–1430

This school was founded by Morikuni [170, 154] another son of Takatsuna of Bizen. It produced blades of all sizes with *itame* and *masame* grain and *hamon* 21.

BUNGO PROVINCE

The School of Yukihira, c. 1160–1280

Sadahide [88, 65], father of Yukihira [43, 32] and founder of the school, was a native of Buzen and (according to tradition) an incarnation of Ryūjin the Dragon King. Yukihira himself worked for the Emperor Go-Toba, and was known as Kishindayu ('Demon-god'). The blades of his school are mostly long, narrow, and of pronounced curve, having *mokume* and *itame* grain, and *hamon* 1.

The Takada School (at Takada) c. 1310–1600 (Pl. 17c)

This long-lived school, founded by Tomomitsu [23, 55], continued right into the Shintō period. Blades of all sizes were made, with small *mokume* grain and *hamon* 7 or 23.

HIGO PROVINCE

The Yenju School (at Kikuchi) c. 1260–1600

Hiromura [29, 60], a native of Yamato, married the daughter of Rai Kuniyuki, and their son Kunimura [154, 60] founded this school. Much of the work follows the Rai tradition. Both long swords and dirks were made, with *mokume* grain and *hamon* 4 or 5.

SATSUMA PROVINCE

The Naminohira School (at Taniyama) c. 980–1600 (Pl. 13b)

This school has one of the longest continuous records of any, and a representative was still working in the 1860's. The founder, Masakuni [31, 154], made a sword for the Emperor Ichijō, and was thus a contemporary of Sanjō Munechika and Tomonari of Bizen. Several notable Naminohira smiths were named Yukiyasu [43, 50] and Yasuyuki [50, 43]. Their blades are characterized by the same regular wavy grain (*ayasugi*) as those of the Gwassan School, though *itame* is also found in the earlier examples. *Hamon* is 2 or 4.

SHINTŌ AND SHINSHINTŌ PERIODS

YAMASHIRO PROVINCE

The Horikawa School (at Kyōto) c. 1580–1700 (Pls. 18a, b, 20b, c)

Umetada Myōju [80, 187], who traced his descent from Sanjō Munechika, and his even more eminent pupil Kunihiro [154, 198] between them trained a considerable proportion of the swordsmiths of Kyōto, Ōsaka, Hizen, and Aki who made the seventeenth century such an outstanding period in the history of the Japanese sword. Myōju's pupils included Tadayoshi [92, 31] of Hizen and Teruhiro [193, 198] of Aki, both of whom founded notable schools in their respective provinces; Kuniyasu [154, 50], Kunitomo [154, 199], and the two Ōsaka smiths Kunisada [154, 114] and Kunisuke [154, 63] were taught by Kunihiro. Both these latter formed their own schools, Kunisada's chief pupil being Inouye Shinkai [140, 59] 'the Masamune of Ōsaka'. Long swords and dirks were mostly produced by this school; the blades often have the engraved design of the dragon and sword, a close *mokume* grain, and *hamon* 9, 14, or 40. The Ōsaka derivatives show *hamon* 24 and 51, often with *yakidashi*.

The Mishina School (at Kyōto) c. 1580–1850 (Pl. 18c)

Kanemichi [131, 183] of Mino, ninth in descent from Masamune's pupil Kaneuji, migrated to Kyōto with his four sons Kinmichi [215, 183], Rai Kinmichi [215, 183], Yoshimichi [51, 183], and Masatoshi [31, 101], towards the end of the sixteenth century. Each founded his own line which continued, in some cases, well into the nineteenth century. Yoshimichi, in particular, had two sons, Yoshimichi [51, 183] and Kanemichi [131, 183], who carried the family tradition to Ōsaka; and Kunikane [154, 39], a pupil of Masatoshi, was the first of a long and eminent line at Sendai in Mutsu. The Mishina smiths made both long and short swords with *mokume* grain and *hamon* 40 or 48.

The Morioka School (at Kyōto) c. 1800–70

Morioka Chōson [161, 163], the founder, was of princely descent, and his pupil Arikoto [53, 28] was a nobleman of the third rank (*Shō-sammi*); his other notable pupil was Keinin [197, 41]. They made blades of all types following mainly the Bizen (Ichimonji) and Sagami traditions.

SETTSU PROVINCE

The Tsuta School (at Ōsaka) c. 1650–1700 (Pl. 20a)

Sukehiro [63, 198] and his son-in-law Sukenao [63, 91] were affiliated through Kunisuke (pupil of Kunihiro) to the Horikawa School of Kyōto. Both are among the very best craftsmen of the Shintō period, and both used a highly individual rounded and flourishing script for their signatures. They made long and short swords with small *mokume* grain and *hamon* 15, 45, or 47, often with *yakidashi*. Sakakura Terukane [193, 39], another outstanding Ōsaka swordsmith, worked in very similar style.

The Hidari Mutsu School (at Ōsaka) c. 1600–1700

Hidari means 'left-handed', and Kaneyasu [39, 100] II, the foremost figure of this group, had the habit of engraving his signature and title (*Mutsu no Kami*) looking-glass fashion, with the characters back to front. His father, Kaneyasu I, was descended from the Tegai School of Yamato. They made both long and short swords with *mokume* grain and *hamon* 40, often with *yakidashi*.

The Ikkanshi School (at Ōsaka) c. 1625–1740

The first Tadatsuna [92, 185] was a native of Himeji in Harima, and also lived at Awataguchi (Kyōto) before settling at Ōsaka; he and his descendants usually incorporated the name Awataguchi in their signatures. Tadatsuna II took the additional name of Ikkanshi, and often engraved dragons on his blades. They made both long and short swords with small *mokume* grain and *hamon* 24, 26, 38, or 47.

THE BLADE

The Owari Seki School (at Kiyosu and Nagoya) c. 1590–1850

There were two branches of this school, both founded by swordsmiths of Mino province working in Seki style. Both lines, of Masatsune [79, 150] and Nobutaka [99, 137] respectively, continued to the ninth generation, the successive generations all bearing the same two names. The Masatsune group made mostly dirks with *mokume* grain and *hamon* 9, 14, or 16; the Nobutaka group made long and short swords with *mokume* grain and *hamon* 34, 37, or 40.

MUSASHI PROVINCE

The Nagasone School (at Yedo) c. 1650–1700 (Pl. 19c)

The founder of this school, Kotetsu Okisato [94, 190, 202, 64], was an armourer up to the age of nearly fifty, but having once taken up sword forging he quickly became the foremost swordsmith of his time; his son Okimasa [202, 31] was a worthy successor. They made both long and short swords, sometimes engraved with the dragon and sword design, with small *mokume* grain and *hamon* 44 or 45.

The Aoi Shimosaka School (at Yedo) c. 1590–1860 (Pl. 19a)

As already noted (p. 23) the favourite swordsmith of Iyeyasu, the first Tokugawa Shōgun, was Shimosaka Yasutsugu [152, 209], originally of Echizen, who settled at Yedo when his patron set up his court there, and was the first of eleven successive swordsmiths of the same name, the last of whom was active in the middle of the nineteenth century. The first character of his name [152] was specially conferred on him by Iyeyasu, being the same as that used for the second part of his own name. The blades of this school were both long and short, with *mokume* grain and *hamon* 9, 11, 13, 14, 38, 39, or 43. They were sometimes engraved with a straight sword, a dragon, or the divinity Fudō, patron of swordsmiths.

The Ishidō School (at Yedo) c. 1650–1860

The senior branch of this school consisted of a line of smiths named Korekazu [109, 1], the first of whom was a native of Ōmi; Korekazu VII (1815–89) was the best of them. The other branch was led by Tsunemitsu [150, 55] and Mitsuhira [55, 32]. Ishidō blades were both long and short, with *mokume* grain and *hamon* 25. Other branches of the Ishidō School flourished in Chikuzen, Kii, Ōmi, and Settsu (Ōsaka).

The Suishinshi School (at Yedo and elsewhere) c. 1780–1860 (Pl. 22b)

Suishinshi Masahide [31, 65], as we have seen, was the leading spirit in the revival of the swordsmith's craft towards the end of the eighteenth century. Both he and his numerous pupils produced blades in great profusion and of wide variety, generally following the old Bizen and Sagami traditions, and the style of Sukehiro (Tsuta) of Ōsaka. They were often engraved with the dragon and sword design.

The Yamaura School (at Yedo) c. 1825–60 (Pls. 22c, 23c)

Kiyomaro [144, 207] was perhaps the most brilliant swordsmith of the Shinshintō period; he committed suicide in 1854. His blades and those of his followers Nobuhide [99, 65] and Kiyondo [144, 3] are mostly long, with a long point, *mokume* or *itame* grain, and *hamon* 12 or 53.

MINO PROVINCE

The Shintō Seki School (Pl. 21a)

The Seki tradition was kept alive in its native province by Ujifusa [20, 93] and a succession of smiths named Jumyō [187, 85]. They made both long and short swords with *mokume* grain and *hamon* 10, 36, or 37. Schools of swordsmiths working in Seki style are also found in Echizen, Kaga, Owari, Mutsu, and Inaba.

INABA PROVINCE

The School of Toshinori, c. 1790–1860

Toshinori [187, 125], whose name is sometimes read as Jukaku, was one of the best of the Shinshintō smiths, and trained many pupils, notably Minryūshi Toshizane [187, 186]. They made both long and short blades with small but pronounced *mokume* grain and *hamon* 27, or occasionally 48.

BIZEN PROVINCE

The Yokoyama School (at Osafune) c. 1580–1860

The Yokoyama smiths were in direct descent from the numerous Sukesadas who were working at Osafune in the sixteenth century, and the most outstanding of them were Kōdzuke no Daijō Sukesada [128, 88] (1577–1674) and Sukenaga [128, 25] (1795–1851). They produced both long and short swords with small precise *mokume* grain and *hamon* 16, 23, 26, or 27, sometimes with *yakidashi*.

BITCHŪ PROVINCE

The Midzuta School (at Midzuta) c. 1580–1740

This school consisted almost entirely of smiths named Kunishige [154, 110], the greatest of whom was the third in the main line, Ōtsuki Yogorō (shortened to Daiyogo) Kunishige. Midzuta blades are both long and short with occasional dirks; they have faint *itame* grain and *hamon* 41 or 50.

KII PROVINCE

The Nanki School (at Meikōzan and Wakayama) c. 1600–1780 (Pl. 21c)

The founder, Shigekuni [110, 154], at first used the name Kanekuni [39, 154], and was descended from the old Tegai School of Yamato; he was followed by three more of the same name, besides collaterals. They made both long and short swords with small *mokume* and *itame* grain and *hamon* 11.

The Chikuzen Nobukuni School (at Fukuoka and Hakozaki) c. 1650–1850 (Pl. 21*b*)

This group of smiths descended from the Nobukuni [99, 154] School of Kyōto, founded by Sadamune's pupil of that name. They made blades of all kinds, with small *mokume* grain and *hamon* 13 or 25. Engraved designs often appear on the blades.

The Shintō Takada School (at Takada) c. 1600–1720

This school was also a continuation from the Kotō period; most of its members used names ending in -*yuki* [43]. Their blades were both long and short, with small but pronounced *mokume* grain and *hamon* 7, 10, 16, 40, or 42.

The School of Tadayoshi (at Saga) c. 1600–1860

As already noted, the first Tadayoshi [92, 51] was a pupil of Myōju, and his direct successors were all named Tadayoshi or Tadahiro [92, 198] down to Tadayoshi IX (d. 1887); each normally used the name Tadahiro until the death of his father or master, after which he succeeded as Tadayoshi. Other members of the school, of which there were many, often used *hiro* [198] as an element in their names. Both long and short swords were made, with small *mokume* grain and *hamon* 9, 10, 13, 15, 24, 40, or 42, and the dragon and sword design is not infrequently found engraved upon them.

The Satsuma School, c. 1580–1860 (Pl. 22*a*)

This school derived from the Seki tradition, and its most important members were Masakiyo [31, 144] and Yasuyo [50, 26]. These two collaborated in 1721 in forging a blade for the Shōgun Yoshimune at Yedo, as a result of which they were allowed the privilege of engraving a single hollyhock leaf on the tangs of their blades (cf. the Aoi Shimosaka School of Musashi, above). Motohira [15, 32] and Masayoshi [31, 67 *or* 89] were both eminent in this province about 1800. Satsuma blades are both long and short with *itame* grain and *hamon* 41, 46, 49, 50, and occasionally 15.

The Greatest Swordsmiths of Japan

The arrangement and classification of the best swordsmiths in order of merit has been a favourite pastime among Japanese amateurs of the subject for several centuries. No two lists agree, and I therefore make no apology for submitting this one. It may provide a basis for argument and discussion, or simply serve as a cockshy.

A. Kotō Period (30 Swordsmiths)

1. Gorō Nyūdō *Masamune* [31, 87] of Sagami (1264–1343).
2. Awataguchi Tōshirō *Yoshimitsu* [51, 55] of Yamashiro (1229–91).
3. Sanjō Kokaji *Munechika* [87, 96] of Kyōto (938–1014).
4. *Tomonari* [23, 73] of Bizen (b. c. 952).
5. Gō *Yoshihiro* [179, 29] of Etchū (1299–1325).
6. Ichimonji *Norimune* [106, 87] of Fukuoka, Bizen (1152–1214).
7. Awataguchi *Hisakuni* [9, 154] of Yamashiro (1149–1216).
8. Saburodayu *Yasutsuna* [50, 185] of Ōhara, Hōki (fl. c. 900).
9. Awataguchi Tōrokurō *Kunitsuna* [154, 185] of Yamashiro and Sagami (1163–1255).
10. Uyemon-no-suke *Sadatsugu* [114, 42] of Aoye, Bitchū (b. 1126).
11. Ichimonji *Sukezane* [63, 140] of Bizen and Sagami (1204–1316(!)).
12. Junkei *Nagamitsu* [83, 55] of Osafune, Bizen (1222–97).
13. Ichimonji *Nobufusa* [99, 93] of Fukuoka, Bizen (fl. c. 1200).
14. Miike Tenta *Motozane* [15, 140] (or *Mitsuyo* [55, 38]) of Chikugo (late eleventh century).
15. Sanjō *Yoshiiye* [51, 138] of Kyōto (953–1023).
16. Tōsaburō *Yukimitsu* [43, 55] of Kamakura, Sagami (1199–1280).
17. *Kanehira* [39, 32] of Bizen (923–1000).
18. *Tsunetsugu* [102, 42] of Aoye, Bitchū (b. 1135).
19. Awataguchi *Kuniyasu* [154, 50] of Yamashiro (fl. c. 1200).
20. Kishindayu *Yukihira* [43, 32] of Bungo (1145–1222).
21. *Mitsutada* [55, 92] of Osafune, Bizen (1194–1271).
22. Ichimonji *Sukemune* [63, 87] of Fukuoka, Bizen (fl. c. 1200).
23. Awataguchi *Kunitomo* [154, 23] of Yamashiro (1146–1214).
24. *Sadamune* [114, 87] of Takagi, Ōmi, and Kamakura, Sagami (1298–1349).
25. Rai Magotarō *Kunitoshi* [154, 101] of Kyōto (1240–1344).
26. Rai *Kunitsugu* [154, 42] of Kyōto (1247–1325).
27. Ōhara *Sanemori* [140, 49] of Hōki (fl. c. 930).

28. Ōshū Tarō *Masatsune* [31, 102] of Bizen (962–1023).
29. Shintōgo *Kunimitsu* [154, 55] of Kamakura, Sagami (1250–1312).
30. Gofuku-Gō Sayeki *Norishige* [106, 110] of Etchū (1290–1366).

B. SHINTŌ PERIOD (15 SWORDSMITHS)

1. Horikawa *Kunihiro* [154, 198] of Hyūga and Kyōto (1531–1614).
2. Hashimoto *Tadayoshi* [92, 51] of Saga, Hizen (1572–1632).
3. Tsuta *Sukehiro* [63, 198] of Ōsaka (1635–82).
4. Inouye *Shinkai* [140, 59] (*Kunisada II* [154, 114]) of Ōsaka (d. 1682).
5. Nagasone *Kotetsu Okisato* [94, 190, 202, 64] of Yedo (1599–1678).
6. Umetada *Myōju Shigeyoshi* [80, 187, 110, 51] of Nishijin, Kyōto (1558–1634).
7. Tsuta *Sukenao* [63, 91] of Ōsaka (b. 1639).
8. Ikkanshi Awataguchi *Tadatsuna* [92, 185] of Ōsaka (late seventeenth–early eighteenth century).
9. Noda Zenshirō *Hankei* [204, 197] of Yedo (d. 1646).
10. Mondo no Shō *Masakiyo* [31, 144] of Satsuma (1670–1730).
11. Ōtsuki Daiyogo *Kunishige* [154, 110] of Midzuta, Bitchū (third quarter of seventeenth century).
12. Nanki *Shigekuni* [110, 154] of Kii (early seventeenth century).
13. Nagasone *Okimasa* [202, 31] of Yedo (third quarter of seventeenth century).
14. Tamba no Kami *Yoshimichi* [51, 183] of Kyōto (early seventeenth century).
15. Shume no Kami Ippei *Yasuyo* [50, 26] of Satsuma (1680–1728).

C. SHINSHINTŌ PERIOD (10 SWORDSMITHS)

1. Kawabe Suishinshi *Masahide* [31, 65] of Dewa and Yedo (1750–1825).
2. Yamaura Tamaki *Kiyomaro* [144, 207] of Yotsuya, Yedo (1813–1854).
3. Shōji Daikei *Naotane* [91, 98] of Yedo (1779–1857).
4. Shōji Jirotarō *Naokatsu* [91, 158] of Yedo (second quarter of nineteenth century).
5. Oku Yamato no Kami *Motohira* [15, 32] of Satsuma (1743–1827).
6. Tegarayama *Masashige* [31, 204] of Mutsu (1754–1824).
7. Hōki no Kami *Masayoshi* [31, 67 *or* 89] of Satsuma (1731–1819).
8. Hosokawa *Masayoshi* [31, 179] of Yedo (mid nineteenth century).
9. Ishidō *Korekazu* [109, 1] VII of Yedo (1815–89).
10. Sa *Yukihide* [43, 65] of Chikuzen and Yedo (1816–85).

PART TWO

The Mounts

Evolution of Styles

The period of serious activity in the making of decorative sword-mounts may be reckoned roughly as the 450 years ending with the third quarter of the nineteenth century, when by the Imperial edict of 1876 the Japanese sword became (apart from the Services) a thing of the past. Some 3,000 craftsmen of note are recorded as having made sword-furniture during this period, and they may be grouped under more than sixty distinct schools, each with its individual style and technical qualities.

We may, however, begin by very briefly tracing the development of Japanese sword-mounts from the earliest times. The form and decoration of the dolmen swords have already been described, and the analogy of their guards with the modern *tsuba* is noteworthy. With Buddhism in the sixth century came the Chinese sword with its quite insignificant type of guard, which the Japanese, however, gradually enlarged and developed. The *shitogi* guard of this early period (resembling in shape the Shintō rice-cake offering of that name) is little more than a short cross-bar bearing decoration on its outer faces only. To this was added later a horizontal loop on either side, forming a type that continued in use for certain solemn court ceremonies down to the Restoration of 1868.

The rise of the military class about the ninth century and the growing disturbances of the time brought with them the development not only of the modern curved type of blade, but also of the modern discoid guard — virtually a return, however unconscious, to the dolmen type. The loops of the *shitogi*-tsuba being filled up and the body diminished, the discoid guard was at once created.

The change in military tactics following the Mongol invasions of 1274–1281 substituted fighting on foot for the cavalry charges of the late Fujiwara and Kamakura periods. The huge *nodachi*, worn at the back like a slung rifle and wielded with both hands, replaced the lighter strongly-curved blade of the horseman. The guards increased proportionately in size and strength, and the material used for them was the finest wrought iron and steel, often forged by swordsmiths and armourers like the great Myōchin family. In the fifteenth century, it would seem, a certain amount of decoration was imported into the iron guard in the form of simple piercing (*sukashi*) or else of primitive inlay (*zōgan*) of brass and copper. About the same period, too, the other mounts (*kōgai, kodzuka, menuki,* etc. — see below) came into use or for the first time received decorative treatment.

Towards 1500 the influence of Buddhist thought and idealism as propagated by the Zen sect gradually elevated the minor crafts, metal working especially, to the dignity of the higher arts, besides increasing the estima-

59

tion in which the sword itself was held. Thus an immense impetus was given to the decoration of the guards and other appurtenances of the now idealized sword. The artist was for the first time proud to sign his work, and the execution of freer designs coupled with the inlaying or incrustation of the softer metals and alloys, as well as the production of exquisite surface-patinas on iron itself, made great strides from this time onwards.

The bloody struggles between the feudal lords during the sixteenth century, culminating in the rise of Oda Nobunaga, led to a further reform in military tactics and, incidentally, to much discussion on the relative merits of round or square, pierced or unpierced guards. *Tsuba* lightened by extensive perforations, or else covered with plaited brass wire were favoured by the famous war-lord Takeda Shingen, and the former type being adopted by the Tokugawa, enjoyed a great vogue in the first part of the Yedo period.

So long as the possibility of war was before men's minds during the early years of the Tokugawa Shōgunate, swords remained practical, and their guards and other mounts were of severe and efficient type. But the continuing years of peace and the lessening prospect of civil conflict led to a general shortening of the blade, accompanied by a gradual elaboration of the guard and mounts. But the way had already been led not only by the great armourers and swordsmiths, the Myōchin and the Umetada, with their bold hammer technique and their broad but sparing inlay as applied to sword-furniture, but particularly by the famous Gotō family, workers to the Shōgunal Court and originators of fine relief-sculpture in gold on the favourite alloy, *shakudō*, with its *nanako* or 'fish-roe' surface. The influence of this family, of which as many as 300 masters are recorded in direct affiliation, was enormous, but that exerted by the Nara was almost as great. This school, taking its rise in the latter half of the seventeenth century at Yedo, broke away from the somewhat rigid traditions of the Gotō, and enlisted in its service a more extensive palette of the coloured alloys, as well as a greater freedom in the choice of subjects, these being adapted chiefly from the more naturalistic designs of the Kano painters.

Another school of far-reaching influence was the Yokoya, founded towards 1650. It pursued the Gotō style until its third master, Sōmin, introduced an entirely new technique of engraving in imitation of brush-strokes (*katakiri-bori*), applied to designs taken largely from the *Ukiyo-ye* or Popular School of drawing. The remaining families or groups of workers will be found for the most part to display either a development or a mixture of the styles above-mentioned. Special attention must be drawn, however, to the foreign influences (Chinese, Korean, Portuguese and Dutch) exerted both in technique and in design upon the workers in the *Namban* ('Southern Barbarian') and enamelling styles of Hizen province and Yedo.

To sum up, it may be said that from 1600 onwards bold relief-sculpture as an adjunct to the simple silhouette piercing or coarse brass inlay of earlier work, made great progress, but gradually yielded in popularity to the *Ye-fū* or pictorial style with its elaborate incrustation of the precious metals and coloured alloys. This became the fashion in the eighteenth century, and reached its decadence in the third quarter of the nineteenth. Even the period of decay, however, was illuminated here and there by the brilliant work of Shummei Hōgen, Hata Nobuyoshi, Gotō Ichijō, and Kanō Natsuo.

Materials and Technique

A. MATERIALS

The commonest basic material for sword-mounts, especially among the earlier examples, is iron, usually of fine quality, and having a good 'ring'. The other metals employed, commonly termed 'soft metals', include silver (*gin*), bronze (*yamagane*), brass (*shinchū*), copper (*akagane*), and the three special copper alloys, *shakudō*, *shibuichi*, and *sentoku*, which are peculiar to Japan and are described below. Guards of solid gold had a vogue in the late seventeenth–early eighteenth century, but their use was prohibited by a sumptuary edict of 1830. Non-metallic guards and other mounts in leather, ivory, wood, and even pottery, are to be found, but must be regarded as freakish and abnormal (Pl. 47).

Shakudō is an alloy of copper with a small proportion of gold; *shibuichi* is an alloy of the same with silver up to 25 per cent (the word *shi-bu-ichi* means literally 'one quarter'); *sentoku* is a variety of brass, the word representing the Japanese pronunciation of Hsüan-tê, the Chinese Emperor in whose reign (1426–36) this alloy is said to have been invented. But none of these, any more than the unalloyed copper itself, attains the beautiful coloration which gives it its peculiar charm unless it has been treated to a special pickling bath, the result of which is to give *shakudō* a lustrous raven or violet-black hue, *shibuichi* a wide range of shades from a rich deep olive-brown to a pale tint resembling oxidized silver, *sentoku* a pleasing chrome yellow colour, and copper itself a fine subdued foxy-red tone quite unlike the sharp metallic gleam of the virgin metal. Although these colours are only skin-deep, they are practically permanent, so long as they are not subjected to scratching or rubbing with abrasives, which will rapidly destroy them and reveal the ugly raw metal beneath.

Pure iron in its bright state seems to have been anathema to the Japanese, who without exception preferred it treated to produce a surface varying in colour from a russet chestnut tint to the deep violet-black (magnetic oxide) characteristic of guards by the later Kinai masters (p. 78). Some guards are made of 'grained iron' (*mokume-tetsu*), exactly corresponding to 'watered' or 'damascened' steel, with the surface etched, so as to throw the 'grain' into relief (Pl. 32).

Occasionally, especially in late work, a guard may be of different metal on the front and the back, or in the central and the outer portion. Others, again, are composite, in the styles known as *mokume* and *guri* (Pls. 34, 35). The former word, besides describing the grained iron just mentioned, is also applied to an analogous process in which sheets of the various copper alloys, as well as silver, and sometimes gold, are soldered together into a single sheet, which is then folded, crumpled, or dented, in a manner reminiscent of geological strata. The resulting uneven surface, on being cut or filed smooth and treated with the necessary 'pickling', presents a section which may be compared to the grain of wood (which is what the word *mokume* means) or to marbled paper. Sometimes this *mokume* is only used as a veneer on a solid copper core, but some pieces are of *mokume* all through. In *guri* (a technique borrowed from lacquer-work) the super-imposed sheets of metals and alloys are kept flat, and the treatment consists merely in cutting bold scrollwork patterns in deep V-shaped grooves, the slopes of which, after pickling, reveal the alternation of patina-colours.

B. METHODS OF DECORATION

1. SURFACES

As often as not, the surface of Japanese sword-fittings is more or less smooth and polished, but the more recent examples (especially those in iron) may be given a minutely granulated gloss by means of etching. Many, however, are varied by punching in different styles. The general term *ishime* ('stone-grain') is applied to surfaces finished with a regular punched pattern, ranging from the minutest stippling with a round-headed tool to the bolder varieties of punching with star-shaped or other devices, in-cluding what is aptly described as 'broken-headed' punch (Pl. 36). But the most characteristically Japanese treatment of a ground — ordinarily found on *shakudō*, but also on other soft metals, and occasionally even on iron — is a close assemblage of tiny granules known as *nanako* ('fish-roe', Pl. 37). In this each single grain is formed by a blow from a cup-headed punch, guided solely by hand and eye, and producing in the best work a ground of absolutely regular rows, straight or curved, of perfect hemispheres, uniform in size and free from any intervening burring of the metal. *Nanako* seems to have been introduced, at first no doubt in a less skilful and finished form, by the Gotō family of masters as early as the fifteenth or sixteenth century, but it was employed in later times by masters of many other schools. Often it was executed by specialists working in collaboration with the artists who produced the other decoration.

2. PIERCING AND OPENWORK

These terms cover a very wide range of treatment, from one or more perforations of simple geometric or conventional form in the solid guard to a complex design of which the details are represented completely in the round, of course with the solid *seppadai* (p. 66) in the middle, and as a rule a narrow continuous border confining the whole. Between these extremes come piercings depicting natural or artificial objects, at first in what is termed 'negative silhouette' (Pl. 39), then in 'positive silhouette' (Pl. 64), that is, like a piece of fret-work with the edges left square. This fret-piercing may be diversified by a few engraved lines to represent texture, plumage, foliage, and the like. Next we may proceed by almost imperceptible stages, beginning with the gentle rounding-off of the edge of the silhouette, to an increasing degree of modelling, until the complete *marubori* ('round carving') is attained (Pl. 38). Special mention must be made of the incredibly fine saw-piercing (*ito-zukashi*) found in some guards of the Itō school; the lines so produced are often little more than a hundredth of an inch wide (Pl. 39).

3. RELIEF-MODELLING AND ETCHING

Carving or modelling on a solid guard may vary from the boldest relief (*takabori*, 'high carving', Pl. 40) down to what is known as *nikuai-bori* or *shishiai-bori* (literally, 'complexion carving'), in which the flat relief is actually sunk below the general level of the surface (Pl. 41).

Ordinarily the chisel (*tagane*) and file (*yasuri*) are employed for relief modelling, whether on iron or a soft metal. But the process of etching with acids is also used; artists of the Jakushi school (p. 79) regularly produced their low reliefs in this manner.

4. INLAY, OVERLAY, AND INCRUSTATION

True inlay (*hon-zōgan*, Pl. 42) consists of the cutting away in the ground metal of a shallow depression of the shape required, into which the metal to be inlaid is hammered; it is often secured in place by the undercutting of the edges of the depression into which it fits, or else it may be soldered or brazed. The resulting surface is flat. Sometimes, however, the inlay may be raised (*taka-zōgan*), which has been called 'incrustation' (Pl. 40). The same effect can be produced by building up the relief with base metal, which is then plated with the surface metal required. In both inlay and incrustation, when a number of different metals and alloys are used, the Japanese term is *iroye* ('coloured picture'). Overlay (*nunome*), which is almost entirely confined to iron mounts, is produced by scoring or cross-hatching the surface so that the softer metal will adhere to it when hammered on in the required design (Pl. 43). The word 'damascening' has sometimes been used for this process. The best examples of inlay will be found among the work of the Kaga schools (p. 79), and of overlay in the Hirata school of Awa (p. 79); incrustation of various kinds is characteristic of many schools, especially, perhaps, the Nara and its derivatives (pp. 79, 80).

Three freak varieties of incrustation, found on comparatively early sword-guards, may be mentioned here: *gomoku-zōgan* ('rubbish incrustation'), whereby the iron guard is largely covered with short lengths or snippets of fine wire (brass, copper, or rarely silver) spread in irregular groups and brazed or soldered in place, the whole being finally polished flat. The resulting designs recall the debris of twigs and pine-needles seen floating on mountain pools. The other variety is called *mukade-zōgan* ('centipede incrustation'), in which a wire (usually iron) following the outline of the guard is held down by numerous little staples of iron or brass wire having their ends let into the iron ground. The propriety of the name is obvious from any example (Pl. 44). The third variety for which, oddly enough, the Japanese do not seem to have invented a technical term, may be described as 'nail-head incrustation'. It is a coarse sort of piqué work, with rows of brass nails or pins hammered into the iron ground, and it may be accompanied by piercings outlined with *hotsuri-zōgan* or incrusted brass wires (Pl. 45). In the seventeenth and eighteenth centuries two further analogous technical processes are worth noting. Certain iron guards exhibit an inlay of *shirome* or *sawari* (hard whitish alloys of copper, darkening with age) fused into hollows in the ground cut to receive it, the whole being polished smooth. The analogy with champlevé enamel is complete. Such work is usually signed *Kunitomo Sadahide* [114, 188], and seems to have been made at Kameyama in the province of Ise. Secondly, *gama-hada* ('toad-skin') is a term applied to iron guards and other mounts which, having been incrusted with small pieces of silver, have then been subjected to a heat sufficient to fuse the silver into globules without allowing it to run away (Pl. 46).

5. ENGRAVING AND CHASING

The difference between these two terms is that in the former metal is removed from the surface engraved, whereas in chasing it is not. Chasing is characterized by the edges of the chased line being slightly raised, as the metal has been displaced by the chisel; it is only found on iron, and usually confined to the work of armourers and swordsmiths. Most of the engraving found on Japanese sword-fittings is of the kind known as *katakiri* ('cutting to one side') in imitation of brush-work; this technique was introduced by Yokoya Sōmin (d. 1733). It will be noticed that, unlike the lines of the ordinary engraving (*kebori*), the V-shaped groove of *katakiri* has one of its sides upright, the other greatly sloping and varying in width according to the depth of the groove (Pl. 79).

Mounting of Katana and Wakizashi

Plates 26–31 give a general idea of the positions, forms, and some of the variations of the fittings found on Japanese blades. In greater detail, starting from the blade end, they are as follows:

A. THE HABAKI

The *Habaki*, or blade-socket, although artistically among the least important of the fittings of a sword, is mechanically indispensable, and is

C. THE FAMOUS SWORDSMAN AND PAINTER
MIYAMOTO MUSASHI (1584–1645) PRACTISING
HIS 'TWO-HANDED VICTORY' STYLE OF
FENCING USING TWO STICKS

Colour-print by KUNIYOSHI, *c.*1848, from the 'Fidelity in Revenge'
series. *Author's Collection.*

found on all Japanese swords, daggers and spears. It is in effect a stout metal collar, its interior fitting accurately over the last quarter-inch of the blade and the first three-quarters of an inch of the tang (these are rough measurements for a weapon of medium size). It has several functions. In the first place, it enables the sword to be tightened in the scabbard, whose cavity is large enough to prevent any undue rubbing of the blade and of the *yakiba* in particular. Furthermore, it serves in a measure to protect the blade from rust at this dangerous point; the portion of the blade under the *habaki* should always be kept slightly oiled. But the most important function it exercises is that of transmitting the stress of a blow through the guard to the hilt itself, instead of directly on to the comparatively weak retaining-peg of bamboo or horn.

The *habaki* is usually made of copper, silvered or gilt, or else loosely overlaid with gold, silver, or *shakudō* foil. The surface is either plainly polished or engraved with oblique burred striations known as *neko-gaki* ('cat scratches'). If the thin foil covering is present, it may be worked into these *neko-gaki*, or else independently decorated with a stamped or repoussé design. *Habaki* of iron, or the precious metals, or even of ivory or wood, are occasionally encountered, but only on swords not mounted for serious use. Where the blade is thinner than average, and so requires a *habaki* of extra stoutness, it may be provided with a *nijū-habaki*, or double *habaki*. This is merely a *habaki* of regular proportions reinforced with a separate but accurately-fitting piece which provides two cheeks to strengthen the lower half (that next to the guard). The *habaki* often provides a guide to the quality of the blade. *Nijū-habaki* and those decorated with a family *mon* in particular are usually associated with fine blades.

B. THE WASHERS

The *Seppa*, or washers, are a pair of oval metal plates encircling the tang on either side of the guard. Almost invariably of copper, plain, gilt, silvered, or loosely overlaid with gold or silver foil, on their outer surfaces they may be plainly polished or covered with light striations; their edges are usually milled or crenellated. Some swords are provided with two or three pairs, and *tachi*, in addition to these ordinary *seppa*, are often fitted with a much larger pair, called *ō-seppa* ('great washers'). These cover the major portion of the guard, and are decorated with engraving, a slender Maltese cross often forming the basis of the design. The use of *seppa* is said to date from the twelfth century. Their function is to protect the *fuchi* (see below) and guard from injury, and to provide a finished appearance.

C. THE GUARD

The *Tsuba*, or guard, the most important of the fittings, is generally in the form of a flat disc; cupped guards are found, but they are not common. Its outline is usually regular and always compact, and in the centre is a wedge-shaped opening to admit the tang. Such of the surrounding field as would be covered by the *seppa* is known as the *seppadai* ('washer-stand'); it is normally quite plain but for the signature, and is as often as not well defined as a regular oval by being slightly raised. On either side of it there may be holes (*ryō-hitsu*) for the *kodzuka* and *kōgai* (see below); where the latter are not present, the *ryō-hitsu* are generally plugged with metal. Iron guards are sometimes pierced in addition with two small round holes of unequal size known as *udenuki-ana* ('sword-knot holes'), through which the sword-knot was formerly passed. These holes may thus indicate an early guard (Pl. 33*b*).

Guards are almost always of metal, though in parade swords they may be of lacquered leather, leather over wood, or pâpier-maché. Iron, steel (especially *namban-tetsu*, or foreign steel), copper of various reddish patinas, and the patinated copper-alloys such as *sentoku* (yellowish), *shakudō* (violet-black), *shibuichi* (silver-grey), *nigurome* (brownish-black), and occasionally bronze of dark green tone (*karakane*) and brass (*shinchū*) pure and simple — such are the usual metals employed for guards, or rather for the base on which the decoration is placed. To these must, however, be added gold and silver, as well as the peculiar juxtaposition of two or more different coloured alloys found in *guri* and *mokume* work (p. 62). Guards and other sword-furniture in solid gold were a feature of the luxurious age of the third Tokugawa Shōgun, Iyemitsu (1623–51), and continued to be used by the *daimyō* (and by the richer *heimin* from about the period Genroku, 1688–1704) until an edict against such extravagance was promulgated in 1830. The edict was frequently evaded by coating the gold with black lacquer. Certain guards are bordered by loose rims of silver, *shakudō*, or other soft metal, and it is not unusual in comparatively recent examples to find the front and back of a guard made of different metals or alloys.

Flat guards are almost invariably decorated on both sides, though the edge is often left plain; cupped guards show decoration on the convex surface only, as a rule. A pictorial design is set so as to be properly viewed when the narrow end of the tang-hole is uppermost, that being its natural position when the sword is thrust through the girdle. If the design on both faces of the guard is not identical, the more important part of it will be on the side next to the hilt and on the right rather than on the left of this, in logical furtherance of the same idea.

If present, the signature is almost always placed on the *seppadai*, on the side next to the hilt (*omote*), overflowing if necessary on to the other side (*ura*). Guards are rarely signed on the exposed part, and then usually on the *ura* side. It is not until the sixteenth century that we find guard-makers placing their signatures on their work.

D. THE HILT

The *Tsuka*, or hilt, of the Japanese sword was always of wood, preferably of the *hō-no-ki* (*Magnolia hypoleuca*), made in two halves glued together.

The bare wood was normally covered with a single piece of white *same*, the noduled skin of a ray-fish (*Rhinobatus armatus*) similar to that used for shagreen in other countries. The seam of this was always placed down the centre of the *ura* side, and the piece was generally chosen so that a central row of three or four larger nodules appeared at the top of the *omote* side.

Over this came the wrapping (*tsuka-ito*, 'hilt-thread') formed of a single length of strong flat silk braid (*uchi-himo*) up to a quarter of an inch in breadth. This was commonly black, but quiet browns, dark blues and greens were sometimes favoured; white wrapping was sometimes used for *katana* by *daimyō* and was a feature of certain types of *tachi*, and leather, cord, and whale-bone are occasionally found. The centre of the wrapping being placed flush with the *omote* side of the *fuchi*, the two ends were wound about the hilt to right and left respectively, being given double twists at regular intervals. The result was that the *same* was completely covered except for a row of lozenge-shaped spaces on either face of the hilt. After passing through the sides of the *kashira* or pommel-cap, the braid was fastened off on either side of the hilt by a neat flat knot. A little below the centre of the hilt on the *omote* side and a little above it on the *ura* side the wrapping partly covered and fastened in place the two *menuki* (see below).

There were many exceptions to this normal method of hilt-wrapping, but they need not be enumerated here. It is, however, perhaps worth mentioning that in the girdle-worn swords carried by *daimyō* wearing the formal dress called *kamishimo* at the Shōgun's court during the Yedo period, the black silk wrapping was crossed over, instead of passing through, the *kashira*, which in this case was of plain black horn; this style is known as *maki-kake no kashira*.

In certain court swords, as in some of the shorter swords and daggers for ordinary wear, the ray-skin hilt was left unwrapped. The *kashira* and the two *menuki* had then to be kept in place by glue, concealed pins, decorative studs, or other suitable means. *Hanashi-menuki* ('free *menuki*') is the term for this style. There are also many other forms of unwrapped hilt, mostly used on dirks and daggers, in which the grip may be covered with polished or carved wood, lacquer, rattan, or metal (Pl. 77*a*).

In shape the hilt is of narrow elliptical section, and generally tapers very slightly from both ends to the middle. In the unwrapped hilts of daggers the *omote* side may be suddenly bevelled off within an inch of the *kashira*; in the case of daggers carried in the bosom of the robe (*kwaiken*) this peculiarity would tell the wearer at once by sense of touch on which side was the edge of the blade (Pls. 27*a*, 77*a*).

E. THE MENUKI

The *Menuki* are a pair of small ornaments in decorated metal placed on either side of the hilt as described above. They are probably vestigial survivals of the decorated ends of the retaining-pegs of ancient swords. They serve to strengthen the grip as well as to adorn the sword. With the *kōgai* and *kodzuka* (p. 69) they may form a uniform set called *mitokoro-mono* ('three places things'). This uniformity may extend to a *soroi-mono* ('uniform thing') or complete set of the metal fittings for a sword, or pair of swords (then called *daishō-soroimono*). A *mitokoro-mono* or a *soroimono* by a well-known metalworker — one of the Gotō for preference — formed a favourite gift on ceremonial occasions among *daimyō* and other high personages.

F. The Fuchi-kashira

The *Fuchi* (collar) and *Kashira* (pommel-cap) have already been referred to; their mechanical function was to strengthen the hilt at each end. The term *kashira*, literally 'head', is a contraction from an original form *tsuka-gashira*, 'hilt-head'; *fuchi* is a general term for a border. The two objects together are commonly called *fuchi-kashira*.

The ordinary *fuchi* consists of a flat band of metal up to half an inch wide that encircles the hilt at the guard end, and is easily removable. Its base is filled with an oval plaque, usually of copper, pierced with a hole to take the tang, which is called *tenjō-gane* ('ceiling-metal').

The *kashira* ordinarily comprises a similar band with a flat or gently rounded top, but *kashira* of completely rounded form are quite common. The whole of the *kashira* and the band of the *fuchi* are normally decorated, often *en suite* and sharing a subject between them. On the latter a pictorial design will almost invariably be arranged so as to be seen properly when the sword is held point downwards, the chief portion of the design being placed on the *omote* side. On the *kashira* the design is properly seen 'end-on' with the blade-edge uppermost.

At each side of the *kashira* is an oval slot (*shitodome-ana*) provided with a removable eyelet (*shitodo-me*, 'bunting's eye') of gilt copper, just large enough to take the hilt braid; the *kashira* is otherwise quite loose on a wrapped hilt. On an unwrapped hilt, however, it is usually fastened not merely by glue, but by two pins with foliated heads large enough to conceal the *shitodome-ana* (from which the eyelets have been removed).

Fuchi are signed on the *omote* side of the outer face of the *tenjō-gane*, or occasionally on their exposed surface; the signature on a *kashira*, in the rare cases when it occurs, is placed on a small metal plaque soldered to its inner surface, or on the outer surface; the same is true of *menuki*.

G. The Mekugi

The *Mekugi* ('eye-nail') or retaining-peg, which, passing through hilt and tang, prevents the blade from dropping out and so binds all the loose parts together, is commonly of bamboo, but dark horn is not unusual; ivory is rare. In a wrapped hilt the slightly tapered *mekugi* enters on the *ura* side in the centre of one of the uncovered lozenges of *same*, so that on the *omote* side its narrower end is hidden beneath the wrapping; but this rule has its exceptions. In the unwrapped hilts of daggers the *mekugi* may pass through metal or ivory eyelets, or through a metal band (*dō-gane*, 'body-metal') encircling the hilt.

The metal *mekugi* is a striking feature of most unwrapped hilts, and comprises a stout copper tube or sleeve with decorative head, often of silver, into which slides or screws from the other side a copper peg with similar head. The screw is often left-handed, and the greatest care must be exercised in dismounting weapons of this type.

H. THE KODZUKA, KŌGAI, ETC.

The *Kodzuka, Kōgai,* and *Umabari* are various implements of knife or skewer form, carried in slots in the sides of the scabbards of certain swords, their hilts being exposed and just rising above the upper surface of the guard, which is pierced to accommodate them, as already explained. Although a *kodzuka* or a *kōgai,* or even both, may very occasionally be found on a sword mounted as a *katana,* they were essentially the proper accompaniments of the smaller weapon; even on these it is not unusual to find only the one or the other (more frequently the *kodzuka*). The *umabari* is only found on weapons mounted in the unconventional style peculiar to the province of Higo, generally replacing the *kodzuka.* None of the three is ever found on swords of *tachi* or *handachi* type.

The word *kodzuka* means, literally, 'little hilt', and there has been some difference of opinion on whether the term should be used for the complete knife, or only for its hilt. The latter use seems to be supported by the etymology of the word, and will be followed here. The whole knife may be called *kogatana,* a term applicable to any small knife. Its place is always on the *ura* side of the scabbard, and its most familiar form, which dates from the sixteenth century, is a thin flat pointed blade thrust into a flat oblong handle. The latter — the *kodzuka* proper — measures up to four inches long by a little over half an inch wide.

This classical type of *kodzuka* is said to have been originated by Tokujō [191, 132] (1549–1631), the fifth master of the Gotō line of sword-furniture makers. The genuineness of the attribution of certain *kodzuka* to masters of an earlier date extends only to the ornaments thereon, which were originally made for other purposes (generally for *kōgai* or *menuki*) and were applied to the *kodzuka* by later craftsmen. Other authorities, however, have maintained that the *kodzuka* dates back to the reign of the Emperor Go-Daigo (early fourteenth century).

At least ninety per cent of *kodzuka* are of the normal plain oblong shape. The commonest variation from it is the rounding off of the butt, but the whole outline may be shaped to some fanciful object, always, however, within the limits of the prescribed oblong. A dried fish (*himono*) or a bridge-post (*obashira*), fashioned more or less in the round, are two of the unconventional forms to which the *kodzuka* may be reduced (Pl. 75*c*).

In material, mode of decoration, and design, the *kodzuku* should correspond with the *kōgai,* and sometimes with the other fittings of the sword.

Besides the usual metals and alloys, wood, polished, carved, or lacquered, is found, as well as ivory and kindred materials. Raised decoration is necessarily confined to the outer face, and is often set within a narrow raised border, the design being worked on a separate plaque (*ji-ita*). The back may be composed of two or even three different alloys joined or spliced together. According to the *Sōken Kishō* (1781), etiquette at one time ruled that on formal occasions the ground (*ji-ita*) of the *kodzuka* and *kōgai*-hilt should be of *shakudō* punched with the fine and regular granulated pattern known as *nanako-ji* ('fish-roe ground'). *Ishime* (diapered grounds) and *ji-migaki* (smooth polished grounds) were used on ordinary occasions.

It is the rule for the design to be placed with its top either at the side corresponding to the edge of the blade (horizontal position), or towards the blade end (vertical position); all early *kodzuka* are of horizontal type, and the vertical type does not seem to have come into use until the mid-eighteenth century, when it was introduced by the Yokoya school. The back is susceptible of flat decoration only, such as inlay or engraving in continuation of, or allusion to, the main design on the front. But commonly it is either plain or covered with striations of the 'cat-scratch' (*neko-gaki*) type. The signature is usually placed on the back near the butt, but it occasionally appears on the butt itself, or on the back edge near the butt.

The blade is set quite freely in the *kodzuka*, being generally held in place by paper wrappings. Many *kodzuka*-blades were the work of swordsmiths of repute, but more often the 'signatures' they bear are no more than decorative. Sometimes they are engraved with the Six Poets and their poems, the 'ascending dragon' (*ama-kurikara*), or with a charm against thunder; this last is, however, most often found on the blades of *umabari*. A number of far-fetched theories on the actual use of the *kodzuka*-knife have been advanced by both Japanese and European writers, but the most likely purpose it served is that of an ordinary pocket-knife.

The *kōgai* is kept on the *omote* side of the scabbard. Its form may be shortly described as a repetition of the *kodzuka*, merging at the blade end into a flat skewer, and having the butt finished with a small forward-curving knob, sometimes fancifully explained as an ear-pick. Materials and decoration are exactly the same. A well-marked variety is the *wari-kōgai*, 'split *kōgai*', which is divided down the middle into two pieces, suggesting a possible use as chop-sticks.

Even more fantastic explanations of the use of the *kōgai* have been put forward than in the case of the *kodzuka*-knife, but it seems clear that in its more modern form it is a survival of a sort of hair-pin for arranging the hair under the helmet and for smoothing and parting it after the removal of the helmet. This explanation has the authority of the *Sōken Kishō*, and is supported by the supposed derivation of the word itself from *kami-kaki*, 'hair-parter'. Authorities are generally agreed that the *kōgai* is of greater antiquity than the *kodzuka*.

The *umabari* ('horse-needle') is a weapon found on swords and daggers mounted by artists of Higo province, and served as a lancet for bleeding horses. Formed of a single piece of steel, it has a two-edged straight blade and an oblong handle something like the classical *kodzuka*. Less conventional sizes and shapes are also found (Pl. 58c).

I. THE SCABBARD

The Scabbard (*Saya*), like the hilt, is made in two halves, usually of *hō-no-ki* wood. Its section is almost always an elongated oval of the same shape and size as the *seppa* (washer) next to it, and this normally remains the same throughout its length. Fine blades not intended for immediate wear were kept in 'preservation scabbards' of plain white wood with guardless hilt to match, a style known as *shira-zaya* ('white scabbard'). The scabbard used for wear, however, is in most cases covered with a very hard lacquer. For the *daishō* or pair of swords worn by the *samurai*, this lacquer is usually of a quiet colour, generally black, and any further decoration is kept at the same subdued level. Bold colours were favoured by swashbucklers, and a strong vermilion, imported from China, was affected on swords worn by the *samurai* of Satsuma and Hyūga, men of notoriously high spirit.

The general surface over which the lacquer is laid may be either wholly plain or varied by wide or narrow flutings running diagonally or transversely. The lacquered ground itself may be either grained or highly polished, of a uniform colour or varied by the *nashiji*, *aogai*, *Wakasa*, *guri-bori*, or other styles, or even decorated in alternate bands of two different colours. Ray-skin lacquer (*same-nuri*) is not unusual (Pls. 28a, 29e). These grounds may further receive any sober form of decoration, but for the *daishō* Japanese taste frowned on elaborate *maki-ye*, or free designs. With daggers, however, the craftsman's fancy is allowed free play, and incrustations of metal ornaments (*kanamono*) are frequent (Pl. 27).

Disregarding the *tachi* type of sword, whose mounts will be described later, the following six points of the scabbard may call for special decorative fittings:

1. The band surrounding the mouth (*koi-guchi*, 'carp's mouth', or *kuchigane* if in metal).

2. The *uragawara*, or strengthening bar set across the base of the *kodzuka*-slot.

3. The lining of the slots for *kodzuka* and *kōgai*.

4. The *kurikata* ('chestnut-shape'), a slotted projection set about a sixth of the scabbard's length below the mouth on the *omote* side, through which passes the *sageo*, or tying-cord.

5. The *sori-tsuno* ('returning-horn') or *origane*, a small hooked projection further down on the same side; directed towards the hilt, it serves to prevent the scabbard from slipping forwards out of the girdle. It is of very infrequent occurrence, and is usually confined to *wakizashi*, but its presence is often the sign of a good blade.

6. The *kojiri*, or chape, covering the butt. This is often omitted,

especially in *wakizashi*, the butt being merely rounded off and lacquered continuously with the rest of the scabbard. In shape, material, and decoration it very often corresponds to the *kashira*.

Excluding no. 3 (which is usually either polished black lacquer, polished natural horn, or soft buff leather) all these fittings are commonly of metal, more or less decorated and *en suite*; but in the quieter mountings they may be in polished black horn of the simplest form and smallest size compatible with their purpose.

Scabbards not lacquered, but merely polished or carved, sometimes *en suite* with the hilt, and decorated with ivory or pearl-shell inlay, are said to have been affected by those who, being below the rank of *samurai*, carried only a single short sword. Such men were priests, physicians, yeomen (*gōshi*), and headmen of villages. Many other fanciful methods of decorating both hilt and scabbard are also found, especially in the shorter weapons, such as a complete overlay of sheet metal variously decorated, of leather in various colours and grainings, or of brocade sunk beneath a transparent lacquer.

The *Sage-o* ('suspension-string') is a length of flat silk braid passed through the *kurikata* (see above) and twisted about the girdle. It varied in length from two to five feet according to the size of the weapon, and could be removed when a fight was impending and used as a *tasuki* to tie back the long sleeves of the civil costume and allow the arms free play; it could also be used to bind a prisoner or vanquished foeman. When a sword is placed on its rack, the *sageo* should be wound neatly round the scabbard at the *kurikata*. The colouring of the *sageo* corresponds to that of the scabbard to which it is attached; if the latter is in good Japanese taste, quiet and sober, the *sageo* will be similar, but gaudy and variegated braid is often found on a flashily mounted weapon. The sword-rack should, if possible, contrast in colour and decoration with the sword placed upon it.

Mounting of Tachi

(Plates 30, 31)

The furniture of a sword mounted as a *tachi* differs in many details from that of all other swords. It has a different nomenclature, is more formal and conventional in its shapes, and of generally richer appearance. The *mon*, or heraldic badge of the wearer, enters very largely into its decoration, in sharp contrast to the ordinary girdle-worn swords.

The guard and *seppa* have already been alluded to; the *habaki*, *fuchi*, and *kuchigane* are identical with the types described above. But the *kashira* and *kojiri* are here replaced respectively by the *kabuto-gane* ('helmet-metal') and the *ishi-dzuki* ('stone attachment'). These are of identical shape and size, being an inch or more in depth, of crested double-ogee outline above, and pierced with a large shaped opening on each face, through which shows the surface of the hilt or scabbard as the case may be. These openings are defined below by a narrow band (which may or may not be of one piece with the rest of the mount), and from those of the *kabuto-gane* issue two short arms of metal, uniting on the edge side, and forming a small loop called *musubi-gane* ('knot-metal') or *saru-te* ('monkey's arms'). These names describe its use and appearance respectively, for it was designed to hold a sword-knot composed of a short leather double cord with metal tassels, and only a moderately vivid imagination is required to picture it as the arms of a tiny monkey, with the hands clasped, issuing from the sides of the pommel.

Sometimes the sides of the *ishi-dzuki* are produced up both edges of the scabbard but for unequal distances, fastened at intervals by metal bands called *seme* ('clasps'). If the chape is short, however, there is simply one ornamental ring, placed about a quarter of the way up the scabbard, and known as *shiba-biki*. Between this and the mouth of the scabbard are set the two sling-bands (*ashi*, literally 'feet') of pear-shaped outline, each having an ornamental projection with oblong slot for the two short strap-loops (of soft deer-skin or gold brocade) called *obitori* ('belt-taking'), and to these was knotted the long narrow belt of soft deer-skin or stiff gold brocade which passed round the waist, fastened by a knot or, more rarely, a metal buckle. In some *tachi* worn with armour the *obitori* are replaced by chains.

On the hilt are the *tsuka-ai* ('hilt-pair') corresponding to the *menuki*, and usually designed as an arrangement of three repetitions of the owner's badge, in gilt metal or gold. The scabbard-implements are never found on *tachi*.

The characteristic style of decoration for the metal mounts of a *tachi* and its scabbard is a *nanako* ground of perfect regularity, broken up into regular panels by plain square borders and bands.

Generally speaking, the *tachi* was worn with court dress by the Imperial family, the court nobility (*kuge*), and *daimyō* or provincial nobility visiting the court. It was also worn with armour by the higher ranks, either as a parade sword or for serious use. In historical times we find the Emperor and *kuge*, the Shōgun, and the higher *daimyō* wearing the richly-mounted *shōzoku-tachi* ('court uniform sword') called also *shin no tachi* ('real *tachi*'). With a straight or slightly curved blade it has a long *same*-covered hilt set with semi-precious stones; the guard is of the *shitogi* form with the loops at each side; the metal mounts generally are of gilt metal or even gold. The *kuge* of lower rank, however, and the majority of the *daimyō* visiting court wore the *kuge-tachi* or *yefu no tachi* ('palace-guard's sword'), generally similar to the above, but without the precious stones, in place of which the hilt was adorned with a number of gilt nail-heads formed as rice-bales (*tawara*), and hence called *tawara-byō* (Pl. 30).

A very strict etiquette ruled the furniture of the court sword for various grades of rank and for different occasions. More than eleven varieties were distinguished by the form and decoration of the guard, the colour and ornamentation of the lacquer on the scabbard, the number and position of the *mon*, and the style of the hilt- and scabbard-mounts.

With armour or on horseback the *itomaki* (thread-wrapped) *no tachi* was worn. This was later known as *saya-maki* (scabbard-wrapped) *no tachi* and, as the name implies, had not only the hilt wrapped with silk braid in the usual manner, but also the upper part of the scabbard to a point just below the sling-bands. This wrapping was usually white, over a ground of purple and gold brocade, and covered the part of the scabbard normally grasped by the left hand when drawing the sword. This type of *tachi*, when not in use, was set vertically, hilt downwards, in a special stand of lacquered wood (Pl. 31); the other types were placed horizontally, edge downwards, on the ordinary sword-rack (*katana-kake*). A sub-species of the *itomaki no tachi* is often shown in representations of great military commanders. This is the *shirizaya no tachi* (literally 'buttock-scabbard sword'), with the entire scabbard below the wrapping covered with the fur of a tiger or boar, spreading out towards the butt.

It is not uncommon to find a sword of the *katana* or *wakizashi* type fitted with hilt- and scabbard-mounts of characteristic *tachi* form, though with the suspension-bands replaced by a *kurikata*. This style of mounting is called *han-dachi* ('half-*tachi*'), and might be used not only for civilian wear, but by a foot-soldier in armour. The guard should always be of *aoi-gata*, or hollyhock-leaf form (e.g. Pls. 46a, 92d).

Mounting of Daggers

(Plate 27)

These are often indistinguishable, so far as their mounts are concerned, from the small *wakizashi*; when differences occur, they centre on the guard. If there is a guard at all, it is generally of the very small type known as *hamidashi-tsuba*, with the *ryō-hitsu* for the accommodation of *kodzuka* and *kōgai* actually cutting into its outline (Pls. 36b, 42e). But a large number of dirks have no guard at all (and therefore no *seppa*) and are called *aikuchi* ('flush-mouth'), the *fuchi* fitting directly against, into, or over the metal-mounted mouth of the scabbard. In this type the *kurikata* is sometimes replaced by a loose ring (Pl. 27b).

Very small daggers, generally less than ten inches in length, often have no metal mounts whatever, being carried in the bosom for secret defence. They are called *kwaiken*, and were especially the weapon carried by the wives and daughters of *samurai*, and might be used in the last resort for *jigai*, or suicide by severing the neck-arteries, the woman's substitute for *seppuku* (vulgarly known as *hara-kiri*). For the ceremonial performance of *seppuku* the dirk was of the prescribed length of 9 *sun* and 5 *bu* (11·3 inches); the blade was of the straight-backed, flat-sided type, and was mounted for the occasion in a plain white wood hilt and scabbard.

The Chief Schools of Sword-Furniture Makers

A. Sixteenth Century onwards

Gotō School (Pls. 4b, 48, 49, 96, 97)

The first Gotō master, Yūjō [128, 132] (1435–1512), worked for the Ashikaga Shōgun Yoshimasa, and established the classical Gotō style — the only correct one for court ceremonial wear right down to 1868. It consists of a ground of *shakudō nanako* with raised designs in gold or gilt. Later Gotō artists deviated considerably from the classical style, notably Seijō [144, 132] (1606–88) and Ichijō [1, 132] (1791–1876), who founded schools of their own. A branch of the family settled in Mino province did work similar to the classical style, but using larger and bolder designs. The Yoshioka School (Inaba no Suke) also worked in a style very close to the classical Gotō from the early seventeenth century.

Myōchin School (Pl. 50)

The Myōchin [80, 245] were the leading family of armourers in Japan, and traced their ancestry to the twelfth century, and even beyond. But the first Myōchin to make sword-furniture was probably Nobuiye [99, 138], the seventeenth hereditary master (d. 1564). Myōchin work is, naturally, always in iron of the finest quality and forging, with designs of great power and dignity. The family continued producing guards into the nineteenth century; other fittings of Myōchin workmanship are rare.

Kaneiye School (Pl. 51)

The founder of this school, Aoki Kaneiye [215, 138], worked at Fushimi, a suburb of Kyōto, about the middle of the century: but much work signed *Kaneiye of Fushimi* was done in the seventeenth and eighteenth centuries. The earlier examples are guards of thin iron, usually worked with Chinese landscapes in low relief, with occasional touches of gold or copper-gilt. Later Kaneiye guards tend to be thicker.

Umetada School (Pl. 52)

The Umetada were a family of swordsmiths, and the twenty-fifth hereditary master, Myōju [80, 187] (1558–1632) was the first to make sword-fittings. His descendants continued working down to the nineteenth century. The Umetada style, centred at Kyōto, shows a skilful combination of chiselling and incrustation, all the usual metals and alloys being used.

THE CHIEF SCHOOLS OF SWORD-FURNITURE MAKERS

Other Sword-Furniture of the Period (Pls. 32, 33, 53, 54, 55)

Iron guards were produced by a number of independent workers including swordsmiths and armourers. Examples of primitive type are found with the signatures Tembō [17, 77], Yamakichi [13, 51], and Sadahiro [114, 198]; of unsigned guards the most noteworthy are those pierced in silhouette called *Owari-sukashi* ('Owari pierced', from the province where they are said to have originated), and a type of thin iron guard worked with various designs in low relief with piercing, called *Kamakura-tsuba*. Iron guards with inlay and incrustation of soft metals, usually brass, also occur; the majority of designs are heraldic. Finally, a few guards were made of a coarse variety of bronze called *yamagane*, which was used concurrently with iron from an early date.

B. SEVENTEENTH CENTURY ONWARDS

Shōami School (Pls. 34d, 56, 57)

This was an offshoot of the Umetada, and during this and the following century established branches in various parts of the country such as Aidzu (Mutsu province), Shōnai (Dewa), Tsuyama (Mimasaka), and especially at Matsuyama and elsewhere in the province of Iyo. Shōami artists practised a variety of styles according to their period and locality. The founder was Shōami Masanori [79, 191] of Nishijin, Kyōto, and the last master, Katsuyoshi [158, 179], died in 1909. In general, the earlier Shōami work is in the softer metals rather than iron, with low relief incrustation of gold, silver, or *shakudō*; a decorated rim is a frequent feature.

The Higo Schools (Pls. 58, 59)

The independent schools of this province owe their foundation to the patronage of the local *daimyō*, Hosokawa Tadaoki (d. 1645), himself a maker of guards. Hirata Hikozō [246, 6] and Nishigaki Kanshirō [255, 224, 252], both of whom founded sub-schools, were among those who worked under him; a little later came Hayashi Matashichi Shigeharu [110, 76] (1608–91) who founded a school at Kasuga. Other Higo schools were the Kamiyoshi, the Shimidzu, and the Kumagai. Each of these adopted an individual style and affected unusual forms, especially for the smaller mounts; the *umabari* (see above, p. 70) is an implement peculiar to this province. Flat piercing, often enriched with broad effects in gold or silver wire inlay, as well as a marked originality of design, are among the characteristics of Higo work. Most of the earlier guards are of well-forged iron of good colour.

The Chōshū (Nagato) Schools (Pls. 60, 61)

The province of Chōshū (Nagato) was the home of eight or more important families engaged in making sword-furniture, of whom the parent was the Nakai group; most of them worked at Hagi, the provincial capital. The most important sub-schools were the Kaneko, the Nakahara, the Inouye, the Yamichi, the Kawaji, the Okada, and the Okamoto. Early

Chōshū work was influenced by the Umetada and Shōami masters; thus examples of the Nakai group often show incrustation of the softer metals on the iron ground. Most Chōshū guards, however, are of iron with a rich black patina, and sharp, powerful, and carefully-modelled relief, either solid or pierced.

Kinai School of Echizen (Pl. 62)

The founder was Ishikawa Kinai (d. 1680), but succeeding masters bore the surname of Takahashi; all signed *Kinai* [105, 219]. The school may possibly be a branch of the Myōchin. They made guards only, of hard well-forged iron, confining themselves to pierced relief of remarkably clean design and execution; dragons were a speciality. Some heightening of the design with gold is found in the later examples, which may be as late as the nineteenth century.

Itō School (Pls. 39a, b, 63)

Itō Masatsugu [31, 42], who may have been a pupil of Umetada Myōju, founded the school at Odawara (Sagami province), but when his descendant Masatsune [31, 102] (d. 1724) was appointed guard-maker to the Shōgun, the family's headquarters was removed to Yedo, where they continued working up to the middle of the nineteenth century. The earlier style is characterized by unmodelled piercing, sometimes using the extremely fine saw-cutting known as *ito-zukashi* ('thread piercing'), but from about 1750 onwards we find modelling, often in the round, or even low relief without piercing. All Itō guards, with a handful of late exceptions, are of iron. Pierced iron guards of slightly different type were also produced at Yedo by the Akao, Akasaka and Sunagawa schools (Pl. 64).

Sōten School (Pl. 66)

The style of Sōten [87, 241] (late seventeenth century) and his successors at Hikone in the province of Ōmi, was developed from the style of guard called *marubori*, in which large and boldly conceived subjects were represented completely in the round within a border. Sōten's designs were smaller, with the addition of elaborate detail in overlay and inlay of gold, silver, and copper; the subjects are generally taken from Chinese and Japanese history. The signature of Sōten has been more extensively forged than that of any other maker. The demand for *Hikone-bori*, as the style was called, was very large, and there was a wholesale manufacture of bad imitations in the Aidzu district of Mutsu province in the early nineteenth century. Sōten guards are almost always of iron.

The Namban and Hirado Schools (Pls. 68, 69)

The term *Namban* ('Southern Barbarian') was applied to all foreigners by the Japanese, and is consequently used to designate a style of sword-furniture in which Chinese and European designs and technique predominate. The work is usually in iron or *sentoku*, either solid or pierced with a maze of floral scrolls interspersed with dragons and other motives.

A type popularized by Mitsuhiro [55, 198] of Yagami often represents the 'Hundred Monkeys' and similar subjects, while Kunishige [154, 110] of Hirado produced guards of *sentoku* enamelled in Korean style. Although initiated in the seventeenth century, these semi-foreign styles mostly occur in work of the eighteenth and nineteenth.

The Jakushi School (Pl. 67)

The founder, Jakushi [116, 242] I of Nagasaki (d. 1707), was a painter in the Chinese style who adapted his painter's technique to metalwork by the use of gold overlay of varying thickness on iron, giving the impression of washes of colour. The favourite subjects of this school, which continued into the nineteenth century, were landscapes and dragons.

The Hirata School of Awa (Pls. 2a, 43, 70)

The school was founded about the middle of the seventeenth century by Hirata Tansai [223, 272], and his successors continued working down to the end of the eighteenth century. Their work, which shows some Shōami and Higo influences, is usually on iron, which is covered with a brilliant overlay of gold leaf or wire in sharply defined patterns with the details lightly engraved. Similar work with geometrical or diaper designs was produced at Kyōto for presentations by visiting *daimyō* to Shōgunal officials at Yedo.

The Kaga Schools (Pls. 1d, 22e, 41d, 42, 71)

Early in the seventeenth century Mayeda Toshiiye, *daimyō* of Kaga province, invited a number of craftsmen of Fushimi to migrate to Kanazawa the provincial capital, and practise their art of flat inlay of soft metals on iron. As time went on, they founded several schools there, the Katsuji, Tsuji, Kuninaga, Kuwamura, Midzuno, and Koichi, gradually replacing the iron base with copper and its alloys, and producing more elaborate and showy designs with an increased use of engraving. Kaga work is hardly ever signed.

The Nara School (Pls. 2f, 3d, 4c, 37b, 41a, b, d, 72–7)

This school, founded in the first half of the seventeenth century at Yedo by Nara Toshiteru [62, 193], exercised an incalculable influence on the fine metalwork of later times. The old Nara style favoured the incrustation of the softer metals on iron grounds in realistic designs taken from nature, but other grounds and methods appeared as the style developed. Nara Toshinaga [240, 67, 62, 187] (1667–1737) first broke away from the tradition, introducing a far greater refinement and variety into both the designs and the materials used. Sugiura Jōi [132, 262] (1700–61), another Nara pupil, originated the technique of sunk relief (*shishiai-bori*); most of the work of his school is in red-patinated copper. Tsuchiya Yasuchika [50, 268], or Tōu [239, 235] (1670–1744), and his successors of the same name specialized in purely decorative designs founded on the impressionistic style of the painter-lacquerer Ogata Kōrin. Hamano Masayuki ['79,

266], sometimes read as Shōzui (1696–1769), a pupil of Toshinaga I, went even further than his master in refinement and elaboration; the Hamano workers seem to have plied an inexhaustible palette of colours, and the exuberance and perfect finish of their decoration reflects the luxury of the age, and foreshadows that decadent straining after effect which mars much of the later nineteenth century work.

The Yokoya School (Pls. 78, 79a, d)

The founder of this important school, Yokoya Sōyo [87, 263] (d. 1691), worked for the Shōgunal Court at Yedo in the classical Gotō style; but his successor Sōmin [87, 244] (d. 1733) broke away and introduced a new style of engraving imitating brush-strokes (katakiri), many of his designs being taken from the work of his friend, the painter Hanabusa Itchō. This style of engraving was adopted by many contemporary and later schools.

The Mito Schools (Pls. 4g, 40, 80–4)

Mito in Hitachi province was the seat of the most powerful cadet branch of the Shōgunal family, several schools of sword-furniture makers being at work there from the late seventeenth century onwards. Their style derives mainly from the Yokoya and Nara masters, and especially from the Hamano branch of the latter. Mito work is fertile in invention, varied in treatment, and brilliant in execution. The most important sub-schools were the Ōyama or Sekijōken, the Hitotsuyanagi, and the Yegawa.

The Hirata School (Pl. 85)

The art of cloisonné enamelling (shippō-yaki) seems to have been introduced from China towards 1600, and Hirata Dōnin [183, 218] (d. 1646), who was in the Shōgun's service, first used it in the decoration of sword-furniture. Hirata work generally consists of small panels of fine enamel set in a base of iron or shakudō. Translucent enamel appears first about 1770. During the nineteenth century many older pieces were redecorated with cloisonné inlays of this nature.

C. EIGHTEENTH CENTURY ONWARDS

The Yanagawa School (Pl. 86)

This notable school almost ranks with the Gotō, the Nara, and the Yokoya in the extent of its influence, the numbers of its pupils, and the importance of the branch schools founded by them. The founder was Yanagawa Naomasa [91, 79] (1691–1757), a pupil of the Yokoya and Yoshioka schools, whose work, and that of his pupils, shows a firm continuity of style combined with great variety in material, technique and design. The subjects are generally taken from the animal and vegetable worlds, and Yanagawa 'lions' (shishi) and prancing horses are famous. Among the many Yanagawa offshoots the most famous are the Sano (inlay covered with nanako, giving the effect of brocade), the Ishiguro, the

D. KAMIYA JIHEI ABOUT TO PERFORM
SEPPUKU WITH HIS *WAKIZASHI* BY SEKI
MAGOROKU KANEMOTO

Colour-print by KUNIYOSHI, *c.*1848, from the series 'Skilfully tempered sharp blades', a set of popular tales featuring swords. *Author's Collection.*
(See page 47.)

Kikuoka, the Inagawa, and, in the nineteenth century, Shummei Hōgen and the Tanabe (Pl. 87, 98).

The Ōmori School (Pl. 88)

The founder, Ōmori Shigemitsu [11, 167, 110, 55] (1693–1726), was a Nara pupil, but the most outstanding member of the school was Teruhide [117, 65] (1729–98), who is credited with the invention of the 'Ōmori waves' with their curling undercut crests, and the gold powdery inlay of haze, recalling the lacquer technique called *nashiji*. The large open paeony in silver with gold centre is another frequent feature of Ōmori work.

The Iwamoto School (Pl. 89)

The most eminent representative of this school was Iwamoto Konkwan [236, 194] (1743–1801) who followed the Nara and Hamano styles, developing them in his own way. Fishes are the favourite subjects, and bold sculpturesque relief on iron or soft metal grounds is a feature of the school. Konkwan's signature has been extensively forged.

The Tetsugendō School (Pl. 90)

Okamoto Naoshige [243, 118], an artist of the Chōshū school (see above, p. 77), came to Kyōto about 1750 and studied under Tetsuya Kuniharu [154, 76] of the Nara school. His work and that of his followers is almost entirely in iron of rich brown patina, with figures in bold relief or in the round. The signatures are usually in the running hand (*sōsho*) accompanied by a seal inlaid in gold.

The Ichinomiya School (Pls. 3e, 91)

Ichinomiya Nagatsune [83, 150] (1719–86) was one of the greatest craftsmen of his time. He belonged to a *samurai* family of Echizen province, and came to Kyōto as a young man, where he studied under the Gotō. Finding their style too rigid, however, he broke away and founded a school of his own. Many of his later designs are borrowed from the work of the famous painter Maruyama Okyō, under whose teaching he became a skilled painter as well as a metalworker. His work illustrates two main techniques: fine *iroye* relief incrustation, and a combination of *katakiri* engraving with the flat inlay of the Kaga school. About 1780 he made a silver brazier ordered by the King of Korea as a gift for the Chinese Emperor Ch'ien Lung; he also enjoyed the favour of the Japanese Court, and was granted the honorary title of Echizen no Daijō. His successors fell away considerably from the high standards he had set.

The Shōnai Schools (Pls. 3f, 79e, 92)

At Shōnai [227, 219] in the northern province of Dewa lived several families of sword-furniture makers, amongst whom were the Funada and the Katsurano. The former was founded in the early eighteenth century by Funada Zaisai [52, 248], a pupil of the Shōami, and the latter by Katsurano Akabumi [230, 221] about 1750. Akabumi was a *samurai* who had studied

81

under Hamano Shōzui. Shōnai work is characterized by great strength and boldness of design.

D. NINETEENTH CENTURY

The Ōtsuki School (Pls. 2c, d, 3b, 94, 95, 99)

This school was established at Kyōto by Ōtsuki Mitsuoki [11, 24, 55, 202] (1766–1834) who was a pupil of the painter Ganku. Some of his best work is in *katakiri* engraving, but he used a great variety of techniques, and his methods were followed by a group of pupils amongst whom Kawarabayashi Hideoki [65, 202], Sasayama Tokuoki [270, 202], and Tenkōdō Hidekuni [65, 154] were the most noteworthy. Kanō Natsuo [253, 159], the last great master of sword-furniture (1828–98) was connected with this school; the wonderful colouring and surface-treatment of his metal grounds and the sympathetic delicacy of his modelling have never been surpassed.

The Tanaka School (Pls. 1c, 4h, 93)

The founder, Tanaka Toryūsai Kiyonaga [144, 187] (living in 1867), was in the main self-taught, but influenced by the Ishiguro. He is credited with introducing the Y-shaped punch to roughen the ground for gold *nunome* overlay. The best amongst a score of his pupils was Morikawa Nagakage [187, 164]. Tanaka work has some affinities with the Jakushi School (see above, p. 79); it is characterized by a raised border with irregular internal outline, soft modelling of the ground in imitation of coarse-grained leather, and the provision from the outset of decoratively treated copper plugs in the tang-hole.

The Greatest Makers of Sword-Furniture

About 1790 Kitao Kōsuisai (Shigemasa) designed a large print entitled *Sankō ni-jū-hachi kishō*, 'Portraits of twenty-eight (metal) drillers' (19 × 14 in.) representing the twenty-eight foremost artists in metal up to that time. It was commissioned by Noda Shirobei Nariaki, a well-known connoisseur of the period, who published *Kinkō Kantei Hiketsu*, a work on the Gotō family, in 1819, and is therefore worth recording as the considered choice of a Japanese expert living in the golden age of the metalworker's craft. A copy of the print, somewhat wormed and rubbed, was published by Joly in the *Behrens Collection Catalogue* (Vol. 1, Part III, Fasc. 1, Pl. XI), and I have reproduced at Pl. 108 a rather enlarged version of it, probably contemporary, painted as a *kakemono*. The artists represented are as follows, beginning at the top centre and working downwards from left to right:

1. Yokoya *Sōmin* [87, 244] (1670–1733)
2. Nara *Toshinaga* [62, 187] (1667–1737)
3. Tsu *Jimpo* [278, 231] (1720–61)
4. Hashinobe *Masasada* [31, 114] (mid-eighteenth century)
5. Nomura *Tomoyoshi* [23, 247] (mid-eighteenth century)
6. Sugiura *Jōi* [132, 262] (1700–61)
7. Ozaki *Naomasa* [91, 79] (d. 1782)
8. Yokoya *Sōyo* [87, 263] (d. 1779)
9. Ichinomiya *Nagatsune* [83, 150] (1722–87)
10. Yanagawa *Naomasa* [91, 79] (1692–1757)
11. Tsuchiya *Yasuchika* [50, 268] (1670–1744)
12. Inagawa *Naokatsu* [91, 274] (1719–61)
13. Yoshioka Buzen (no Suke *Shigehiro* [110, 198], d. 1753)
14. Ōmori *Terumasa* [117, 84] (1705–72)
15. Hamano *Masayuki* [79, 266] (1696–1769)
16. Murakami *Jochiku* [226, 273] (mid-eighteenth century)
17. Hamano *Noriyuki* [251, 266] (d. 1787)
18. Mito *Michinaga* [183, 187] (d. 1768)
19. Gotō *Seijō* [144, 132] (1663–1734)
20. Nara *Tsuneshige* [150, 110] (mid-eighteenth century)
21. Nara *Toshimitsu* [62, 55] (early eighteenth century)
22. Nara Sōyū [87, 53] (*Toshiharu* [62, 113], late seventeenth century)
23. Ishikawa (Ishiyama) *Mototada* [151, 279] (1669–1734)

83

THE MOUNTS

24. Nara *Masanaga* [31, 83] (early eighteenth century)
25. Iwamoto *Ryōkwan* [67, 194] (mid-eighteenth century)
26. Hosono Sōzayemon (*Masamori* [31, 49], *c.* 1700)
27. Furukawa *Genchin* [15, 245] (mid-eighteenth century)
28. Umetada *Naritsugu* [257, 275] (1678–1752)

It will be noticed that all the artists represented were workers in soft metals, and at the other extreme of Japanese opinion stands the author of the *Tōban Shimpin Dzukan* and several other eighteenth-century authorities who had no use for anything but stout iron guards of archaic simplicity and severely practical type. Even iron Chōshū guards are dismissed by these purists as 'very peculiar and vulgar'.

European collectors usually manage to compromise, and to admire both the functional austerity of 'old iron' and the richness and technical perfection of the admittedly less practical soft metal fittings. They would probably wish to remove certain names from Noda's list, and to substitute others, and would in any case like to see it expanded to include Kanō Natsuo, Shummei Hōgen, Gotō Ichijō, and other great nineteenth-century masters. In fact, like the list of the 'greatest' swordsmiths on p. 55 it may stimulate collectors and others to draw up lists of their own.

Appendix A

THE NENGŌ, OR YEAR-PERIODS, FROM A.D. 800

[Numbers in square brackets correspond to the characters in the accompanying table]

782 Yenryaku [17, 53]	1028 Chōgen [22, 5]	1161 Ōhō [54, 27]
806 Daidō [2, 16]	1037 Chōryaku [22, 53]	1163 Chōkwan [22, 47]
810 Kōnin [10, 3]	1040 Chōkyū [22, 1]	1165 Yeiman [9, 40]
824 Tenchō [6, 22]	1044 Kwantoku [47, 46]	1166 Ninan [3, 14,]
834 Jōwa [23, 21]	1046 Yeishō [9, 23]	1169 Kaō [45, 54]
848 Kashō [45, 34]	1053 Tengi [6, 38]	1171 Jōan [23, 14]
851 Ninju [3, 44]	1058 Kōhei [36, 12]	1175 Angen [14, 5]
854 Saikō [43, 50]	1065 Jiryaku [18, 53]	1177 Jishō [18, 23]
857 Tenan [6, 14]	1069 Yenkyū [17, 1]	1181 Yōwa [48, 21]
859 Jōgwan [29, 56]	1074 Jōhō [23, 27]	1182 Juyei [44, 9]
877 Gwangyō [5, 49]	1077 Shoryaku [23, 53]	1184 Genryaku [5, 53]
885 Ninna [3, 21]	1081 Yeihō [9, 27]	1185 Bunji [7, 18]
889 Kwampyō [47, 12]	1084 Ōtoku [54, 46]	1190 Kenkyū [30, 1]
898 Shōtai [24, 32]	1087 Kwanji [47, 18]	1199 Shōji [11, 18]
901 Yengi [17, 37]	1094 Kahō [45, 27]	1201 Kennin [30, 3]
923 Yenchō [17, 22]	1096 Yeichō [9, 22]	1204 Genkyū [5, 1]
931 Shōhei [23, 12]	1097 Shōtoku [23, 46]	1206 Kenyei [30, 9]
938 Tengyō [6, 49]	1099 Kōwa [36, 21]	1207 Jōgen [23, 5]
947 Tenryaku [6, 53]	1104 Chōji [22, 18]	1211 Kenryaku [30, 53]
957 Tentoku [6, 46]	1106 Kashō [45, 23]	1213 Kempō [30, 27]
961 Ōwa [54, 21]	1108 Tennin [6, 3]	1219 Jōkyū [23, 1]
964 Kōhō [36, 27]	1110 Tenyei [6, 9]	1222 Jōō [29, 54]
968 Anna [14, 21]	1113 Yeikyū [9, 1]	1224 Gennin [5, 3]
970 Tenroku [6, 39]	1118 Genyei [5, 9]	1225 Karoku [45, 39]
973 Tenyen [6, 17]	1120 Hōan [27, 14]	1227 Antei [14, 29]
976 Jō-gen [29, 5]	1124 Tenchi [6, 18]	1229 Kwanki [47, 38]
978 Tengen [6, 5]	1126 Daiji [2, 18]	1232 Jōyei [29, 9]
983 Yeikwan [9, 56]	1131 Tenshō [6, 23]	1233 Tempuku [6, 41]
985 Kwanna [47, 21]	1132 Chōshō [22, 23]	1234 Bunryaku [7, 53]
987 Yeiyen [9, 17]	1135 Hōyen [27, 17]	1235 Katei [45, 42]
989 Yeiso [9, 31]	1141 Yeiji [9, 18]	1238 Ryakunin [53, 3]
990 Shōryaku [11, 53]	1142 Kōji [36, 18]	1239 Yenō [17, 54]
995 Chōtoku [22, 46]	1144 Tenyō [6, 48]	1240 Ninji [3, 18]
999 Chōhō [22, 27]	1145 Kyūan [1, 14]	1243 Kwangen [47, 5]
1004 Kwankō [47, 10]	1151 Nimpei [3, 12]	1247 Hōji [55, 18]
1012 Chōwa [22, 21]	1154 Kyūju [1, 44]	1249 Kenchō [30, 22]
1017 Kwannin [47, 3]	1156 Hōgen [27, 5]	1256 Kōgen [36, 5]
1021 Jian [18, 14]	1159 Heiji [12, 18]	1257 Shōka [11, 45]
1024 Manju [40, 44]	1160 Yeiryaku [9, 53]	1259 Shōgen [11, 5]

1 久	9 永	17 延	25 享	33 授	41 福	49 慶
2 大	10 弘	18 治	26 武	34 祥	42 禎	50 衡
3 仁	11 正	19 政	27 保	35 乾	43 齊	51 興
4 化	12 平	20 明	28 昭	36 康	44 壽	52 龜
5 元	13 至	21 和	29 貞	37 國	45 嘉	53 曆
6 天	14 安	22 長	30 建	38 喜	46 德	54 應
7 文	15 吉	23 承	31 祚	39 祿	47 寬	55 寶
8 中	16 同	24 昌	32 泰	40 萬	48 養	56 觀

1260 Bunō [7, 54]	1394 Ōyei [54, 9]	1570 Genki [5, 52]
1261 Kōchō [10, 22]	1428 Shōchō [11, 22]	1573 Tenshō [6, 11]
1264 Bunyei [7, 9]	1429 Yeikyō [9, 25]	1592 Bunroku [7, 39]
1275 Kenji [30, 18]	1441 Kakitsu [45, 15]	1596 Keichō [49, 22]
1278 Kōan [10, 14]	1444 Bunan [7, 14]	1615 Genna [5, 21]
1288 Shōō [11, 54]	1449 Hōtoku [55, 46]	1624 Kwanyei [47, 9]
1293 Yeinin [9, 3]	1452 Kyōtoku [25, 46]	1644 Shōhō [11, 27]
1299 Shōan [11, 14]	1455 Kōshō [36, 11]	1648 Keian [49, 14]
1302 Kengen [35, 5]	1457 Chōroku [22, 39]	1652 Shōō [23, 54]
1303 Kagen [45, 5]	1460 Kwanshō [47, 11]	1655 Meireki [20, 53]
1306 Tokuji [46, 18]	1466 Bunshō [7, 11]	1658 Manji [40, 18]
1308 Yenkei [17, 49]	1467 Ōnin [54, 3]	1661 Kwambun [47, 7]
1311 Ōchō [54, 22]	1469 Bummei [7, 20]	1673 Yempō [17, 55]
1312 Shōwa [11, 21]	1487 Chōkyō [22, 25]	1681 Tenna [6, 21]
1317 Bumpō [7, 27]	1489 Yentoku [17, 46]	1684 Teikyō [29, 25]
1319 Genō [5, 54]	1492 Meiō [20, 54]	1688 Genroku [5, 39]
1321 Genkō [5, 25]	1501 Bunki [7, 52]	1704 Hōyei [55, 9]
1324 Shōchū [11, 8]	1504 Yeishō [9, 11]	1711 Shōtoku [11, 46]
1326 Kareki [45, 53]	1521 Taiyei [2, 9]	1716 Kyōhō [25, 27]
1329 Gentoku [5, 46]	1528 Kyōroku [25, 39]	1736 Gembun [5, 7]
1331 Genkō [5, 10]	1532 Tembun [6, 7]	1741 Kwampō [47, 27]
1334 Kemmu [30, 26]	1555 Kōji [10, 18]	1744 Yenkyō [17, 25]
1336 Yengen [17, 5]	1558 Yeiroku [9, 39]	1748 Kwanyen [47, 17]
		1751 Hōreki [55, 53]
N. Court	*S. Court*	1764 Meiwa [20, 21]
1338 Ryakuō [53, 54]	(Yengen)	1772 Anyei [14, 9]
1342 Kōyei [36, 9]	1340 Kōkoku [51, 37]	1781 Temmei [6, 20]
1345 Teiwa [29, 21]	1346 Shōhei [11, 12]	1789 Kwansei [47, 19]
1350 Kwanō [56, 54]		1801 Kyōwa [25, 21]
1352 Bunna [7, 21]		1804 Bunkwa [7, 4]
1356 Yembun [17, 7]		1818 Bunsei [7, 19]
1361 Kōan [36, 14]		1830 Tempō [6, 27]
1362 Jōji [29, 18]		1844 Kōkwa [10, 4]
1368 Ōan [54, 14]	1370 Kentoku [30, 46]	1848 Kayei [45, 9]
	1372 Bunchu [7, 8]	1854 Ansei [14, 19]
1375 Yeiwa [9, 21]	1375 Tenju [6, 33]	1860 Manyen [40, 17]
1379 Kōreki [36, 53]		1861 Bunkyū [7, 1]
1381 Yeitoku [9, 46]	1381 Kōwa [10, 21]	1864 Genji [5, 18]
1384 Shitoku [13, 46]	1384 Genchū [5, 8]	1865 Keiō [49, 54]
1387 Kakei [45, 49]		1868 Meiji [20, 18]
1389 Kōō [35, 54]		1912 Taishō [2, 11]
1390 Meitoku [20, 46]		1926 Shōwa [28, 21]

APPENDIX A

INDEX OF NENGŌ BY CHARACTERS

[The two numbers of the characters on the accompanying table that form each *nengō* are followed by the date when it began; reference can then be made to the preceding chronological list to determine how the characters should be read and how long the *nengō* in question lasted.]

1,14:1145	6,27:1830	9,53:1160	18,14:1021	29,9 :1232	45,42:1235
– 44:1154	– 33:1375	– 56: 983	– 23:1177	– 18:1362	– 49:1387
2,9 :1521	– 38:1053	10,3 : 810	– 53:1065	– 21:1345	– 53:1326
– 11:1912	– 39: 970	– 4 :1844	20,18:1868	– 25:1684	– 54:1169
– 16: 806	– 41:1233	– 14:1278	– 21:1764	– 54:1222	46,18:1306
– 18:1126	– 46: 957	– 18:1555	– 46:1390	– 56: 859	47,3 :1017
3,12:1151	– 48:1144	– 21:1381	– 53:1655	30,1 :1190	– 5 :1243
– 14:1166	– 49: 938	– 22:1261	– 54:1492	– 3 :1201	– 7 :1661
– 18:1240	– 53: 947	11,5 :1259	22,1 :1040	– 9 :1206	– 9 :1624
– 21: 885	7,1 :1861	– 8 :1324	– 5 :1028	– 18:1275	– 10:1004
– 44: 851	– 4 :1804	– 12:1346	– 18:1104	– 22:1249	– 11:1460
5,1 :1204	– 8 :1372	– 14:1299	– 21:1012	– 26:1334	– 12: 889
– 3 :1224	– 9 :1264	– 18:1199	– 23:1132	– 27:1213	– 17:1748
– 7 :1736	– 11:1466	– 21:1312	– 25:1487	– 46:1370	– 18:1087
– 8 :1384	– 14:1444	– 22:1428	– 27: 999	– 53:1211	– 19:1789
– 9 :1118	– 18:1185	– 27:1644	– 39:1457	35,5 :1302	– 21: 985
– 10:1331	– 19:1818	– 45:1257	– 46: 995	36,5 :1256	– 27:1741
– 18:1864	– 20:1469	– 46:1711	– 47:1163	– 9 :1342	– 38:1229
– 21:1615	– 21:1352	– 53: 990	– 53:1037	– 11:1455	– 46:1044
– 25:1321	– 27:1317	– 54:1288	23,1 :1219	– 12:1058	48,21:1181
– 39:1688	– 39:1592	12,18:1159	– 5 :1207	– 14:1361	49,14:1648
– 46:1329	– 52:1501	13,46:1384	– 12: 931	– 18:1142	– 22:1596
– 49: 877	– 53:1234	14,5 :1175	– 14:1171	– 21:1099	– 54:1865
– 52:1570	– 54:1260	– 9 :1772	– 21: 834	– 27: 964	51,37:1340
– 53:1184	9,1 :1113	– 19:1854	– 27:1074	– 53:1379	53,3 :1238
– 54:1319	– 3 :1293	– 21: 968	– 46:1097	– 54:1389	– 54:1338
6,3 :1108	– 11:1504	– 29:1227	– 53:1077	40,17:1860	54,3 :1467
– 5 : 978	– 17: 987	17,1 :1069	– 54:1652	– 18:1658	– 9 :1394
– 7 :1532	– 18:1141	– 5 :1336	24,32: 898	– 44:1024	– 14:1368
– 9 :1110	– 21:1375	– 7 :1356	25,21:1801	43,50: 854	– 21: 961
– 11:1573	– 22:1096	– 22: 923	– 27:1716	44,9 :1182	– 22:1311
– 14: 857	– 23:1046	– 25:1744	– 39:1528	45,5 :1303	– 27:1161
– 17: 973	– 25:1429	– 38: 901	– 46:1452	– 9 :1848	– 46:1084
– 18:1124	– 27:1081	– 46:1489	27,5 :1156	– 15:1441	55,9 :1704
– 20:1781	– 31: 989	– 49:1308	– 14:1120	– 23:1106	– 18:1247
– 21:1681	– 39:1558	– 53: 782	– 17:1135	– 27:1094	– 46:1449
– 22: 824	– 40:1165	– 54:1239	28,21:1926	– 34: 848	– 53:1751
– 23:1131	– 46:1381	– 55:1673	29,5 : 976	– 39:1225	56,54:1350

Appendix B

The Numerals			The "Ten Stems" (Jikkan)		The "Twelve Signs" (Jū-ni-shi)	
1	Ichi	一	Kinoye	甲	Ne : rat	子
2	Ni	二	Kinoto	乙	Ushi : ox	丑
3	San	三	Hinoye	丙	Tora : tiger	寅
4	Shi	四	Hinoto	丁	U : hare	卯
5	Go	五	Tsuchinoye	戊	Tatsu : dragon	辰
6	Roku	六	Tsuchinoto	己	Mi : snake	巳
7	Shichi	七	Kanoye	庚	Uma : horse	午
8	Hachi	八	Kanoto	辛	Hitsuji : goat	未
9	Ku	九	Midzunoye	壬	Saru : monkey	申
10	Jū	十	Midzunoto	癸	Tori : cock	酉
11	Jū-ichi	十一			Inu : dog	戌
12	Jū-ni	十二			I : wild boar	亥
15	Jū-go	十五				
20	Ni-jū	廿				
25	Ni-jū-go	廿五				

Appendix C

THE PROVINCES

Note: The numbers in square brackets after each name correspond with the characters on the adjoining table. In each case the character which is used in combination with *-shū* to form the shortened or colloquial name of the province (see p. 40) has its number printed in *italics*.

A. *Kinai*

'The Home Provinces'

1. Yamashiro [6, *52*]
2. Yamato [*5*, *36*]
3. Kawachi [*32*, 7]
4. Idzumi [36, *47*]
5. Settsu [*93*, 44]

B. *Tōkaidō*

'The Eastern Sea Circuit'

6. Iga [*15*, 70]
7. Ise [15, *75*]
8. Shima [*29*, 82]
9. Owari [*30*, 58]
10. Mikawa [*1*, 32]
11. Tōtōmi [*77*, 16]
12. Suruga [*88*, 32]
13. Kai [*13*, 72]
14. Idzu [15, *27*]
15. Sagami [*45*, 81]
16. Musashi [*39*, 91]
17. Awa [19, *38*]
18. Kadzusa [*4*, 87]
19. Shimosa [2, *87*]
20. Hitachi [*62*, 59]

C. *Tōsandō*

'The Eastern Mountain Circuit'

21. Ōmi [40, *16*]
22. Mino [49, *83*]
23. Hida [*51*, 80]
24. Shinano [*42*, 83]
25. Kōdzuke [*4*, 60]
26. Shimotsuke [2, *60*]
27. Mutsu [*59*, 67]
28. Dewa [14, *17*]

D. *Hokurikudō*

'The Northern Land Circuit'

29. Wakasa [*50*, 53]
30. Echizen [*73*, 48]
31. Kaga [*11*, 70]
32. Noto [*54*, 71]
33. Etchū [*73*, 8]
34. Echigo [*73*, 43]
35. Sado [*24*, 64]

E. *Sanindō*

'The Mountain Shade Circuit'

36. Tamba [*9*, 31]
37. Tango [*9*, 43]
38. Tajima [*21*, 55] [*9*]
39. Inaba [*20*, 78]
40. Hōki [*23*, 56]
41. Idzumo [14, *66*]
42. Iwami [*12*, 28]
43. Oki [*86*, 25]

F. *Sanyōdō*

'The Mountain Sunny Circuit'

44. Harima [*79*, 85]

45. Mimasaka [49, *22*]
46. Bizen [*63*, 48]
47. Bitchū [*63*, 8]
48. Bingo [*63*, 43]
49. Aki [19, *92*]
50. Suō [41, *26*]
51. Nagato [*37*, 35]

G. *Nankaidō*

'The Southern Sea Circuit'

52. Kii [*46*, 15]
53. Awaji [*57*, 74]
54. Awa [*33*, 31]
55. Sanuki [*94*, 25]
56. Iyo [15, *84*]
57. Tosa [*3*, 24]

H. *Saikaidō*

'The Western Sea Circuit'

58. Chikuzen [*69*, 48]
59. Chikugo [*69*, 43]
60. Buzen [*89*, 48]
61. Bungo [*89*, 43]
62. Hizen [*34*, 48]
63. Higo [*34*, 43]
64. Hyūga [*10*, 18]
65. Ōsumi [5, *65*]
66. Satsuma [*90*, 82]
67. Iki [*68*, 25]
68. Tsushima [*76*, 55]

1 三	13 甲	25 岐	37 長	49 美	61 參	73 越	85 磨
2 下	14 出	26 防	38 房	50 若	62 常	74 路	86 隱
3 土	15 伊	27 豆	39 武	51 飛	63 備	75 勢	87 總
4 上	16 江	28 見	40 近	52 城	64 渡	76 對	88 駿
5 大	17 羽	29 志	41 周	53 狹	65 隅	77 遠	89 豐
6 山	18 向	30 尾	42 信	54 能	66 雲	78 幡	89 豐
7 內	19 安	31 波	43 後	55 馬	67 奧	79 播	90 薩
8 中	20 因	32 河	44 津	56 耆	68 壹	80 彈	91 藏
9 冊	21 但	33 阿	45 相	57 淡	69 筑	81 模	92 藝
10 日	22 作	34 肥	46 紀	58 張	70 賀	82 摩	93 攝
11 加	23 伯	35 門	47 泉	59 陸	71 登	83 濃	94 讚
12 石	24 佐	36 和	48 前	60 野	72 斐	84 豫	

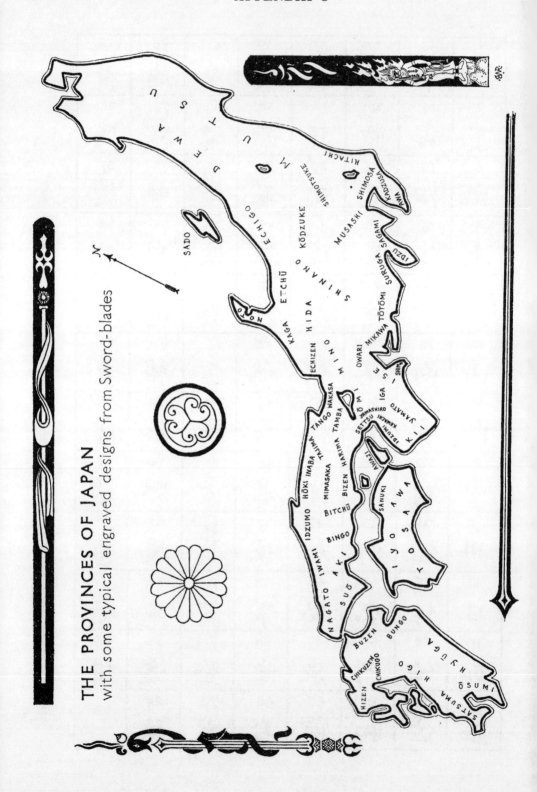

THE PROVINCES OF JAPAN
with some typical engraved designs from Sword-blades

Appendix D

CARE AND CLEANING

In dealing with both blades and mounts two golden rules should always be observed: never be in a hurry, and always under-clean rather than over-clean. In general, blades should never be touched with the bare hand. When in doubt, leave well alone.

The first thing for a collector to do when a sword comes into his possession is to 'strip' it. Normally this should involve no more than the removal of the retaining-peg, when the hilt, washers, guard and *habaki* may be easily withdrawn. Sometimes, however, rust or some other obstruction prevents this, in which case holding the sword in the left hand by the end of the hilt at an angle of about 45 degrees, the edge uppermost, strike the left forearm or wrist sharply with the open right hand. If this fails to loosen the blade, tap or strike all round the blade side of the guard as near the *habaki* as possible with a wooden mallet or a piece of wood and a hammer. If the guard is of soft metal or delicate workmanship it should, of course, be carefully wrapped in cloth or soft leather during this process. Once the blade is stripped it may be cleaned of superficial dirt or grease with a soft cloth and spirit (good lighter fuel will do very well). Ignorant possessors of Japanese blades often keep them permanently dripping with oil, or coated with grease, or even varnish, and when these are finally removed by a more discerning owner, they are often found to have left stains and discolorations on the surface of the blade.

'Duraglit' impregnated wool may be used to remove such surface discolorations, and is also effective on minor rust-patches. If the rust is active, it is as well to remove the red efflorescence, taking the greatest care not to scratch the surrounding unrusty surface. This can be done with the edge of a halfpenny (the metal being softer than that of the blade), and subsequent patient rubbing with 'Duraglit' wool will eventually remove the corrosion and leave the pit clean. In the case of deep pits and 'spider' rust, a strong brass or even iron pin can be safely used to remove the rust. An excellent tool can be made for this purpose by driving a long panel-pin into a small piece of hard wood up to a third of its length; snip off the head of the pin, and sharpen it to a fine point by filing. The point can be renewed after use by further filing, and as the metal of the pin is comparatively soft it can do no harm if carefully used. But these are only makeshift measures, and the proper restoration and repolishing of a damaged, scoured, or rusted blade can only be effected by a professional Japanese polisher.

Ideally a blade should be kept, polished and dry, in *shirazaya* (p. 71) neatly tied in a lined bag of silk brocade and resting, edge upwards, on a rack. Unless the sword is actually being worn or used, the mounts and scabbard belonging to it should be kept separately, if possible on a dummy wooden blade made to fit them. The blade can then be examined without the attention being distracted by the mounts (and vice versa). This, however, is admittedly a counsel of perfection, and some collectors actually prefer to keep their blades fully mounted.

Where there is any danger of damp, blades should be given a *thin* coating of pure oil of cloves, which should be periodically cleaned off and renewed; mineral oils and grease should not be used, because they tend to stain the blade. Whenever a blade is unsheathed, before it is replaced in its scabbard it should be dusted with an *uchiko* (a small bag with a handle, containing powdered limestone) and then wiped with soft Japanese paper. If this is not obtainable, a silk handkerchief will do; 'Kleenex' paper handkerchiefs and 'Andrex' lavatory paper are also excellent for the purpose. An *uchiko* can easily be made in the following manner: loosely bind a small ball of cotton-wool about an inch in diameter to a bit of stick or bamboo; then get half an ounce of *Wiener Kalk* (finely powdered limestone) from a chemist's, put it into a piece of thin silk folded double, and bind this over the cotton-wool at the end of the stick, not too tightly. The result is like a little mop — an exact replica (especially if red silk be used) of the Japanese *uchiko*.

Soft metal mounts may be gently cleaned of superficial dirt with a soft cloth or brush and spirit, and then very lightly waxed before a final rub with a clean chamois-leather; the Japanese make a special cloth impregnated with vegetable wax for this purpose. But in general, the less done to them the better. It should be unnecessary to add that all abrasives and metal-polishes of any kind whatsoever must be utterly eschewed where soft metal mounts are concerned (see p. 61).

The following additional notes have been kindly supplied by Engineer Commander A. R. Newman, R.N. (retd.), whose practical knowledge and experience of the subject are unrivalled:

'Guards and other mounts of plain iron may be soaked in dilute caustic soda, and then washed and scrubbed with a stiff scrubbing-brush and soap; they should then be waxed. This process will produce fair results with a minimum of danger. Rough iron *tsuba* of the kind made by armourers and swordsmiths which are in really bad condition (as so many are) can be given a new lease of life by placing them in the clear part of an open household fire, raising them to a dull red, and then putting them in the ashes to anneal by slowly cooling. When they are cold they should be scrubbed with soap and water, particular attention being given to piercings and apertures, and afterwards heated on a hot-plate to drive out moisture and wax. The method of waxing is as follows: Make a mixture of paraffin wax and beeswax with any fag-ends of shoe-polish tins (excluding black) in a small saucepan. Heat this gently until it is fluid. Now heat the *tsuba* until it is too hot to handle. Hold it horizontally over the wax with a pair of dental forceps (which are easy to obtain, and often cost only a few pence), dip it, shake violently, and leave it on blotting-paper. Next day rewarm it and wipe with cloth and tissues until no wax adheres, and finally brush it well with a clean soft shoe-brush.

'Some iron guards of the Chōshū, Bushū, and Tetsugendō types (see above, pp. 77f, 81) have a burnished finish. Rust specks and particles may be removed from these with a very sharp scalpel. They should then be rubbed gently with wire wool, heated on a hot-plate, and quenched in thin oil. Dry them, and finish with a touch of clean oil.

'Soft metal mounts are as a rule in fair condition, and should not be treated without advice. They may, however, be washed between the hands with soap and water, dried, and then perhaps finished with a light touch of a cloth impregnated with plate-powder. If a *shakudō* guard, while in moderate condition, has somehow lost large areas of its blue-black surface, then all must be polished off right up to the gold or silver inlay, and the higher the polish, the better your chances. Degrease carefully, and pickle in a solution of Cupr. Sub-Acetas; this is not readily soluble, so perhaps it is better filtered before use. To every four parts add one part of copper sulphate and a pinch of salt. If no effect is visible after the guard has been in the solution for some time, add a spoonful of vinegar. Further details may be found in the Japan Society of London *Transactions*, Vol. XIII, pp. 90ff., but Professor Gowland skates over the subject somewhat. At best, the results are not always satisfactory, nor is the film produced always durable. *Shibuichi* may be treated in the same way, but only after considerable thought, because sometimes time alone will improve a degreased and perfectly clean guard. *Sentoku* behaves much better: remove the corrosion, polish, degrease, and leave to the hand of time, though boiling in weak soda will hasten the process. Patinated copper may be treated in the same way as *sentoku*, but up to a year may be required before the guard looks reasonable, and copper is best left alone, apart from giving it a wash.

'Do not use ammonia, and use sulphur with great care, and then but seldom. Never be in a hurry. You can, of course, work on a number of pieces at a time — for instance, three soaking, three rinsing, and three drying. Later on the task may be eased by the acquisition of a jeweller's buffing-spindle and a dental flexible shaft with wire and hair brushes, and confidence will be gradually acquired as a result of experience. Keep a few old guards of no value and try your ideas on them first.

'For the storage of *tsuba*, shallow trays, cloth-covered, are the best. Brocade bags are pleasant for your treasures, but not essential. Guards should not rest on bare wood or even lacquer surfaces, and must never lie on top of each other.'

Lastly, the lacquer scabbard can be polished with any good furniture wax or cream. Ideally, it should only be handled with a silk handkerchief, and any finger-marks should be immediately wiped off. Lacquer should not be kept exposed to the light, which causes the colours to fade and dries up the texture.

Appendix E

TABLES OF CHARACTERS USED IN THE NAMES
OF SWORDSMITHS AND MAKERS
OF SWORD-FITTINGS

#		#		#		#		#		#		#		#		#	
1	一 ICHI:KAZU	2	了 RIŌ	3	入 NIU	4	力 RIKI	5	卜 BOKU	6	三 SAN:MITSU	7	下 SHITA:SHIMO	8	千 SEN:CHI	9	久 HISA
19	戸 TO	20	氏 UJI	21	介 SUKE	22	方 KATA	23	友 TOMO	24	月 GWATSU	25	永 YEI:NAGA	26	代 YO	27	加 KA
37	左 SA	38	世 YO	39	包 KANE	40	用 YU:MOCHI	41	任 TOMO	42	次 TSUGI-:-TSUGU	43	行 GIŌ:YUKI	44	汎 HIRO	45	西 SAI
55	光 MITSU	56	辻 TSUJI	57	作 SAKU	58	阪 SAKA	59	改 KAI	60	村 MURA	61	邦 KUNI	62	利 TOSHI	63	助 SUKE
73	成 NARI	74	戒 KAI	75	国 KUNI	76	治 JI:HARU	77	法 NORI:HŌ	78	阿 A	79	政 MASA	80	明 MEI:MIŌ:AKI	81	門 MON:KADO
91	直 NAO	92	忠 TADA	93	房 BŌ:FUSA	94	虎 KO:TORA	95	武 TAKE	96	近 CHIKA	97	周 CHIKA	98	胤 TANE	99	信 SHIN:NOBU
109	是 KORE	110	重 SHIGE	111	泉 SEN	112	宣 NOBU	113	春 HARU	114	貞 SADA	115	美 YOSHI	116	若 WAKA	117	英 FUSA:HIDE
127	神 SHIN	128	祐 SUKE:YŪ	129	師 MORO:SHI	130	能 YOSHI	131	兼 KANE	132	乗 JŌ:NORI	133	島 SHIMA	134	鬼 KI:ONI	135	息 SOKU
145	陳 CHIN:NOBU	146	祥 YOSHI	147	敎 NORI	148	野 NO	149	章 AKI	150	常 TSUNE	151	基 MOTO	152	康 YASU	153	通 MICHI
163	尊 SON	164	景 KAGE	165	奥 OKU	166	爲 TAME	167	森 MORI	168	堯 TAKA	169	貴 TAKA	170	盛 MORI	171	菊 KIKU
181	照 TERU	182	遊 YŪ	183	道 MICHI	184	圓 YEN	185	綱 TSUNA	186	實 SANE	187	壽 JU:TOSHI	188	榮 YEI	189	遠 TŌ
199	儔 TOMO	200	謹 SHIN	201	賴 YORI	202	興 OKI	203	憲 NORI	204	繁 HAN	205	鎭 SHIGE	206	藏 KURA:ZŌ	207	麿 MARO

10 上 KŌ(DZUKE)	11 大 DAI:Ō	12 丸 MARU	13 山 SAN:YAMA	14 水 SUI:MIDZU	15 元 GEN:MOTO	16 王 Ō	17 天 TEN:AMA	18 手 TE:JU
28 功 KOTO	29 弘 HIRO	30 外 TO	31 正 MASA	32 平 HEI:HIRA	33 生 SHŌ	34 冬 FUYU	35 本 HON:MOTO	36 末 SUYE
46 舟 FUNE	47 先 -ZAKI	48 充 MITSU	49 守 MORI	50 安 YASU	51 吉 YOSHI	52 在 ARI	53 有 ARI	54 旨 MUNE
64 里 SATO	65 秀 HIDE	66 谷 TANI	67 良 RIŌ:YOSHI	68 完 KWAN:SADA	69 克 YOSHI	70 孝 TAKA	71 辰 TATSU	72 延 YEN:NOBU
82 刻 TOKI	83 長 CHŌ:NAGA	84 昌 MASA	85 命 MIŌ	86 京 KEI	87 宗 SŌ:MUNE	88 定 SADA	89 幸 YUKI:YOSHI	90 奇 KI
100 保 HŌ:YASU	101 俊 TOSHI	102 恒 TSUNE	103 持 MOCHI	104 秋 AKI	105 紀 KI	106 則 NORI	107 軍 GUN	108 盈 MITSU
118 茂 SHIGE	119 屋 YA:IYE	120 風 KAZE:FŪ	121 倫 TOMO	122 城 KI:JŌ:SHIRO	123 峰 HŌ	124 院 IN	125 格 KAKU:NORI	126 時 TOKI
136 冑 MUNE	137 高 TAKA	138 家 IYE	139 泰 YASU	140 真 SHIN:SANE	141 峯 HŌ	142 座 ZA	143 御 GO	144 清 KIYO
154 國 KUNI	155 順 JUN	156 隆 TAKA	157 植 UYE	158 勝 KATSU	159 雄 O	160 統 MUNE	161 朝 TOMO	162 雲 UN
172 賀 YOSHI	173 進 SHIN	174 傳 TEN:DEN	175 經 TSUNE	176 路 MICHI	177 歳 TOSHI	178 業 NARI	179 義 YOSHI	180 資 SUKE
190 徹 TETSU	191 德 TOKU:NORI	192 隣 RIN:CHIKA	193 輝 TERU	194 寬 KWAN:HIRO	195 蓮 REN	196 髮 KAMI	197 慶 KEI:YOSHI	198 廣 HIRO
208 藤 FUJI:TŌ	209 繼 TSUGI:-:BUGE	210 寶 HŌ	211 續 TSUGI:-:TSUGU	212 鶴 TSURU	213 顯 AKI	214 鷹 TAKA	215 金 KIN:KANA	216 惠 KEI

217	218	219	220	221	222	223
子	仁	內	之	文	太	冊
KO	NIN	NAI	YUKI	FUMI	TA	TAN
224	225	226	227	228	229	230
四	仲	如	庄	兵	孚	赤
SHI	NAKA	JO	SHŌ	HEI	SANE	AKA
231	232	233	234	235	236	237
甫	序	味	知	雨	昆	易
HO	TSUNE	MI	TOMO	U	KON	YASU
238	239	240	241	242	243	244
宜	東	奈	典	芝	尚	珉
YOSHI	TŌ	NA	TEN	SHI	NAO	MIN
245	246	247	248	249	250	251
珍	彦	喜	哉	幽	悦	矩
YOSHI	HIKO	YOSHI	SAI	YŪ	YETSU	NORI
252	253	254	255	256	257	258
郎	夏	笫	勘	貫	就	善
RŌ	NATSU	CHŪ	KAN	TSURA	NARI	YOSHI
259	260	261	262	263	264	265
琴	登	幹	意	與	墨	樂
KIN	NARI	MOTO	I	YO	BOKU	RAKU
266	267	268	269	270	271	272
隨	龍	親	霍	篤	盧	齋
YUKI:ZUI	TATSU	CHIKA	KWAKU	TOKU	YOSHI	SAI
273	274	275	276	277	278	279
竹	克	受	俗	理	尋	董
CHIKU	KATSU	TSUGU	YO	MASA	JIN	TADA

INDEX OF READINGS FOR THE TABLES OF CHARACTERS USED IN THE NAMES OF SWORDSMITHS AND MAKERS OF SWORD-FITTINGS

A, 78
Aka, 230
Aki, 80, 104, 149, 213
Ama, 17
Ari, 52, 53
Bō, 93
Boku, 5, 264
Chi, 8
Chika, 96, 97, 192, 268
Chiku, 273
Chō, 83
Chū, 254
Dai, 11
Den, 174
Fū, 120
Fuji, 208
Fumi, 221
Fune, 46
Fusa, 93, 117
Fuyu, 34
Gen, 15
Go, 143
Gun, 107
Gwatsu, 24
Gyō, 43
Han, 204
Haru, 76, 113
Hei, 32, 228
Hide, 65, 117, 188
Hiko, 246
Hira, 32
Hiro 29, 44, 194, 198
Hisa, 9
Ho, 231
Hō, 77, 100, 123, 141, 210
Hon, 35
I, 262
Ichi, 1
In, 124
Iye, 119, 138
Ji, 76
Jin, 278
Jo, 226
Jō, 122, 132

Ju, 18, 187
Jun, 155
Ka, 27
Kado, 81
Kage, 164
Kai, 59, 74
Kaku, 125
Kami, 196
Kan, 255
Kana, 215
Kane, 39, 131
Kata, 22
Katsu, 158, 274
Kaze, 120
Kazu, 1
Ki, 90, 105, 122, 134
Kei, 86, 197, 216
Kiku, 171
Kin, 215, 259
Kiyo, 144
Ko, 94, 217
Kō, 10
Kon, 236
Kore, 109
Koto, 28
Kuni, 61, 75, 154
Kura, 206
Kwaku, 269
Kwan, 68, 194
Maro, 207
Maru, 12
Masa, 31, 79, 84, 277
Mei, 80
Mi, 233
Michi, 153, 176, 183
Midzu, 14
Min, 244
Mitsu, 6, 48, 55, 108
Mochi, 40, 103
Mon, 81
Mori, 49, 167, 170
Moro, 129
Moto, 15, 35, 151, 261
Mune, 54, 87, 136, 160

Mura, 60
Myō, 80, 85
Na, 240
Naga, 25, 83
Nai, 219
Naka, 225
Nao, 91, 243
Nari, 73, 178, 257, 260
Natsu, 253
Nin, 218
No, 148
Nobu, 72, 99, 112, 145
Nori, 77, 106, 125, 132, 147, 191, 203, 251
Nyū, 2
O, 159
Ō, 11, 16
Oki, 202
Oku, 165
Oni, 134
Raku, 265
Ren, 195
Riki, 4
Rin, 192
Rō, 252
Ryō, 2, 67
Sa, 37
Sada, 68, 88, 114
Sai, 45, 248, 272
Saka, 58
Saku, 57
San, 6, 13
Sane, 140, 186, 229
Sato, 64
Sen, 8, 111
Shi, 129, 224, 242
Shige, 110, 118, 205
Shima, 133
Shimo, 7
Shin, 99, 127, 140, 173, 200
Shiro, 122
Shita, 7
Shō, 33, 227

101

Index

INDEX

INDEX

INDEX

INDEX

INDEX

Yasutsugu, Shimosaka, 23, 52

Yasutsuna, Ōhara, 17, 44, 47, 55

Yasuyo, Ippei, 23, 54, 56

Yasuyoshi, Sa, 49

Yasuyuki, Naminohira, 22, 50

Yegawa School of Mito, 80

Yenju School, 22, 44, 50

Yenshin, Jōunsai, 24

Yokoyama School, 53

Yokoya School, 60, 70, 80

Yorimitsu, *see* Raikō

Yoritomo, Minamoto no, 19

Yoriyoshi, Minamoto no, 18

Yoroi-tōshi, 28

Yoshifusa, 20

Yoshihiro, Gō, 21, 55

Yoshii School, 44, 49

Yoshiiye, Minamoto no, 18

Yoshiiye, Sanjō, 18, 45, 55

Yoshimasa, Ashikaga Shōgun, 22, 38, 76

Yoshimichi, Mishina, 23, 51, 56

Yoshimitsu, Ashikaga Shōgun, 22

Yoshimitsu, Awataguchi, 21, 45, 55

Yoshimune, Tokugawa Shōgun, 54

Yoshioka (Inaba no Suke) School, 76, 80

Yoshitoki, Hōjō, 19

Yūjō, Gotō, 76

Yūkei, *see* Daishimbō

Yukihide, Sa, 24, 56

Yukihira, Kishindayu, 20, 44, 49 f., 55

Yukihira, School of, 49

Yukikuni, 19 f.

Yukimitsu, 21, 46, 55

Yukinobu, Senju-in, 18, 45

Yukiyasu, Naminohira, 24, 50

Zaisai, Funada, 81

Zen sect, 59

NOTE: The orthography of the Japanese words and names throughout this book is that used by Koop in his collectors' manual *Japanese Names and how to read them*, with one exception — the use of *y* rather than *i* in such syllables as *hyo*, *ryū*, *myō*, etc., in which I follow Brinkley, Hepburn, and the other standard dictionaries. As *Japanese Names* is, or should be, the 'bible' of all European and American amateurs of Japanese art, this orthography will be more familiar to them than the various jarring systems evolved in Japan and elsewhere during the last thirty years, besides being a far more accurate transcription of the *kana* syllabary as used in the pre-Meiji period — the period with which collectors are mainly concerned. Thus the modern systems use *z* indifferently for the *nigori* of both *ts* and *s*, and make no distinction between *ka* and *kwa*, *ga* and *gwa*. Of the Japanese Government sponsored system that would substitute the egregious *zyuzyutu* and *Huzi* for the *jujutsu* and *Fuji* we all know, the less said the better.

1. MISCELLANEOUS SWORD-FITTINGS

(a) *Fuchi-kashira* (copper): pine-saplings in the mist. Signed, *Jochū* [226, 254] with *kakihan* (Murakami School). VAM, M.1601–1931 (ex Hildburgh Coll.).

(b) *Tsuba (shakudō)* 'lion' and cub. Signed, *Kikuoka Mitsumasa* [55, 79] with *kakihan*. VAM, M.66–1914 (ex Church Coll.).

(c) *Kodzuka* (iron): a 'smooth dragon'. Tanaka School. M.265–1936 (ex Ransom Coll.).

(d) *Tsuba* (copper): wave-birds *(chidori)* and pines. Kage School, Oxford, Museum of Eastern Art (ex Church Coll.).

(e) *Fuchi-kashira (shakudō)*: eagles. Signed, *Kiyosada* [144, 88] of *Sendai* (Kusakari School). VAM, M.62,a–1957.

2. MISCELLANEOUS SWORD-FITTINGS

(a) *Tsuba* (iron): a mass of flowers. Hirata School. Oxford, Museum of Eastern Art (ex Church Coll.).

(b) *Fuchi-kashira (shibuichi):* wild geese, reeds, and the moon. Signed, *Ōishi Akichika* [80, 268] (School of Shummei Hōgen) and dated for 1850. VAM, M.104,a–1955.

(c) *Kodzuka* (copper): Fukurokuju. Seal, *Mitsuoki* [55, 202] (Ōtsuki School). VAM, M.184–1910.

(d) *Kodzuka (sentoku)*: a tiger. Signed, *Kishōtei Mitsuhiro* [55, 29] with *kakihan* (Otsuki School). VAM, M.333–1936 (ex Ransom Coll.).

(e) *Fuchi-kashira (shakudō):* cissus foliage. Kaga School. VAM, M.936–1931 (ex Hildburgh Coll.).

(f) *Tsuba (sentoku)*: wolf on the battle-field of Musashi-no. Signed, *Ōoka Masataka* [79, 70] with *kakihan* (Hamano School). VAM, M.456–1916 (ex Alexander Coll.).

3. MISCELLANEOUS SWORD-FITTINGS

(a) *Kodzuka* (copper): grasses under the moon. Signed with a *kakihan*. VAM, M.78–1952.

(b) *Kodzuka* (silver): a gold-fish. Signed, *Yoshiyuki* [179, 220] with *kakihan* (Ōtsuki School). VAM, M.2137–1931 (ex Hildburgh Coll.).

(c) *Tsuba (shibuichi)*: the foxes' wedding procession. Tsuji School. VAM, M.33–1920 (ex Gaskell Coll.).

(d) *Kodzuka (shibuichi)*: a temple-guardian *(Ni-ō)*. Signed, *Masayuki* [79, 266] (Hammano School). VAM, M.120–1936 (ex Ransom Coll.).

(e) *Fuchi-kashira (shibuichi)*: snails. Signed, *Tsunenae* [150, 91] with *kakihan* (Ichinomiya School). VAM, M.60,a–1957.

(f) *Tsuba* (gold plated copper): carp in the waves. Signed, *Sasaki Shōhei* [227, 228] (Shōnai Schools). VAM, M.58–1919 (ex Naunton Coll.).

(g) *Fuchi-kashira (shakudō)*: butterflies, Signed, *Nobutatsu* [99, 267] (Murakami School). VAM, M.63,a–1957.

4. MISCELLANEOUS SWORD-FITTINGS

(a) *Tsuba* (copper): butterflies. Signed, *Wada Isshin Masatatsu* [1, 140, 79, 267] *Bizan Kakuō* (pupil of Gotō Ichijō) and dated Ansei 4 (1857). VAM, M.32–1920 (ex Gaskell and Behrens Coll.).

(b) *Fuchi-kashira (shakudō)*: crabs. Signed, *Tsu Shumpo* [113, 321] (Gotō branch school). VAM, M.51,a–1957.

(c) *Kodzuka (shibuichi)*: tiger-lily. Signed, *Tsuchiya Masaharu* [31, 113], *pupil of Shōmin* /Tsuchiya School). VAM, M.113–1936 (ex Ransom Coll.).

(d) *Kodzuka (shakudō)*: bamboos. Kaga School. VAM, M.531–1911 (ex Hawkshaw Coll.).

(e) *Kodzuka* (copper): egret and willow. Signed, *Funada Ikkin Yoshinaga* [1, 259, 179, 83] with *kakihan* (pupil of Gotō Ichijō) and dated Kayei 3 (1851). VAM, M.137–1910.

(f) *Kodzuka (shibuichi)*: sun and waves. Signed, *Katsurano Fumio* [221, 159] *of Tsurugaoka in Dewa province* with seal, *Fumi* (pupil of Natsuo). VAM, M.1481–1931 (ex Hildburgh Coll.).

(g) *Fuchi-kashira (shakudō)*: the three heroes of Shu (Gentoku, Kwanu, and Chōhi). Signed, *Unno Yoshimori* [115, 170] *of Mito* with *kakihan*. VAM, M.1313–1931 (ex Hildburgh Coll.).

(h) *Tsuba* (copper): Mount Fuji and sailing-boats in a shower. Signed, *Tōryū* [239, 267] *Hōgen*, i.e. Tanaka Kiyonaga. VAM, M.952–1910 (ex Salting Coll.).

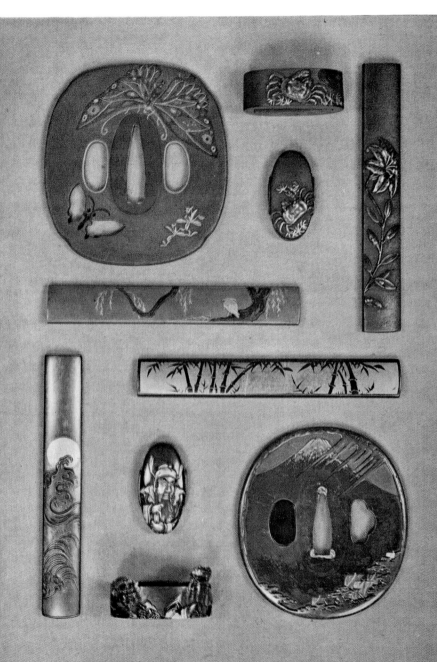

5. THE SWORDSMITH MUNECHIKA

The swordsmith Sanjō Kokaji Munechika [87, 96] forging the blade *Kogit-sune Maru* ('Little Fox') aided by the Fox-Spirit in the form of a youth. Drawing for an unpublished colour-print, signed *Drawn by Ichiyūsai Kuni-yoshi*. About 1835. VAM, E.2250–1990 (ex Happer Coll.).

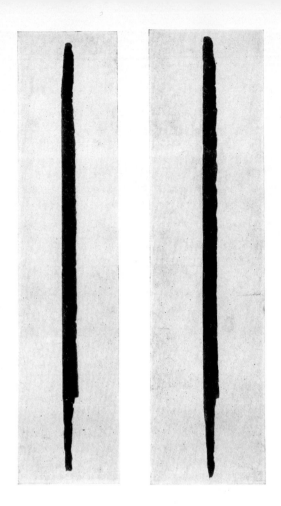

**6. SWORD BLADES AND POMMEL
OF THE DOLMEN PERIOD**

Blades: 3 ft. 6¾ in., and 3 ft. 9½ in. British
Museum, Franks Bequest (ex Gowland
Coll.).

7. BLADE-TYPES OF THE EARLY HISTORICAL PERIOD

(a) Reproduction of a blade, the original formerly the property of the Emperor Shōmu (724–749) and now preserved in the Imperial Repository of Shōsō-in, Nara. 2 ft. 7¼ in. VAM, M.60–1954.

(b) Blade of *Ken* or *Tsurugi* type. 2 ft. 3 in. VAM, M.20–1915.

(c) *Tachi* blade signed *Yasutsuna* [50, 185]. 3 ft. 5 in. Stowe School, Buckingham.

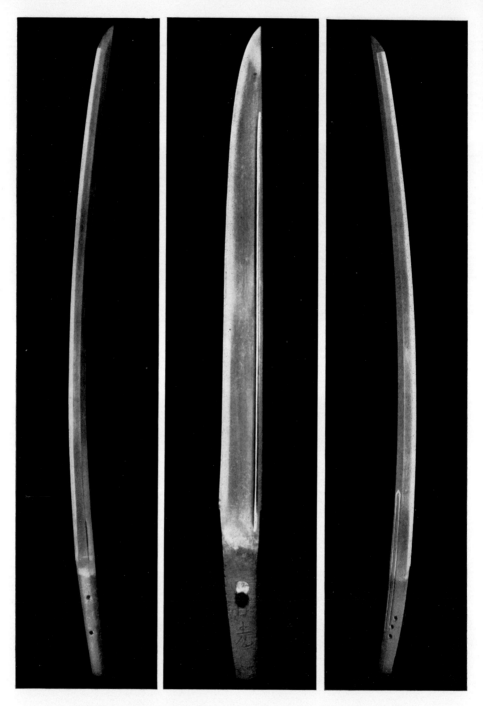

8. THE FIVE TRADITIONS (i) YAMASHIRO-DEN

(a) *Tachi* blade signed *Hisakuni* [9, ·154] (Awataguchi, 1149–1216), the tang cut down and now of Bizen shape. 2 ft. 11¾ in. Ex Craig Collection.

(b) *Tantō* blade signed *Yoshimitsu* [51, 55] (Awataguchi, 1229–1291). 1 ft. Festing Collection.

(c) *Tachi* blade signed *Kuniyasu* [154, 50] (Awataguchi, early 13th century). 2 ft. 8½ in. Ex Craig Collection.

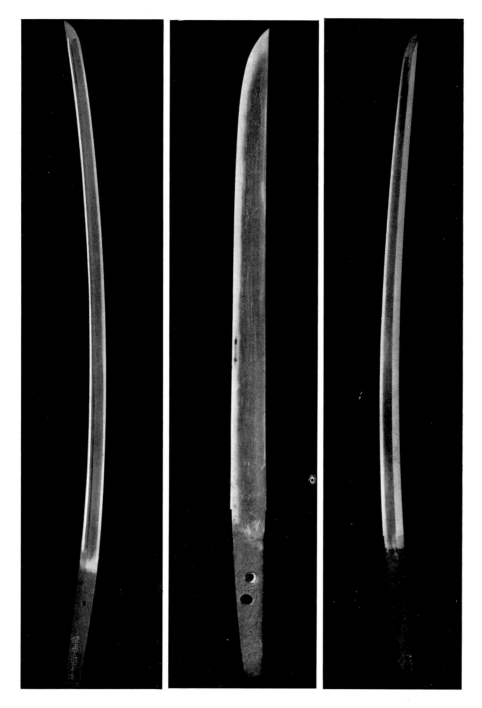

9. THE FIVE TRADITIONS (ii) YAMATO-DEN

(a) *Tachi* blade attributed to Hōshō Gorō Sadamune [114, 87] (early 14th century). 2 ft. 10 in. Ex Craig Collection.

(b) *Tantō* blade signed *Kunitsugu* [154, 42] (Yamato, early 14th century). 1 ft. 2 in. VAM, 697–1908 (ex Davison Coll.).

(c) *Katana* blade attributed to Shikkake Norinaga [106, 83] (14th century). 2 ft. 10¾ in. British Museum, 1959–7–30–11 (ex Lloyd Coll.).

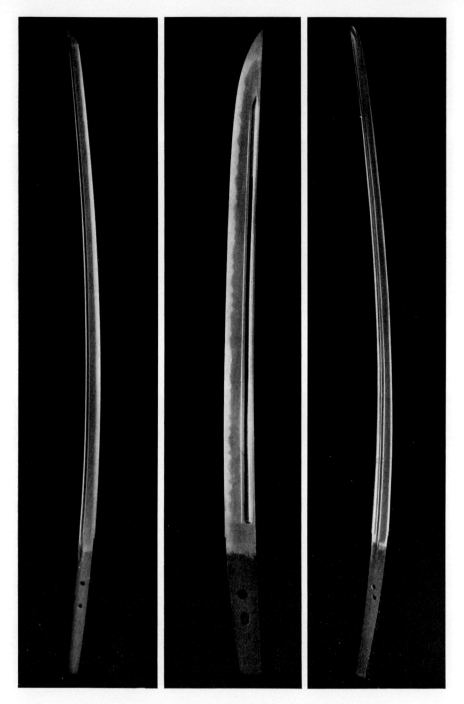

10. THE FIVE TRADITIONS (iii) BIZEN-DEN

(a) *Tachi* blade signed *made by Chikakage* [96, 164] *of Osafune in Bizen province* and dated Bumpō 1 (1317). 3 ft. 0½ in. Ex Craig Collection.

(b) *Tantō* blade signed *Yasumitsu* [152, 55] *of Osafune in Bizen province* and dated Ōyei 12 (1405). 1 ft. 6 in. VAM, M.67–1952.

(c) *Tachi* blade signed *Nagamitsu* [83, 55] (Osafune, 1222–1297). 2ft. 9 in. Ex Craig Collection.

11. THE FIVE TRADITIONS (iv) *SŌSHŪ-DEN*

(a) *Tachi* blade signed *Masamune* [31, 87] (1264–1343). 3 ft. 1¼ in. British Museum, 1958–7–30–20 (ex Lloyd Coll.).

(b) *Tantō* blade signed *Sadamune* [114, 87] (1298–1349). 1 ft. 0¾ in. Ex Craig Collection.

(c) *Katana* blade attributed to Shidzu Saburō Kaneuji [131, 20] (1284–1344) and inlaid in gold with its name, *Sasa no tsuyu* ('Dew on the Grass'). 2 ft. 11¼ in. Formerly Author's Collection.

12. THE FIVE TRADITIONS (v) *SEKI-DEN* (*MINO-DEN*)

(a) *Katana* blade attributed to Seki Magoroku Kanemoto [131, 15] (early 16th century); the tang has been shortened, and *of Seki in Mino province* is all that remains of the signature. Presented to Queen Victoria in 1860 by the Shōgun Iyemochi. 3 ft. VAM, 262-1865.

(b) *Tantō* blade signed *Kanemoto* [131, 15] (early 16th century) with later engraving of the divinity Monju on the lion. 1 ft. 6¼ in. VAM, M.28–1912 (ex Dobree Coll.).

(c) *Katana* blade signed *Kanemoto* [131, 15] (16th century). 3 ft. 1½ in. Author's Collection.

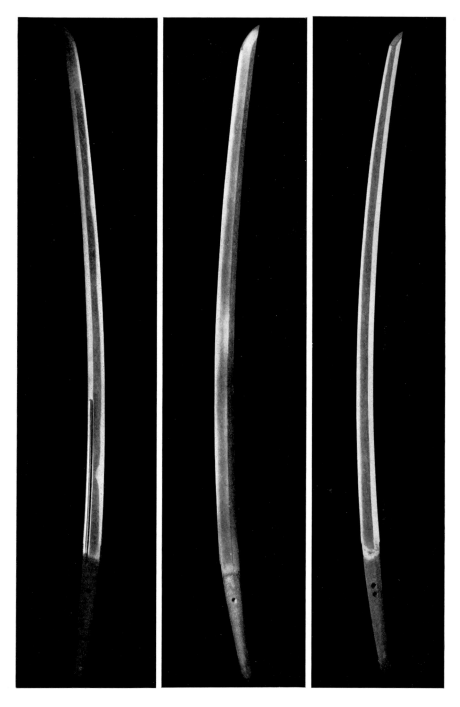

13. THE AOYE, NAMINOHIRA, AND GWASSAN SCHOOLS

(a) *Tachi* blade signed (Aoye) *Tsunetsugu* [102, 42] (early 13th century). 2 ft. 10½ in. British Museum, 1958–7–30–172 (ex Lloyd Coll.).

(b) *Tachi* blade signed *Naminohira Yasuyuki* [50, 43] (14th century). 2 ft. 11 in. VAM, M.10–1947 (ex Jahn Coll.).

(c) *Katana* blade signed *Gwassan* [24, 13] (12th–13th century). 2 ft. 8 in. Ex Craig Collection.

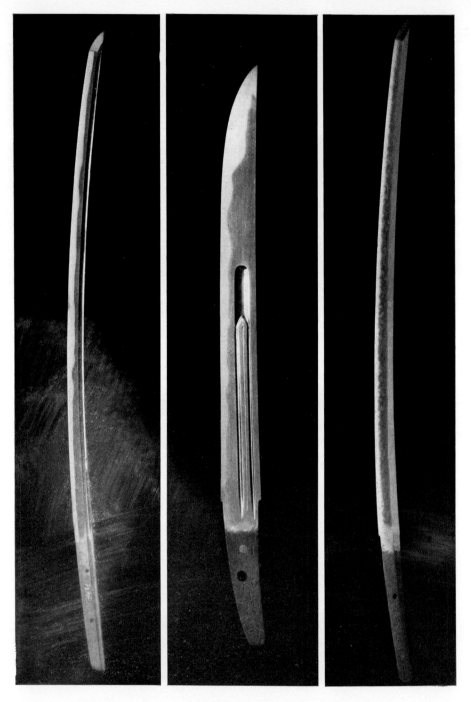

14. MASAMUNE, YUKIMITSU, AND SUKEZANE

(a) *Katana* blade with gold inlaid attribution to Masamune [31, 87]. 2 ft. 11½ in. Festing Collection.

(b) *Tantō* blade signed *Yukimitsu* [43, 55]. 1 ft. 3 in. Festing Collection.

(c) *Katana* blade signed *Sukezane* [63, 140] *of Osafune in Bizen province*. 2 ft. 10½ in. Ex Craig Collection. (This is not Ichimonji Sukezane, but a mid 14th century smith of the same name working under the influence of Masamune and his school.)

15. THE SCHOOL OF MASAMUNE

(a) *Ka ana* blade signed *Akihiro* [104, 198] *of Sagami province* and dated Oan 2 (1369). 2 ft. 10¾ in. Ex Craig Collection.

(b) *Tantō* blade with attribution in red lacquer to Hasebe Kunishige [154, 110]. 1 ft. 3¾ in. Festing Collection.

(c) *Katana* blade signed *Sadamune* [114, 87] *of Sagami province* and dated Gentoku . . . (1329–1331). 3 ft. 2¾ in. Ex Craig Collection.

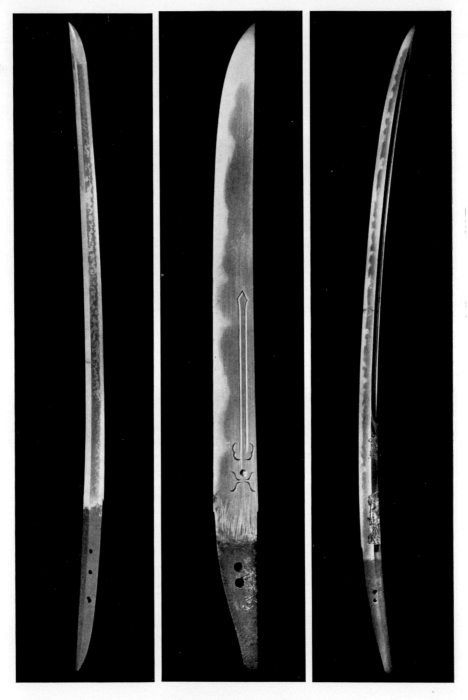

16. MURAMASA OF ISE

(a) *Tachi* blade signed *Muramasa* [60, 31] (late 14th century). 3 ft. 4 in. Author's Collection.

(b) *Tantō* blade signed *Muramasa* [60, 31] (15th century). 1 ft. 3¾ in. VAM, M.429–1924.

(c) *Katana* blade signed *Muramasa* [60, 31] (15th century). 3 ft. 3¾ in. VAM, M.340–1940 (ex Tomkinson Coll.).

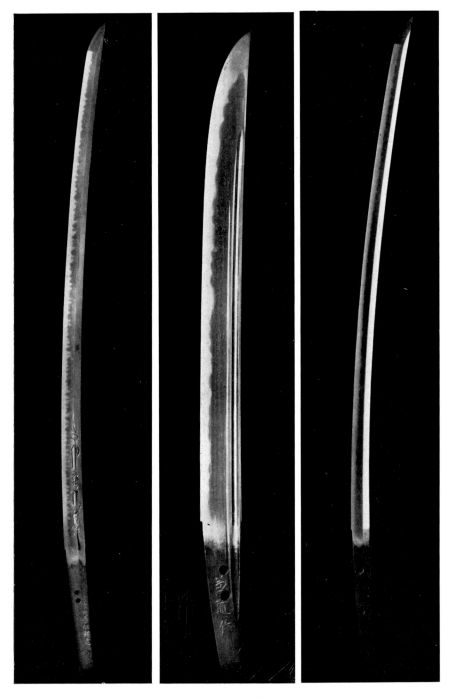

17. BLADES OF THE SENGOKU PERIOD

(a) *Katana* blade signed *Sukesada* [128, 88] *of Osafune in Bizen province*
(early 16th century). 2 ft. 10½ in. VAM, 633–1908 (ex Davison Coll.).
(b) *Tantō* blade signed *Kanemichi* [131, 183] (Seki, late 16th century).
1 ft. 3½ in. VAM, M.140–1929.
(c) *Katana* blade signed *Taira no Shige* [205] ... *of Takada in Hōshū*
(Bungo province), the second character of the name lost through shortening
of the blade (mid 16th century). 3 ft. 1½ in. Ex Author's Collection.

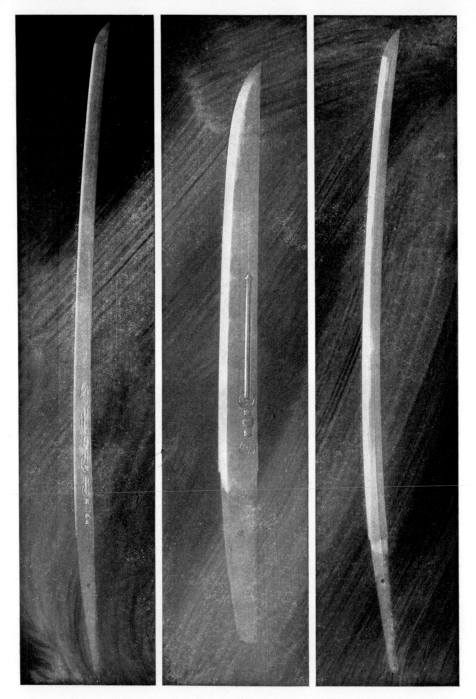

18. *SHINTŌ* BLADES OF KYŌTO

(a) *Katana* blade attributed to Umetada Myōju [80, 187] (early 17th century). 3 ft. 1½ in. VAM, M.21–1912 (ex Dobree Coll.).

(b) *Tanto* blade signed *Kunihiro* [154, 198] (early 17th century). 1 ft. 6½ in. Festing Collection.

(c) *Katana* blade signed *made by Mishina Tamba no Kami Yoshimichi* [51, 183] *in Settsu* (early 17th century). 3 ft. 0½ in. VAM, M.924–1916 (ex Alexander Coll.).

19. *SHINTŌ* BLADES OF YEDO

(a) *Wakizashi* blade signed *Yasutsugu* [152, 209] *of Echizen at Yedo in Musashi province* (early 17th century). 1 ft. 11½ in. VAM, M.24–1912 (ex Dobree Coll.).

(b) *Katana* blade signed *Hankei* [204, 197] (early 17th century). 3 ft. 1¼ in. VAM, M.6–1947 (ex Jahn Coll.).

(c) *Wakizashi* blade signed *Nagasone Kotetsu Nyūdō Okisato* [202, 64]. 2 ft. 2¼ in. Ex Craig Collection.

20. *SHINTŌ* BLADES OF ŌSAKA

(a) *Wakizashi* blade signed *Tsuta Echizen no Kami Sukehiro* [63, 198] and dated Kwambun 11 (1671). 2 ft. 2½ in. Yamada Collection.
(b) *Katana* blade signed *Kawachi no Kami Kunisuke* [154, 63] (mid 17th century). 3 ft. 1 in. Author's Collection.
(c) *Wakizashi* blade signed *Inouye Shinkai* [140, 59] and dated Kwambun 13 (1673). 2 ft. 2 in. VAM, 643–1908 (ex Davison Coll.).

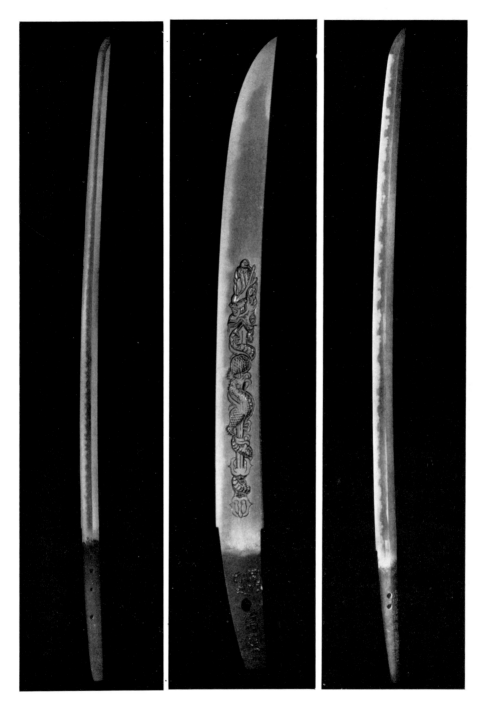

21. MISCELLANEOUS *SHINTŌ* BLADES

(a) *Katana* blade signed *Mutsu no Kami Ōmichi* [11, 183] . . . sometimes read as *Daidō*. 2 ft. 11¼ in. British Museum, 1958–7–30–176 (ex Lloyd Coll.).

(b) *Tantō* blade signed *made and engraved by Nobukuni* [99, 154] *in the precincts of the Temple of Hachiman at Hakozaki in Chikuzen province* and dated Shōtoku 3 (1713). 1 ft. 3 in. VAM, M.31–1912 (ex Dobree Coll.).

(c) *Katana* blade signed *this was made by Monju Shigekuni* [110, 154] *in the province of Kii* (early 18th century). 2 ft. 7¾ in. Ex Craig Collection.

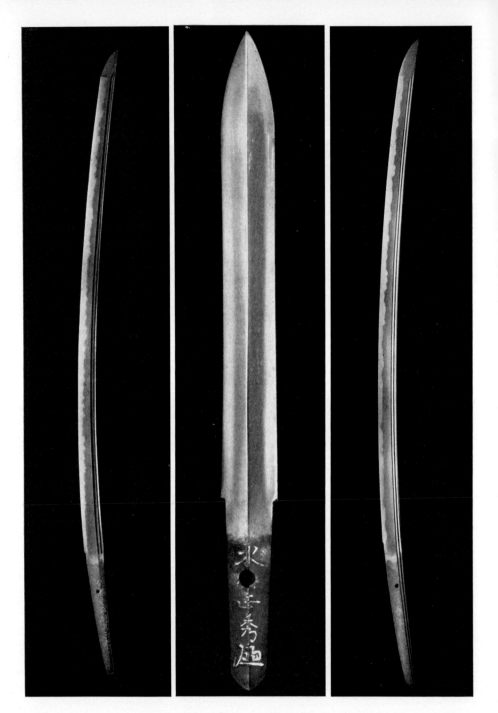

22. *SHINSHINTŌ* BLADES (i)

(a) *Katana* blade signed *Hōki no Kami Taira no Ason Masayoshi* [31, 89] (of Satsuma) and dated Bunkwa 4 (1807). 3 ft. 1¼ in. VAM, 601–1908 (ex Davison Coll.).

(b) Dagger blade of *ken* form signed *Suishin*(shi) *Masahide* [31, 65] with *kakihan* (early 19th century). 8¼ in. VAM, M.3–1932.

(c) *Katana* blade signed *Yamaura Tamaki Masayuki* [31, 43] (i.e. Kiyomaro, [144, 207] 1813–1854) and dated Tempō 10 (1839); made to the order of Ban Kagenori. 3 ft. Festing Collection.

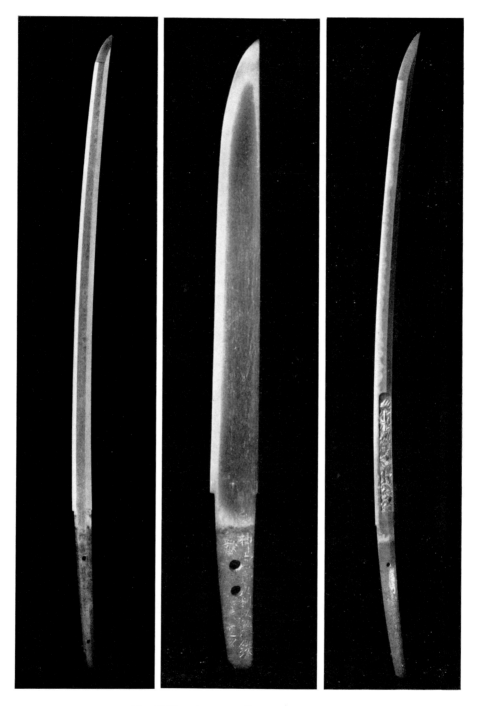

23. *SHINSHINTŌ* BLADES (ii)

(a) *Katana* blade signed *this was made at Naniwa* (Ōsaka) *by Gwassan Sadayoshi* [114, 51] *to the order of Mr. Iinuma of the Matsumoto daimyate* and dated Keiō 1 (1865). The blade is named on the scabbard *Sugukata Maru* ('Direct Method'). 3 ft. 2¼ in. Festing Collection.

(b) *Tantō* blade signed *Miyamoto Noto no Kami Kanenori* [39, 106], *made in the precincts of the Ise Temples out of iron left over from the sacred temple blade* (late 19th century). 11¾ in. VAM, M.97–1912 (ex Davison Coll.).

(c) *Katana* blade signed *Kurihara Kenshi Nobuhide* [99, 65], made for the Emperor Meiji. 2 ft. 11½ in. Author's Collection.

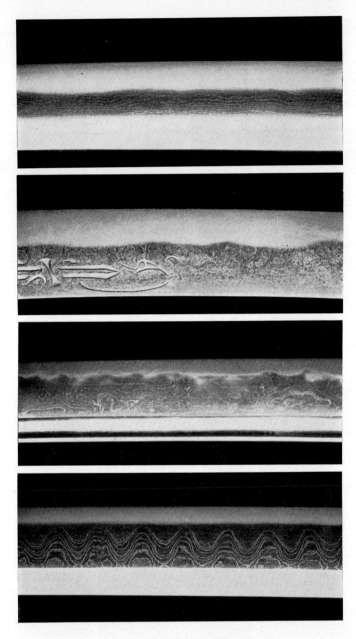

24. TYPES OF *JIHADA*

(a) *Masame*, from a blade by Michiharu (1866). Ex Craig Collection.

(b) *Mokume*, from a blade by Masamune of Yama-nouchi (early 16th century). Ex Craig Collection.

(c) *Itame*, from a blade by Kanemitsu of Bizen (pupil of Masamune: mid 14th century). Ex Craig Collection.

(d) *Ayasugi*, from a blade by Gwassan Sadayoshi (Pl. 23a).

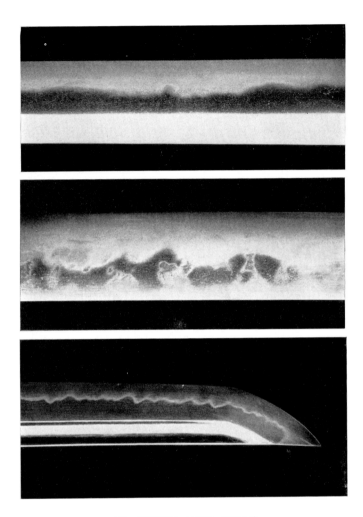

25. *NIYE* AND *NIOI*

(a) A cloud of *niye* at the edge of the *yakiba*, from a blade by Kunisada of Ōsaka (early 17th century). Ex Craig Collection.

(b) Clouds of *niye* on a *hitatsura* (*Hamon* 33) blade by Masahiro of Sagami (end of the 14th century). Ex Craig Collection.

(c) *Nioi* on a blade by Gwassan Sadakazu (1836–1918). Ex Craig Collection.

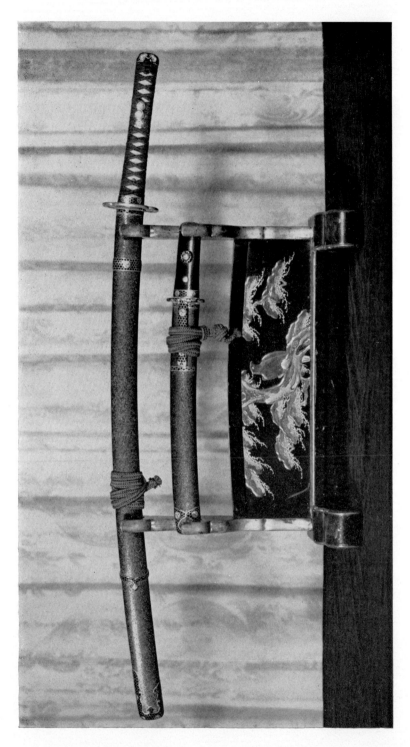

26. *DAISHŌ* ON A SWORD-RACK

Mounted in *handachi* style. Festing Collection.

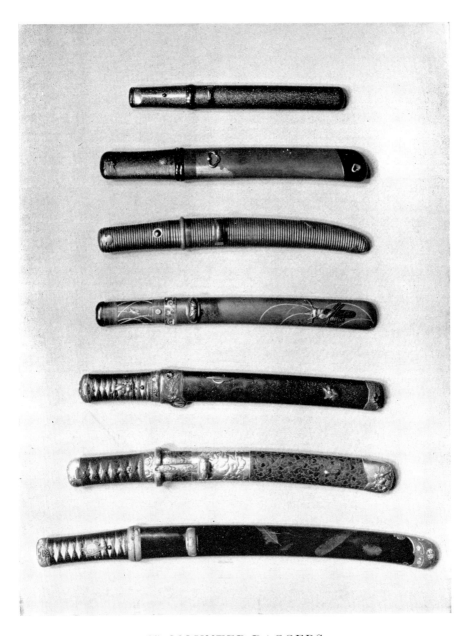

27. MOUNTED DAGGERS

(a) *Kwaiken* with hilt and scabbard of *aogai* lacquer. 10½ in. VAM, 701–1908 (ex Davison Coll.).

(b) *Aikuchi* with ring *kurikata*. 1 ft. 0¾ in. VAM, 699–1908 (ex Davison Coll.).

(c) *Hamidashi* 1 ft. 1 in. VAM, 698–1908 (ex Davison Coll.):

(d) *Aikuchi* with mounts of champlevé enamel. 1 ft. 1½ in. VAM, M.329–1910.

(e) *Aikuchi*. 1 ft. 2¾ in. VAM, M.983–1910 (ex Salting Coll.).

(f) *Hamidashi*. 1 ft. 3½ in. VAM, M.20–1947 (ex Jahn Coll.).

(g) *Aikuchi* with enamelled mounts by Kono Yoshikatsu (metal) and Hirata Hikoshirō [246, 224, 252] (enamel). 1 ft. 7 in. VAM, M.17–1947 (ex Jahn Coll.).

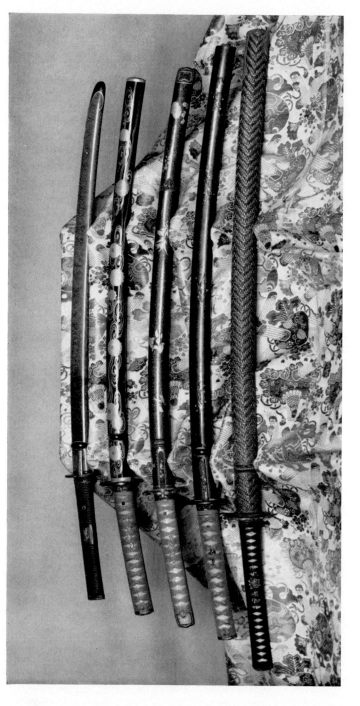

28. MOUNTED *KATANA*

(a) Leather-wrapped hilt and scabbard of fine *same-nuri*; a gift from the city of Kagoshima to Sir Claude Macdonald. 3 ft. 1½ in. VAM, M.137–1929.

(b) Scabbard of black and gold lacquer (for the blade, see Pl. 9b). 3 ft. 2½ in. VAM, M.10–1947 (ex Jahn Coll.).

(c) Mounted in *handachi* style. 3 ft. 3¾ in. VAM, M.923–1916 (ex Alexander Coll.).

(d) Mounted in quiet, formal style; presented to Queen Victoria by the Shōgun Iyemochi (cf. Pl. 8a). 3 ft. 6 in. VAM, 263–1865.

(e) Scabbard entirely covered in basket-work. 3 ft. 8½ in. VAM, M.112–1928 (ex Lee Coll.).

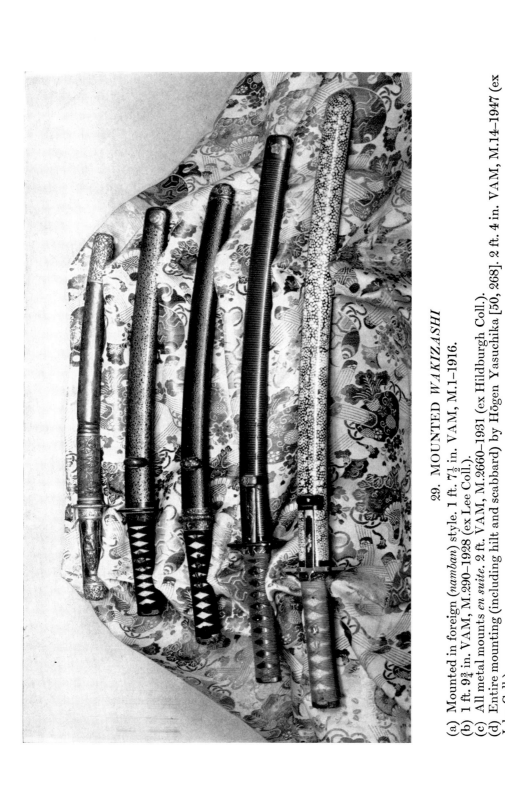

29. MOUNTED *WAKIZASHI*

(a) Mounted in foreign (*namban*) style. 1 ft. 7½ in. VAM, M.1–1916.
(b) 1 ft. 9¾ in. VAM, M.290–1928 (ex Lee Coll.).
(c) All metal mounts *en suite*. 2 ft. VAM, M.2660–1931 (ex Hildburgh Coll.).
(d) Entire mounting (including hilt and scabbard) by Hōgen Yasuchika [50, 268]. 2 ft. 4 in. VAM, M.14–1947 (ex Jahn Coll.).
(e) Scabbard of *same-nuri*, 2 ft. 7½ in. VAM, M.926–1916 (ex Alexander Coll.).

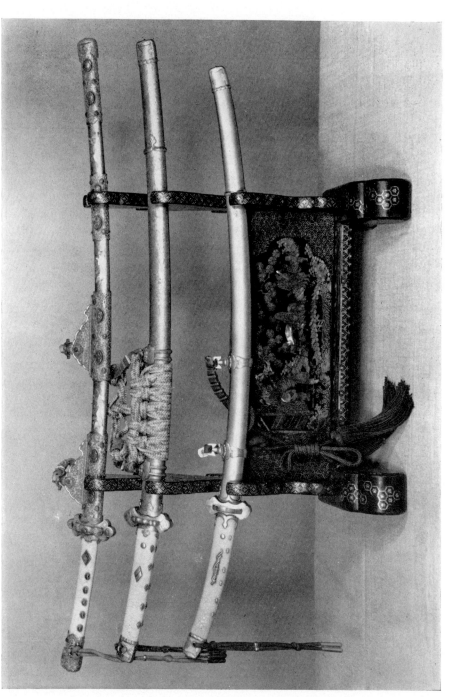

30. COURT *TACHI*

(a) *Shōzoku-tachi*. 3 ft. 1¾ in. VAM, M.144–1915 (ex Behrens Coll.).
(b) *Yefu-no-tachi* with badge of the Nambu family. 3 ft. 0½ in. VAM, M.1081–1927.
(c) *Yefu-no-tachi* of plainer style. 2 ft. 11 in. VAM, M.332–1910.

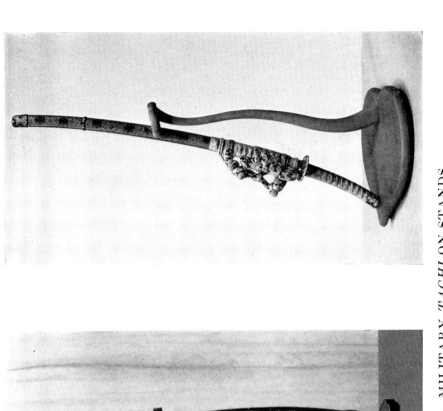

31. MILITARY *TACHI* ON STANDS

(a) Festing Collection.

(b) VAM, M.139–1929.

32. ETCHED IRON GUARDS

(a) Signed, *Kuninaga* [154, 25]. VAM, M.156–1915 (ex Church Coll.).

(b) Signed, *Kei* [175] *of Kii province* with *kakihan*. VAM, M.632–1931 (ex Hildburgh Coll.).

(c) Signed, *Ōmi no Kami Tsugihide* [209, 65] (a late 18th century swordsmith of Yedo). VAM. M.71–1931 (ex Hildburgh Coll.).

33. EARLY PIERCED IRON GUARDS

(a) Armourer's work. VAM, M.30–1915 (ex Church Coll.).
(b) Swordsmith's work. VAM, M.171–1923 (ex Tassel Coll.).

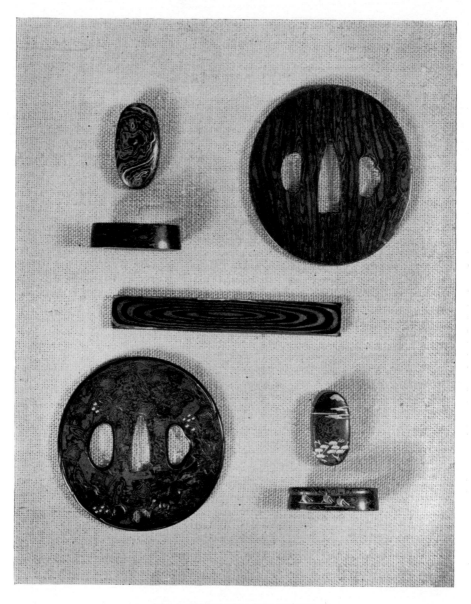

34. *MOKUME* MOUNTS

(a) *Fuchi* and *kashira*. VAM, M.66, 67–1957.

(b) *Tsuba: mokume* veneer. VAM, M.338–1911 (ex Hawkshaw Coll.).

(c) *Kodzuka.* VAM, M.387–1910.

(d) *Tsuba:* squirrel and vine. Signed, *Shōami Morikuni* [170, 154] *of Matsuyama in Iyo province.* VAM, M.65–1954 (ex Hope and Gilbertson Coll.).

(e) *Fuchi-kashira:* Mount Fuji, pines and sailing boats. VAM, M.65,a–1957.

35. *GURI*

Tsuba. Signed, *Takahashi Okitsugu* [202, 42] with *kakihan*. VAM, M.260–1912. (Photographed at a slight angle to show the layers of different alloys of which it is composed.)

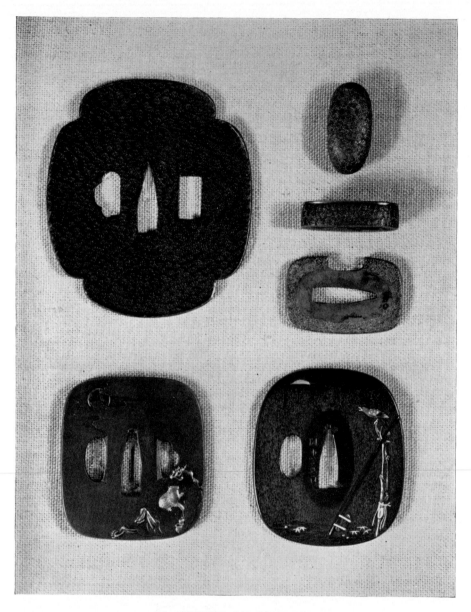

36. TYPES OF *ISHIME*

(a) *Tsuba* (iron). VAM, M.1751–1931 (ex Hildburgh Coll.).

(b) *Fuchi-kashira* and *hamidashi-tsuba* (brass). VAM, M.2648–1931 (ex Hildburgh Coll.).

(c) *Tsuba* (copper): Gama Sennin and his toad. Signed. *Yūmeiken Kwakusen* with seal, *Masahiro* [31, 29]. VAM, M.2051–1931 (ex Hildburgh Coll.).

(d) *Tsuba* (*shakudō*): birds. VAM, M.591–1916 (ex Alexander Coll.).

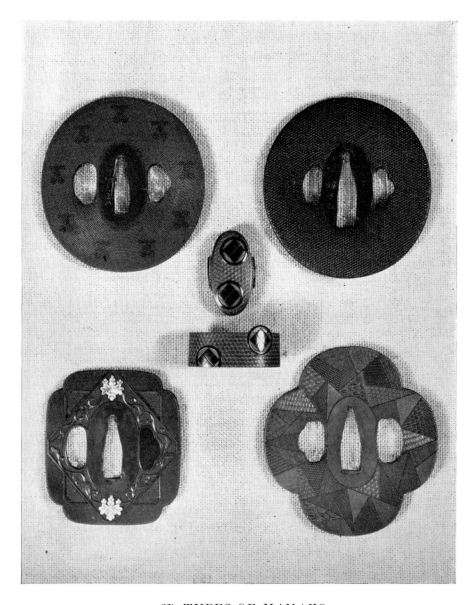

37. TYPES OF *NANAKO*

(a) *Tsuba* (copper): badge of the Nagai family. Signed, *Sano Naonobu* [91, 99] with *kakihan*. VAM, M.1408–1931 (ex Hildburgh Coll.).

(b) *Tsuba* (iron). Signed, *Masayuki* [79, 220] with *kakihan*. VAM, M.1753–1931 (ex Hildburgh Coll.).

(c) *Fuchi-kashira* (*shibuichi*): heraldic badges. Signed, *Ōoka Masatsugu* [79, 42] with *kakihan*. VAM, M.233–1921 (ex Joly Coll.).

(d) *Tsuba* (*shibuichi*): *kiri* badges. VAM, M.351–1911 (ex Hawkshaw Coll.).

(e) *Tsuba* (copper). VAM, M.348–1911 (ex Hawkshaw Coll.).

38. *MARUBORI* GUARDS

(a) (Iron) Purse, *inrō*, and *netsuke*. VAM, M.153–1915 (ex Church Coll.).
(b) (*Shakudō*) Kanzan and Jittoku. VAM, M.684–1931 (ex Hildburgh Coll.).
(c) (Iron) A 'lion'. Signed, *Kinhiko* [246] with *kakihan*. VAM, 705–1908 (ex Davison Coll.).

39. *ITO-SUKASHI*

(Iron). Egret and lotus-pond. VAM, M.151–1911 (ex Hawkshaw Coll.).

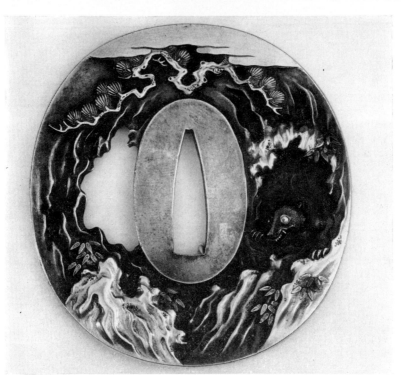

40. *TAKABORI* (HIGH RELIEF) AND *TAKAZŌGAN*
(INCRUSTATION)

Tsuba, silver with relief incrustation of gold and *shakudō*. Bear in a
cave; reverse, a waterfall. Signed, *Kiunsai Yasukuni* [100, 75].
VAM, M.21–1913 (ex Seymour Trower Coll.).

41. *SHISHIAI-BORI* (SUNK RELIEF)

(a) *Tsuba* (copper)*:* tiger and bamboo. Signed, *Tōu* [239, 235] with *kakihan*. VAM, M.243–1911 (ex Hawkshaw Coll.).

(b) *Fuchi-kashira* (copper)*:* Gama Sennin and another *sennin*. Signed, *Jōi* [132, 262]. VAM, M.1121–1931 (ex Hildburgh Coll.).

(c) *Kodzuka* (silver)*:* cranes. VAM, M.168–1936 (ex Behrens and Ransom Coll.).

(d) *Tsuba* (copper)*:* Kanzan and Jittoku. Signed, *Jōi* [132, 262] with seal. VAM, M.70–1952.

42. HON-ZŌGAN (INLAY)

(a) *Tsuba* (*shakudō*): chrysanthemum and *kiri* and *kiku* badges. VAM, M.70–1919 (ex Hawkshaw and Naunton Coll.).

(b) *Fuchi-kashira* (*shakudō*). VAM, M.50,a–1957.

(c) *Tsuba* (*shakudō*): willow, plum-tree, and bamboo-grass by a fence. VAM, M.28–1920 (ex Gaskell Coll.).

(d) *Fuchi-kashira* (*shakudō*). VAM, M. 937a–1931 (ex Hildburgh Coll.).

(e) *Hamidashi-tsuba* (*shakudō*). VAM, M.909–1931 (ex Hildburgh Coll.).

43. *NUNOME* (OVERLAY) (all iron)

(a) *Tsuba.* VAM, M.882–1931 (ex Hildburgh Coll.).
(b) *Fuchi-kashira.* VAM, M.321–1931 (ex Hildburgh Coll.).
(c) *Tsuba:* cock and chickens. VAM, M.878–1931 (ex Hildburgh Coll.).
(d) *Tsuba:* 'smooth dragons' and scrolls. VAM, 1434–1888.

44. *MUKADE* AND *GOMOKU* GUARDS (all iron)

    (a) VAM, M.81–1911 (ex Hawkshaw Coll.).
    (b) VAM, M.152–1931 (ex Hildburgh Coll.).
    (c) VAM, M.50–1915 (ex Fox Coll.).

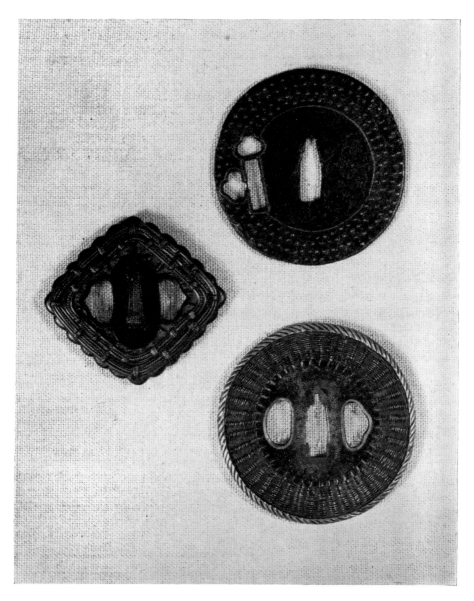

45. SHINGEN AND 'NAIL-HEAD
INCRUSTATION' GUARD (all iron)

(a) Bridge-post and quatrefoil. VAM, M.201–1921 (ex Joly Coll.).
(b) VAM, M.133–1914 (ex Behrens Coll.).
(c) VAM, 1447–1888.

46. *SAWARI* AND *GAMA-HADA* (all iron)

(a) *Tsuba:* a turnip. Signed, *Sadahide* [114, 188]. VAM, M.332–1911 (ex Hawkshaw Coll.).

(b) *Fuchi-kashira.* VAM, M.408–1911 (ex Hawkshaw Coll.).

(c) *Kojiri.* VAM, M.243–1924.

(d) *Tsuba:* a lotus-leaf. VAM, M.27–1920 (ex Gaskell Coll.).

47. NON-METALLIC MOUNTS

(a) *Tsuba,* lacquered tortoiseshell: crossed hawk's feathers. VAM, M.226–1921 (ex Joly Coll.).

(b) *Tsuba,* carved ivory: waves and wave-birds (*chidori*). Signed, *made by Tadatoshi* [92, 62]. VAM, M.1667–1931 (ex Hildburgh Coll.).

(c) *Kodzuka,* wood, with Shibayama inlay: toys. Signed, *Kwampo* [194, 231]. VAM, M.311–1936 (ex Lee and Ransom Coll.).

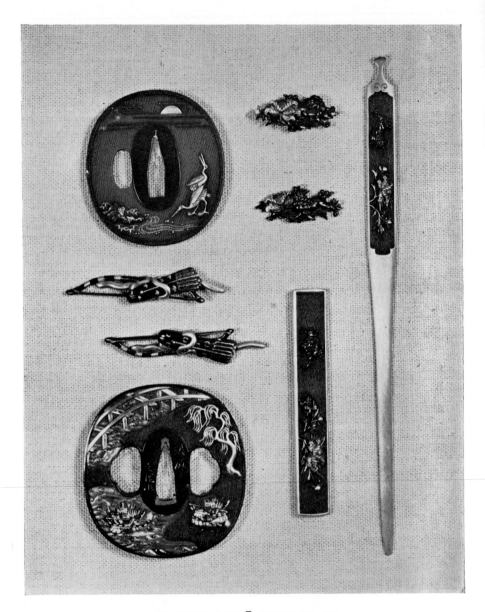

48. THE GOTŌ SCHOOL (i)

(a) *Tsuba* (copper): cranes at sunset. Signed, *Tsu Jimpo* [278, 231] with *kakihan*. VAM, M.1044–1931 (ex Hildburgh Coll.).

(b) Pair of *menuki* (*shakudō*): bows and arrows. Signed, *Gotō Mitsuyo* [55, 276] with *kakihan* (= Jōha, d. 1724). VAM, M.138,a–1924 (ex Marcus Coll.).

(c) *Tsuba* (*shakudō*): the rival generals at the Uji river (cf. Pl. 77b). Signed, *Gotō Mitsumasa* [55, 277] with *kakihan* (= Jujō, d. 1742). VAM, M.79–1919 (ex Hawkshaw and Crewdson Coll.).

(d) Set of *kodzuka kōgai* and pair of *menuki* (*shakudō*): 'lions' and paeonies. VAM, M.975,a,b,c–1931 (ex Hildburgh Coll.).

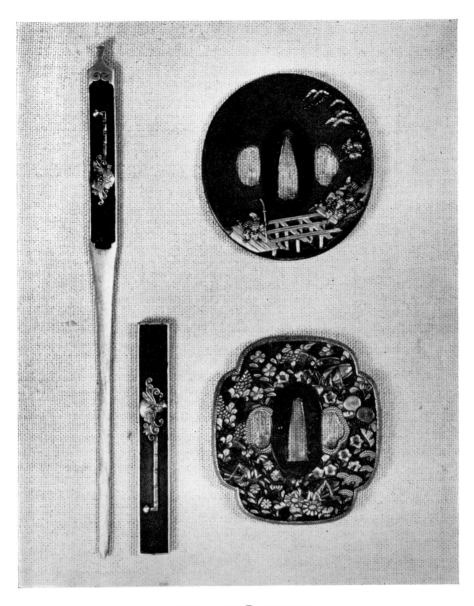

49. THE GOTŌ SCHOOL (ii)

(a) *Kodzuka* and *kōgai* (all *shakudō*): long-handled wine-pots for the marriage-ceremony. Signed, *Gotō Kwakujō* [269, 132] with *kakihan*. VAM, M.964,a–1931 (ex Hildburgh Coll.).

(b) *Tsuba:* Ichirai Hōshi and Tsutsui Jōmyō at the battle of the Uji Bridge (1180). Signed, *Gotō Yetsujō* [250, 132] with *kakihan* (d. 1687). VAM, M.329–1921 (ex Crewdson Coll.).

(c) *Tsuba:* mantis and autumn plants. Signed, *Mitsunaka* [55, 225] *of Mino.* VAM, M.4–1923 (ex Bjorck Coll.).

50. THE MYŌCHIN SCHOOL (all iron)

(a) *Tsuba*. Signed, *Nobuiye* [99, 138]. VAM. M.363–1923 (ex Bjorck Coll.).
(b) *Kashira* in the form of a court-cap. VAM, M.393–1911 (ex Hawkshaw Coll.).
(c) *Kashira* in the form of a helmet-bowl. VAM, M.477–1910.
(d) *Tsuba*. VAM, M.90–1911 (ex Hawkshaw Coll.).

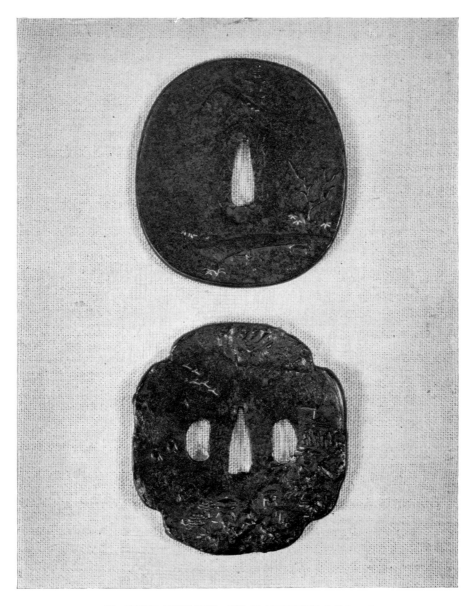

51. THE SCHOOL OF KANEIYE (all iron)

(a) *Tsuba:* a Chinese landscape. Signed, *Kaneiye* [215, 138] *of Fushimi in Yamashiro province.* VAM, M.250–1912.

(b) *Tsuba:* a Chinese landscape. Signed, *Kanemitsu* [215, 55]. VAM, M.166–1913 (ex Behrens Coll.).

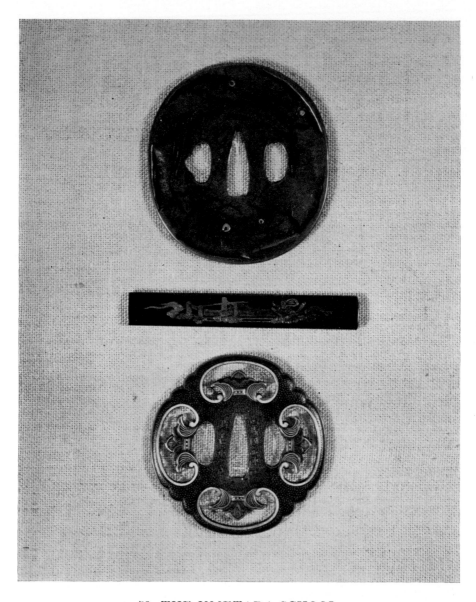

52. THE UMETADA SCHOOL

(a) *Tsuba* (copper): gourd-leaves. Signed, *Umetada Myōju* [80, 187]. VAM, M.5–1920 (ex Garbutt Coll.).

(b) *Kodzuka* (*shakudō*): the Weaving Princess at her loom. Signed. *Umetada Shigeyoshi* [110, 179], VAM, M.14–1936 (ex Lee and Ransom Coll.).

(c) *Tsuba* (*shakudō*). Signed, *Umetada Shigeyoshi* [110, 179] *of Nishijin* (Kyōto) *in Yamashiro province*. VAM, M.1143–1926 (ex Behrens Coll.).

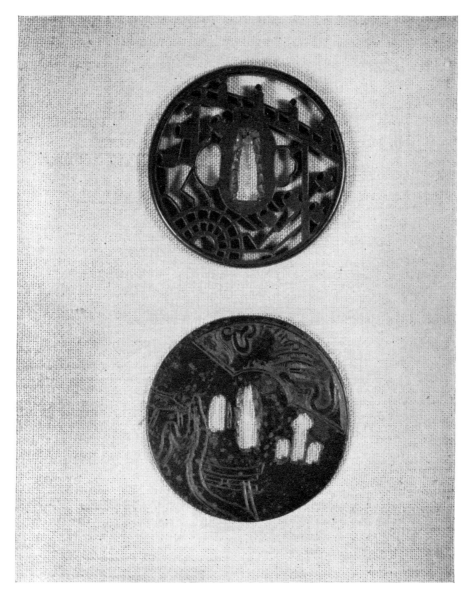

53. OWARI AND KAMAKURA GUARDS (all iron)

(a) Bridge and water-wheel. VAM, M.2–1923 (ex Bjorck Coll.).
(b) Temple, *torii* and rock; fan-mount. VAM, M.149-1913 (ex Behrens Coll.).

54. TEMBŌ

(Iron). Signed, *Tembō* [17, 77] *of Yamashiro*. VAM, M.253–1912.

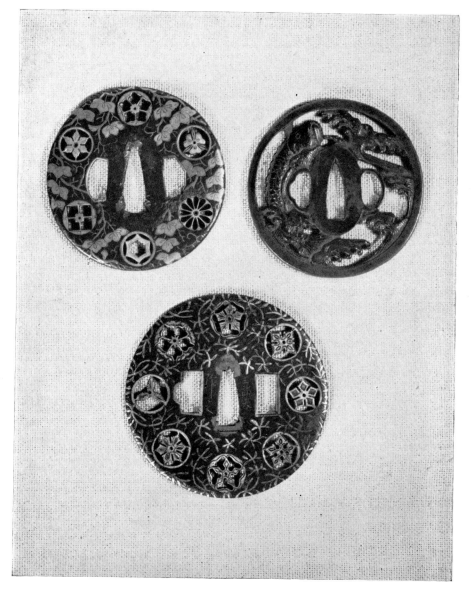

55. *MON-ZUKASHI* AND *YAMAGANE* GUARDS

(a) (Iron). VAM, M.237–1916 (ex Alexander Coll.).

(b) (*Yamagane*). Carp and waterfall. VAM, M.186–1916 (ex Eumorfopoulos Coll.).

(c) (Iron). Signed, *this was made by . . . ya Saburota* [6, 252, 222] *of Okayama in Bizen province*. VAM, M.203–1921 (ex Joly Coll.).

56. THE SHŌAMI SCHOOL (i)

(a) *Tsuba* (iron): geese and reeds. Signed *Tō(hei) Shigemitsu* [110, 55]. VAM, M.41–1957.

(b) *Tsuba* (copper): nightingale and plum-tree. Signed, *Shōami Tōji Nobushige* [99, 110]. VAM, M.236–1923 (ex Guest Coll.).

(c) *Tsuba* (iron): the cyclical characters. Signed, *Shōami Moritsugu* [167, 42] *of Matsuyama*. VAM, M.114–1928 (ex Lee Coll.).

57. THE SHŌAMI SCHOOL (ii)

(a) *Kodzuka* (iron): plum-blossom. VAM, M.15–1936 (ex Ransom Coll.).

(b) *Tsuba* (copper): stream with floating *omodaka* (water-plantain) leaves. VAM, M. 103–1911 (ex Hawkshaw Coll.).

(c) *Tsuba* (iron): mushrooms. Signed, *Shōami Shigehiro* [110, 198]. VAM, M.97–1911 (ex Hawkshaw Coll.).

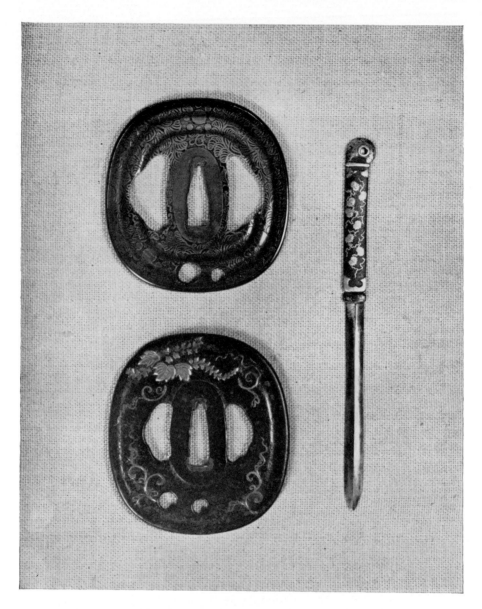

58. THE HIGO SCHOOLS (i)

(a) *Tsuba* (*sentoku*): badges of the Hosokawa family. VAM, M.23–1919 (ex Huish Coll.).

(b) *Tsuba* (iron): paulownia scrolls. VAM, M.174–1913 (ex Behrens Coll.).

(c) *Umabari* (steel): cissus-vine. VAM, M.22–1936 (ex Ransom Coll.).

59. THE HIGO SCHOOLS (ii) (all iron)

(a) *Kodzuka:* paulownia scrolls. VAM, M.266–1916 (ex Alexander Coll.).
(b) *Tsuba.* VAM, M.36–1924 (ex Marcus Coll.).
(c) *Tsuba.* VAM, M.107–1911 (ex Hawkshaw Coll.).
(d) *Kodzuka:* paper cranes, clouds and young pines. VAM, M.30–1936 (ex Naunton and Ransom Coll.).

60. THE CHŌSHŪ SCHOOLS (i) (all iron)

(a) *Tsuba:* maple, cottages, and deer. Signed, *Nakai Tomotsune* [23, 102] *of Hagi in Chōshū.* VAM, M.116–1911 (ex Hawkshaw Coll.).

(b) *Tsuba:* pine-needles and cones. Signed, *Inouye Kiyotaka* [144, 137] *of Hagi in Chōshū.* VAM, M.17–1914 (ex DeAth Coll.).

(c) *Tsuba:* chrysanthemum badge and leaves. Signed, *Yaji Sakunoshin Tomohisa* [23, 9] *of Hagi in Chōshū.* VAM, M.42–1957.

61. THE CHŌSHŪ SCHOOLS (ii)

(Iron). *Tsuba:* bamboos. Signed, *Masayuki* [31, 89] *of Hagi in Chōshū.* VAM, M.1277–1926 (ex Brooks Coll.).

62. THE KINAI SCHOOL OF ECHIZEN (all iron)

(a) *Tsuba: aoi* leaves. Signed, *Kinai* [105, 219] *of Echizen*. VAM, M.141–1914 (ex Behrens Coll.).

(b) *Tsuba:* chrysanthemum blossoms and leaves. Signed, *Kinai* [105, 219] *of Echizen 'an old gentleman of seventy-three'*. VAM, M.43–1957.

(c) *Tsuba:* Tadatsune and the boar, an incident of Yoritomo's hunting party under Mount Fuji (1193). Signed, *Kinai* [105, 219] *of Echizen*. VAM, M.113–1911 (ex Hawkshaw Coll.).

(d) *Tsuba:* a dragon. Signed, *Kinai* [105, 219] *of Echizen*. VAM, 704–1901 (ex Bowes Coll.).

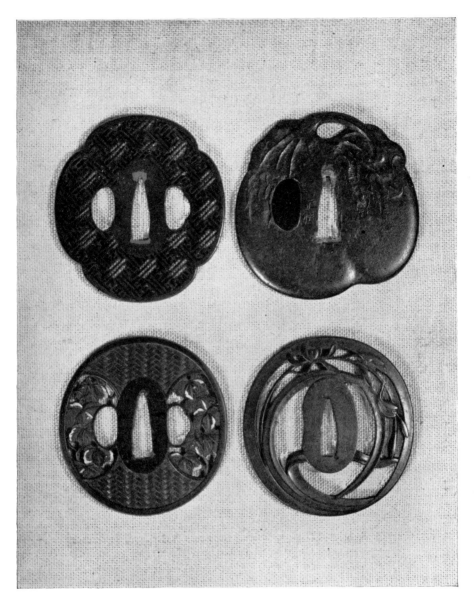

63. THE ITŌ, OR ODAWARA BUSHŪ SCHOOL (all iron)

(a) *Tsuba.* VAM, M.457–1931 (ex Hildburgh Coll.).

(b) *Tsuba:* an egg-fruit. Signed, *Masatsune* [31, 102]. VAM, M.39–1937 (ex Dobree Coll.).

(c) *Tsuba:* cissus-vines and matting. Signed, *Masayoshi* [31, 51] *of Bushū.* VAM, M.1281–1926 (ex Brooks Coll.).

(d) *Tsuba:* a spray of orchid. Signed, *Yoshinaga* [238, 187] *of Kōfu* (Yedo). VAM, M.292–1916 (ex Alexander Coll.).

64. THE AKAO AND AKASAKA SCHOOLS (all iron)

(a) *Tsuba:* grasses under the moon ('the battle-fields of Musashi'). Signed, (Akasaka) *Tadatoki* [92, 126]. VAM, M.64–1914 (ex Church Coll.).

(b) *Tsuba:* wild geese and ships' masts. Signed, *Akao Yoshitsugu* [51, 42] *of Kōfu* (Yedo). VAM, M.144–1914 (ex Behrens Coll.).

(c) *Tsuba:* paddle and tradesman's weight. Signed, *Akao Yoshitsugu* [51, 42] *of Yedo.* VAM, M.217–1912 (ex Hayashi Coll.).

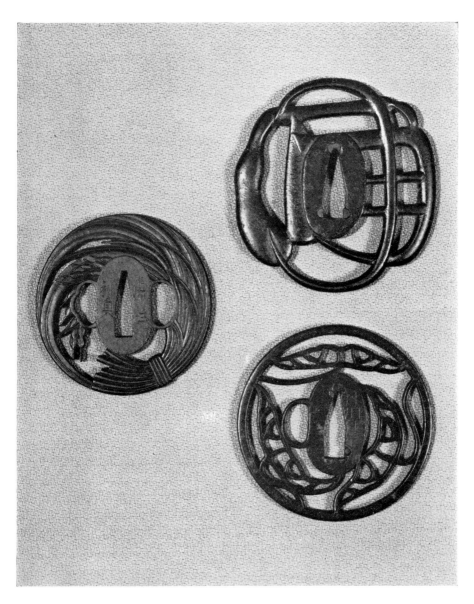

65. THE SCHOOLS OF SATSUMA,
TAMBA, AND SADO (all iron)

(a) *Tsuba:* bean-pod with stems and tendrils forming the character *ura* ('sea-shore'). Satsuma School. VAM, M.211–1921 (ex Joly Coll.).

(b) *Tsuba:* a sheaf of rice. Signed, *Toshisada* [62, 114] *of Sado province.* VAM, M.305–1916 (ex Alexander Coll.).

(c) *Tsuba:* lotus-leaves. Signed, *Sadamasa* [88, 31] *of Tamba province.* VAM, M.634–1931 (ex Hildburgh Coll.).

66. THE SCHOOL OF SŌTEN (*HIKONE-BORI*)

(a) *Tsuba* (*shakudō*): Li Po admiring the waterfall. Signed, *Sōheishi Nyūdō Sōten* [87, 241] *of Hikone in Ōmi province*. VAM, M.709–1931 (ex Hildburgh Coll.).

(b) *Fuchi-kashira* (*shibuichi*): Chinese sage and attendant. Signed, *Sōheishi Nyūdō Sōten* [87, 241]. VAM, M.742–1931 (ex Hildburgh Coll.).

(c) *Tsuba* (iron): scene from the Wars of Gempei (late 12th century). Signed, *Sōheishi Nyūdō Sōten* [87, 241] *of Hikone in Ōmi province*. VAM, M.74–1919 (ex Hawkshaw and Crewdson Coll.).

(d) *Tsuba* (iron): scene from the Wars of Gempei (late 12th century). Signed, *Sōheishi Nyūdō Sōten* [87, 241]. VAM, M.59–1924 (ex Marcus Coll.).

(e) *Fuchi-kashira* (iron): dragon and clouds. Signed, *Sōheishi Sōten* [87, 241] *of Hikone in Ōmi province*. VAM, M.743a–1931 (ex Hildburgh Coll.).

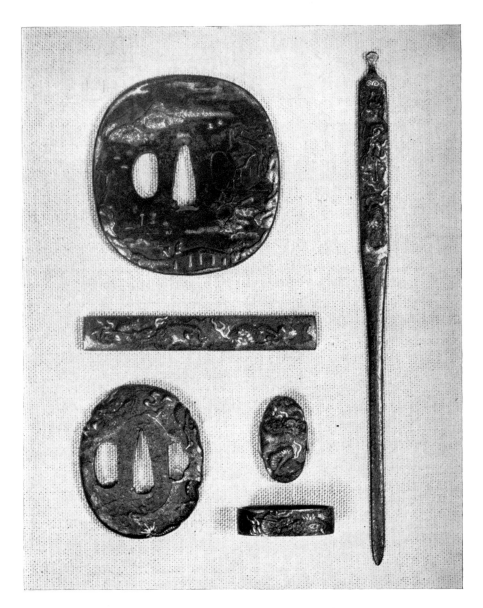

67. THE SCHOOL OF JAKUSHI (all iron)

(a) *Tsuba:* a Chinese landscape. Signed, *Jakushi* [116, 242]. VAM, M.824–1931 (ex Hildburgh Coll.).

(b) Set of *tsuba fuchi-kashira kodzuka* and *kōgai:* dragons and clouds. Signed, *Kiyō sanjin Fūdōyen Jakushi* [116, 242] (*kodzuka* and *kōgai*); *Kiyō sanjin Fūunsai Jakushi* [116, 242] (*fuchi-kashira*); and *Kiyō sanjin Jakushi* [116, 242] *Fūdōsai Minamoto no Koremitsu* with *kakihan,* made for *Nakao Shigeyasu at the castle-town of Akita in the late summer of the Hare year in the period Tempō* (1831) (*tsuba*). VAM, M.201,400,529,530–1911 (ex Hawkshaw Coll.).

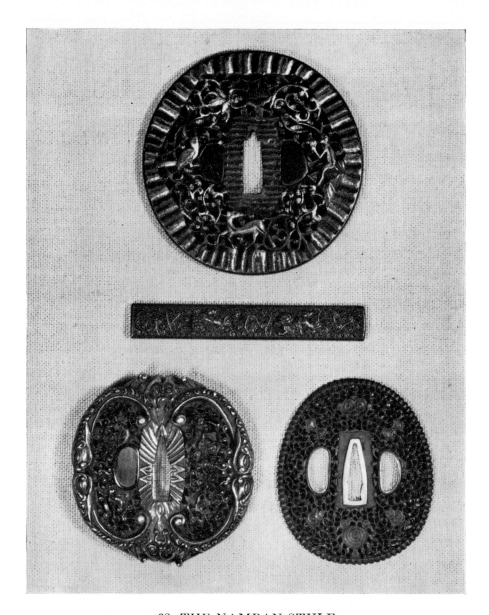

68. THE NAMBAN STYLE

(a) *Tsuba* (iron): wasp and nest, wagtail, stag and monkey amid scrolls. VAM, 183–1911 (ex Hawkshaw Coll.).

(b) *Kodzuka* (iron): 'lions' amid scrolls. VAM, M.316–1916 (ex Alexander Coll.).

(c) *Tsuba (sentoku)*: imitating a European sword-guard. VAM, M.315–1916 (ex Alexander Coll.).

(d) *Tsuba* (iron): fine scroll-work. VAM, M.773–1931 (ex Hildburgh Coll.).

69. THE HIRADO (HIZEN) SCHOOLS (all *sentoku*)

(a) *Tsuba:* 'lion' and paeonies. VAM, M.321–1916 (ex Alexander Coll.).
(b) *Tsuba:* 'the thousand monkeys'. Signed, *Mitsuhiro* [55, 198] *of Yagami in Hizen province.* VAM, M.193–1911 (ex Hawkshaw Coll.).
(c) *Tsuba:* paeony sprays. Signed, *Kamiko* [127, 217] *of Nagasaki* and dated Taiyei 3 (1523), but probably later. VAM, M.64–1924 (ex Marcus Coll.).

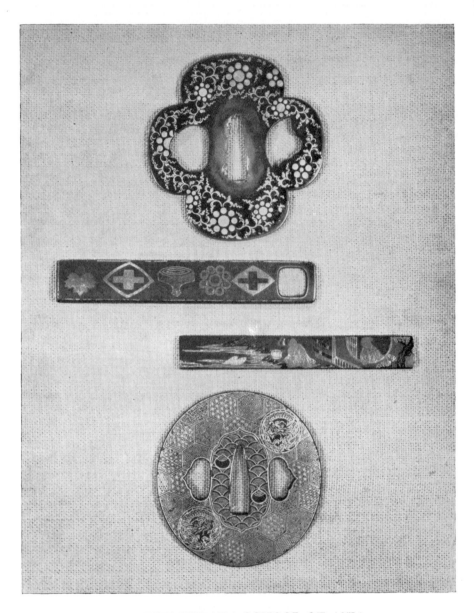

70. THE HIRATA SCHOOL OF AWA

(a) *Tsuba* (*sentoku*)*:* badges of the Mayeda and Hosokawa families. VAM,
M.105–1911 (ex Hawkshaw Coll.).

(b) *Kodzuka* (iron)*:* heraldic designs. VAM, M.273–1910.

(c) *Kodzuka* (iron)*:* one of the Chinese Paragons of Filial Piety. Signed,
Kiyonori [144, 106] with seal, *Ryū*. VAM, M.32–1936 (ex Ransom Coll.).

(d) *Tsuba* (iron). VAM, 214–1911 (ex Hawkshaw Coll.).

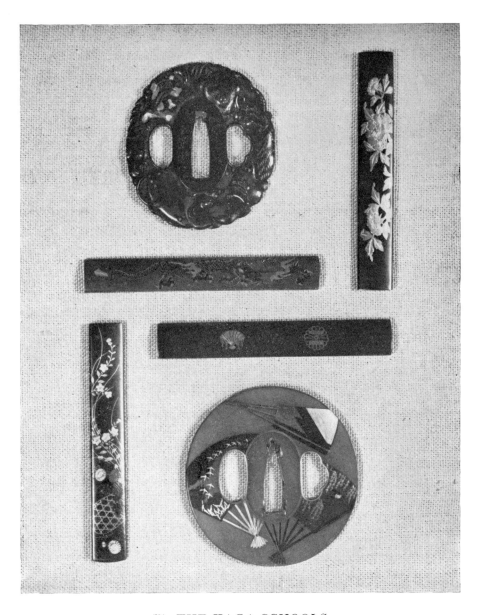

71. THE KAGA SCHOOLS

(a) *Tsuba* (*shakudō*): oxen. Signed, *Yasukawa Masakiyo* [31, 144] *of Kaga province* with *kakihan*. VAM, M.364–1923.

(b) *Kodzuka* (*shakudō*): a paeony-bush. VAM, M.36–1936 (ex Ransom Coll.).

(c) *Kodzuka* (*shibuichi*): a dragon. VAM, M.40–1936 (ex Ransom Coll.).

(d) *Kodzuka* (*shibuichi*): badges of the Niwa family. VAM, M.919–1931 (ex Hildburgh Coll.).

(e) *Kodzuka* (*shibuichi*): basket and autumn flowers. VAM, M.43–1936 (ex Ransom Coll.).

(f) *Tsuba* (copper): fans. VAM, M.30–1920 (ex Gaskell Coll.).

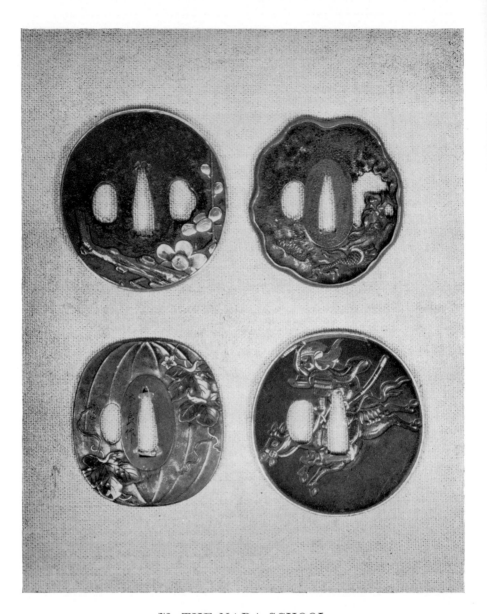

72. THE NARA SCHOOL

(a) *Tsuba* (iron)*:* plum-blossom. Signed, *made by Nara* [240, 67]. VAM, M.263–1916 (ex Alexander Coll.).

(b) *Tsuba* (copper)*:* a dragon, Signed, *Nara Tomomitsu* [234, 55]. VAM, M.1085–1931 (ex Hildburgh Coll.).

(c) *Tsuba* (*shibuichi*)*:* a melon. Signed, *made by Nara* [240, 67]. VAM, M.366–1916 (ex Alexander Coll.).

(d) *Tsuba* (*shakudō*)*:* Uyesugi Kenshin attacking Takeda Shingen (on reverse) at the battle of Kawanakajima (*c.* 1564). Signed, *Nara Shigechika* [110, 268]. VAM, M.141–1928 (ex Lee Coll.).

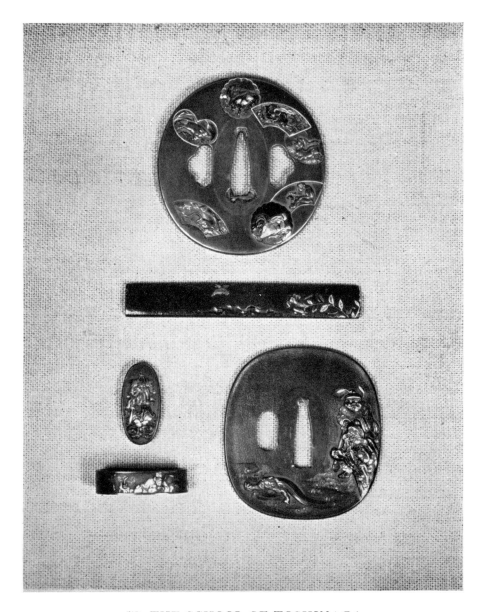

73. THE SCHOOL OF TOSHINAGA

(a) *Tsuba* (*shakudō* front, *shibuichi* back): the animals of the Zodiac. Signed, *Nara Toshishige* [62, 110] with *kakihan*. VAM, M.1110–1931 (ex Hildburgh Coll.).

(b) *Kodzuka* (*shakudō*): wagtail and sparrow. Signed, *Toshinaga* [62, 187] with *kakihan*. VAM, M.380–1916 (ex Alexander Coll.).

(c) *Fuchi-kashira* (*shibuichi*): the Chinese Emperor Gensō dreaming of Shōki the demon-queller. Signed, *Toshinaga* [62, 187] with *kakihan*. VAM, M.1104–1931 (ex Hildburgh Coll.).

(d) *Tsuba* (*shibuichi*): Shōki the demon-queller. Signed, *Toshinaga* [62, 187] with *kakihan*. VAM, M.233–1911 (ex Hawkshaw Coll.).

74. THE SCHOOL OF JŌI

(a) *Tsuba* (copper): Shōki riding a 'lion'. Signed, *Jōi* [132, 262] with seal, *Nagaharu* [25, 113]. VAM, M.85–1924 (ex Marcus Coll.).

(b) *Fuchi-kashira* (*sentoku*): Chōkwarō conjuring a horse from his gourd. Signed, *Jōi* [132,.262] *Nagaharu* [25, 113]. VAM, M.1124–1931 (ex Hildburgh Coll.).

(c) *Kodzuka* (*shibuichi*): the Eight Immortals. Signed, *Issandō Jōi* [132, 262]. VAM, M.106–1936 (ex Ransom Coll.).

(d) *Tsuba* (*sentoku*): Hotei on horseback. Signed, *Nagaharu* [25, 113]. VAM, M.425–1916 (ex Alexander Coll.).

(e) *Fuchi-kashira* (copper): Gama Sennin and another *sennin*. Signed, *Jōi* [132, 262]. VAM, M.1122–1931 (ex Hildburgh Coll.).

75. THE TSUCHIYA SCHOOL OF YASUCHIKA

(a) *Tsuba* (iron): a medley of characters. Signed, *Ysauchika* [50, 268]. VAM, M.245–1911 (ex Hawkshaw Coll.).

(b) *Kodzuka* (copper): a flower arrangement. Signed, *Tōu* [239, 235] with seal, *Yasuchika* [50, 268]. VAM, M.404–1916 (ex Alexander Coll.).

(c) *Kodzuka* (iron): a writer's brush. Signed, *Yasuchika* [50, 268] with *kaki-han*. VAM, M.403–1916 (ex Alexander Coll.).

(d) *Kodzuka* (sentoku): dragon and clouds. Signed, *Yasuchika* [50, 268]. VAM, M.517–1911 (ex Church Coll.).

(e) *Tsuba* (shakudō): a trailing plant. Signed, *Yasuchika* [50, 268] with *kakihan*. VAM, M.1149–1913 (ex Hildburgh Coll.).

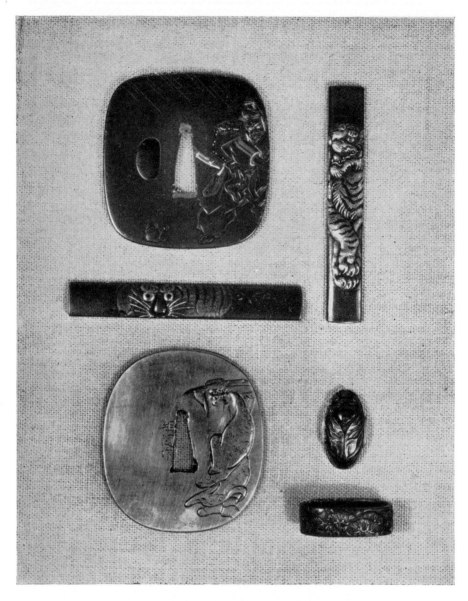

76. THE HAMANO SCHOOL (i)

(a) *Tsuba:* Tadamori and (on reverse) the oil-thief. Signed, *Otsuryūken Masayuki* [79, 266]. VAM, M.334–1921 (ex Crewdson Coll.).

(b) *Kodzuka:* a tiger. Signed, *Otsuryūken Miboku* [233, 264] with *kakihan.* VAM, M.1169–1931 (ex Hildburgh Coll.).

(c) *Kodzuka:* a tiger. Signed, *Masayuki* [79, 266] 'aged seventy-three'. VAM, M.118–1936 (ex Ransom Coll.).

(d) *Tsuba* (gilt): Shōki. Signed, *Noriyuki* [251, 266] *saku.* VAM, M.700–1916 (ex Alexander Coll.).

(e) *Fuchi-kashira:* cicada and pine-trunk. Signed, *Masayuki* [79, 266]. VAM M.1172–1931 (ex Hildburgh Coll.).

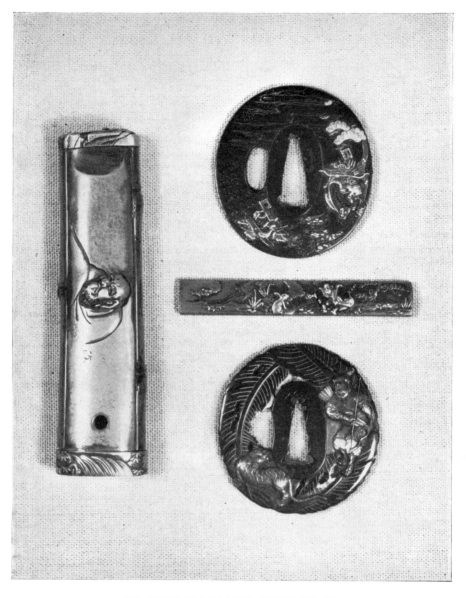

77. THE HAMANO SCHOOL (ii)

(a) Hilt for a dirk (*sentoku*): Daruma. Signed, *Masayuki* [79, 266]. VAM, M.424–1916 (ex Alexander Coll.).

(b) *Tsuba* (*shakudō*): the rival generals Sasaki Takatsuna and Kajiwara Kagesuye at the Uji river crossing (1184). Signed, *Hamano Naoyuki* [91, 266] with *kakihan*. VAM, M.445–1916 (ex Alexander Coll.).

(c) *Kodzuka* (*shibuichi*): Momotarō the boy-hero offering a cake to the hare. Signed, *Hamano Hōyūsai Naotsune* [91, 175] with *kakihan*. VAM, M.150–1936 (ex Ransom Coll.).

(d) *Tsuba* (*shakudō*): Chinaman hunting a tiger. Signed, (Hata) *Nobuyoshi* [99, 271] with *kakihan*. VAM, 1207–1931 (ex Hildburgh Coll.).

78. THE YOKOYA SCHOOL

(a) *Tsuba* (bronze): Tiger and bamboo. Signed, *Sōmin* [87, 244]. VAM, M.1255–1931 (ex Hildburgh Coll.).

(b) *Kodzuka* (*shakudō*): Soga Gorō arrested by Goromaru (1193). Signed, *Sōmin* [87, 244] with *kakihan* 'after a design by Hokuso-ō Hanabusa Itchō'. VAM, M.175–1936 (ex Ransom Coll.).

(c) *Kodzuka* (*shibuichi*): a woman of Ohara carrying firewood. Inscribed, *Hanabusa Itchō* with seal, and signed, *Sōmin* [87, 244] with *kakihan*. VAM, M.345–1936 (ex Ransom Coll.).

(d) *Kodzuka* (*shibuichi*): Shōki the demon-queller. Signed, *Sōmin* [87, 244] with *kakihan*. VAM, M.174–1936 (ex Ransom Coll.).

(e) *Kodzuka* (silver): Monju the Bodhisatva. Signed, *Sōyo* [87, 263] with *kakihan*. VAM, M.177–1936 (ex Ransom Coll.).

(f) *Tsuba* (*shakudō*): tigers and bamboo. Signed *Sōyo* [87, 263] with *kakihan*. VAM, M.20–1913 (ex Seymour Trower Coll.).

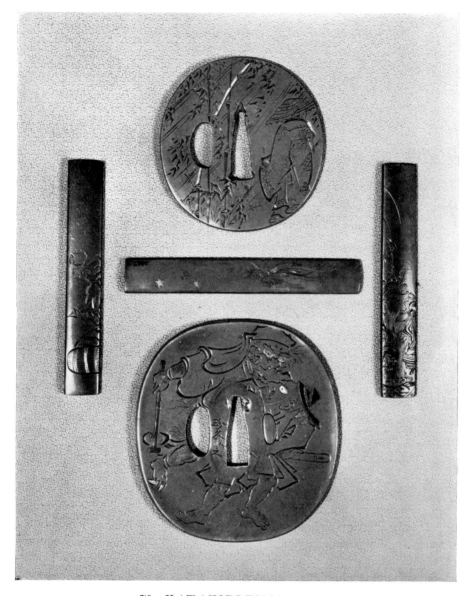

79. *KATAKIRI* ENGRAVING

(a) *Kodzuka* (*shibuichi*): Daikoku. Signed, *Sōmin* [87, 244] with *kakihan*. VAM, M.172–1936 (ex Naunton and Ransom Coll.).

(b) *Tsuba* (copper): the Chinese poet Toba in a shower of rain. Signed, *Ishiyama Sammi*. VAM, M.87–1915 (ex Seymour Trower Coll.).

(c) *Kodzuka* (*shibuichi*): the Chinese hero Kwanu. Signed, *Tsūtembō Naga-yuki* [25, 266]. VAM, M.132–1936 (ex Ransom Coll.).

(d) *Kodzuka* (*shibuichi*): bird of paradise (*fūchō*). Signed, *Sōmin* [87, 244]. VAM, M.124–1910.

(e) *Tsuba* (copper): scene from the *Nō* drama *Momiji-gari* (the witch leaping on Taira no Koremochi). Signed, *this was carved by Yoshihisa* [245, 9] (Shōnai Schools). VAM, M.326–1911 (ex Hawkshaw Coll.).

80. THE MITO SCHOOLS (i)

(a) *Tsuba (shibuichi):* two Chinese sages playing checkers in a landscape. Signed, *Ichijōsai Hironaga* [29, 187] with *kakihan*. VAM, M.267–1911 (ex Hawkshaw Coll.).

(b) *Fuchi-kashira (shakudō):* chrysanthemums. Signed, *Unno Yoshimori* [115, 170]. VAM, M.54,a–1957.

(c) *Kodzuka (shakudō):* the Eight Views (*Hakkei*) of Lake Biwa. Signed, *Katsuhira* [153, 32] *of Mito*. VAM, M.192–1936 (ex Ransom Coll.).

(d) *Tsuba* (copper)*:* Shōki and Chōkwarō. Signed, *Hiroyasu* [29, 139] with *kakihan*. VAM, M.270–1911 (ex Hawkshaw Coll.).

(e) Pair of *menuki* (gold)*:* the Bodhisattvas Monju and Fugen. Signed, *Moritoshi* [170, 187]. VAM, M.476,a–1916 (ex Alexander Coll.).

81. THE MITO SCHOOLS (ii)

(a) *Kodzuka (shibuichi):* village by the shore. Signed, *Hirochika* [29, 268]. VAM, M.191–1936 (ex Ransom Coll.).

(b) *Tsuba (shibuichi):* tiger by a cascade. Signed, *Motohira* [151, 32] with *kakihan.* VAM, M.466–1916 (ex Alexander Coll.).

(c) *Kodzuka (shibuichi):* a cock. Signed, *Masaharu* [79, 113]. VAM, M.2144–1931 (ex Hildburgh Coll.).

(d) *Kodzuka (shibuichi):* fishes, Signed, *Yamagawa Yoshinaga* [51, 83] with *kakihan.* VAM, M.469–1916 (ex Alexander Coll.).

82. THE SEKIJŌKEN SCHOOL OF MITO

(a) *Tsuba* (iron): the giant centipede of Seta bridge. Signed. *Sekijōken Motozane* [15, 229]. VAM, M.272–1911 (ex Hawkshaw Coll.).

(b) *Kodzuka* (copper): Yemma-ō, King of Hell. Signed, *Shihō-usō Sadamoto* [114, 261] with *kakihan* 'at Yedo'. VAM, M.197–1936 (ex Lee and Ransom Coll.).

(c) *Fuchi-kashira* (*shibuichi*): Plum and paeony. Signed, *Sekijōken Ōyama Motoyasu* [15, 237] with *kakihan*. VAM, M.491–1916 (ex Alexander Coll.).

(d) *Fuchi-kashira* (*shibuichi*): Pheasants and cherry-blossom. Signed, *Sekijōken Motozane* [15, 299] with *kakihan*. VAM, M.56,a–1957.

(e) *Kodzuka* (copper): Kanzan and Jittoku. Signed; *this was carved by Shihō-usō Sadamoto* [114, 261] *at Suifu* (Mito). VAM, M.1345–1931 (ex Hildburgh Coll.).

(f) *Tsuba* (iron): bird on a branch. Signed, *Sekisoken Motohiro* [15, 198]. VAM, M.26–1920 (ex Gaskell Coll.).

83. THE HITOTSUYANAGI SCHOOL OF MITO

(a) *Fuchi-kashira* (*shibuichi*): geese by a fence. Signed, *made by Hirano Izayemon* (i.e. Tomoyoshi IV [23, 258]) and dated Tempō 5 (1834). VAM, M.55,a–1957.

(b) *Tsuba* (iron): a dragon. Signed, *made by Hitotsuyanagi Tomoyoshi* [23, 258]. VAM. 1416–1888.

(c) *Kodzuka* (*shibuichi*): dragon and jewel. Signed, *Hitotsuyanagi Tomoyoshi* [23, 258] with *kakihan*. VAM, M.198–1936 (ex Ransom Coll.).

(d) *Tsuba* (*shibuichi*): the grass-cutter's boy and his ox. Signed, *made by Hitotsuyanagi Michinaga* [183, 187]. VAM, M.497–1916 (ex Alexander Coll.).

(e) *Kodzuka* (*shibuichi*): a temple-guardian (*Ni-ō*). Signed, *this was made by Hitotsuyanagi Tomonaga* [23, 187]. VAM, M.200–1936 (ex Ransom Coll.).

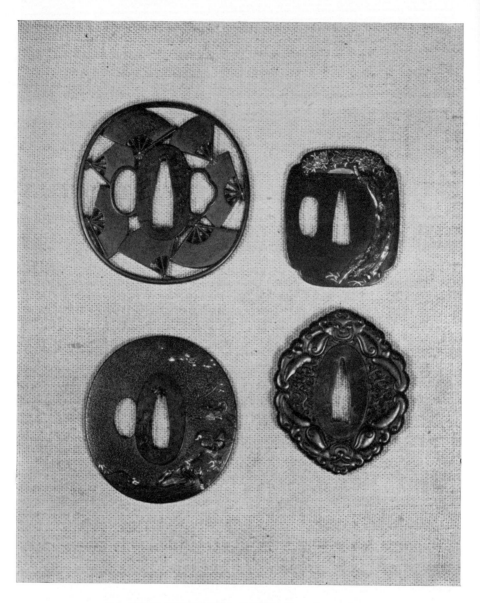

84. THE YEGAWA SCHOOL OF MITO

(a) *Tsuba* (iron)*:* fans. Signed, *Yegawa Muneyoshi* [87, 179] with *kakihan*, and dated for 1859. VAM, M.32–1919 (ex Hawkshaw and Naunton Coll.).

(b) *Tsuba* (*shakudō*)*:* cherry-tree. Signed, *Yegawa Toshimasa* [62, 79]. VAM, M.279–1911 (ex Hawkshaw Coll.).

(c) *Tsuba* (*shibuichi*)*:* mandarin ducks by a stream. Signed, *Toshimasa* [62, 79]. VAM, M.501–1916 (ex Alexander Coll.).

(d) *Tsuba* (iron)*.* Signed, *Yegawa Toshimasa* [62, 79] with *kakihan*. VAM, M.280–1911 (ex Hawkshaw Coll.).

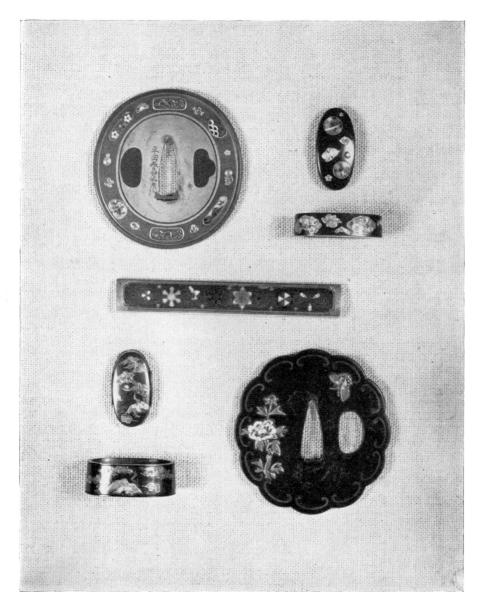

85. THE HIRATA SCHOOL (CLOISONNÉ ENAMEL)

(a) *Tsuba* (*sentoku*)*:* Signed, *Hirata Harunari* [113, 257] with *kakihan.* VAM, M.596–1916 (ex Alexander Coll.).

(b) *Fuchi-kashira* (*shakudō*). VAM, M.407–1911 (ex Hawkshaw Coll.).

(c) *Kodzuka* (copper-gilt)*:* snow crystals. VAM, M.285–1936 (ex Lee and Ransom Coll.).

(d) *Fuchi-kashira* (*shibuichi*)*:* a waterside landscape. VAM, M.64,a–1957.

(e) *Tsuba* (iron)*:* butterfly and paeony. VAM, M.111–1924 (ex Marcus Coll.).

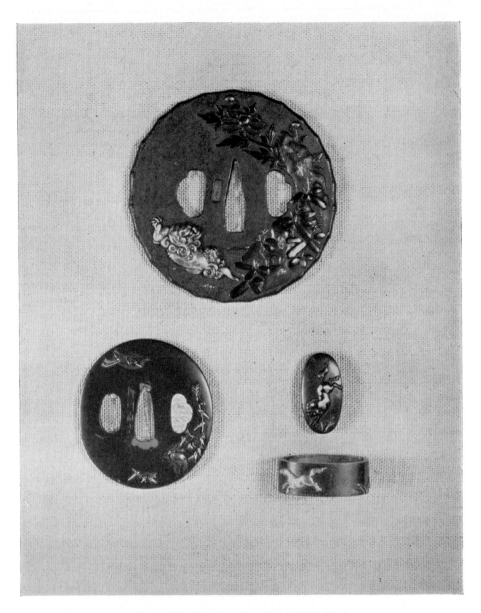

86. THE YANAGAWA SCHOOL

(a) *Tsuba* (iron): 'lion' and paeony. Signed, *Naoharu* [91, 113]. VAM, M.285–1911 (ex Hawkshaw Coll.).

(b) *Tsuba* (*shibuichi*): egrets and reeds. Signed, *Yanagawa Naomitsu* [91, 55] with *kakihan*. VAM, M.504–1916 (ex Alexander Coll.).

(c) *Fuchi-kashira* (*shibuichi*): horses. Signed, *Yanagawa Naomasa* [91, 79] with *kakihan*. VAM, M.1367–1931 (ex Hildburgh Coll.).

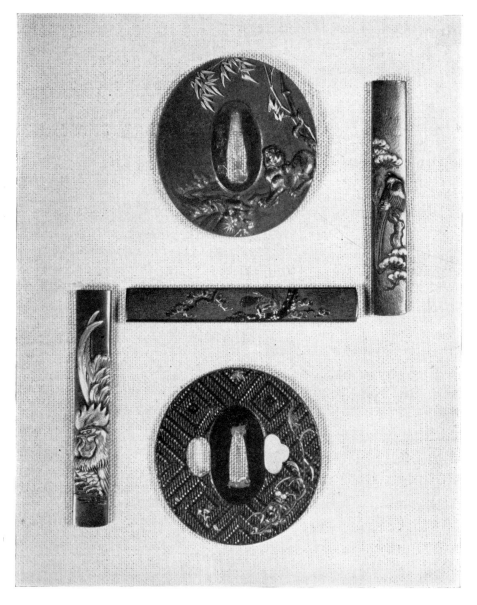

87. THE ISHIGURO SCHOOL

(a) *Tsuba (shibuichi):* tiger and bamboo. Signed, *Ishiguro Masayoshi* [79, 115] with *kakihan.* VAM, M.296–1911 (ex Hawkshaw Coll.).

(b) *Kodzuka (shibuichi):* pheasant on a pine-tree. Signed, *Shōjutei Ishiguro Masatsugu* [79, 209] with *kakihan.* VAM, M.224–1936 (ex Ransom Coll.).

(c) *Kodzuka (shakudō):* hawk on a pine-tree. Signed, *Ishiguro Yoshikatsu* [115, 158] with *kakihan.* VAM, M.1321–1926 (ex Brooks Coll.).

(d) *Kodzuka (shibuichi):* a cock. Signed, *Ishiguro Masatsune* [79, 150] with *kakihan.* VAM, M.221–1936 (ex Lee and Ransom Coll.).

(e) *Tsuba (shakudō):* butterfly and autumn plants. Signed, *Ishiguro Masayoshi* [79, 115]. VAM, M.518–1916 (ex Alexander Coll.).

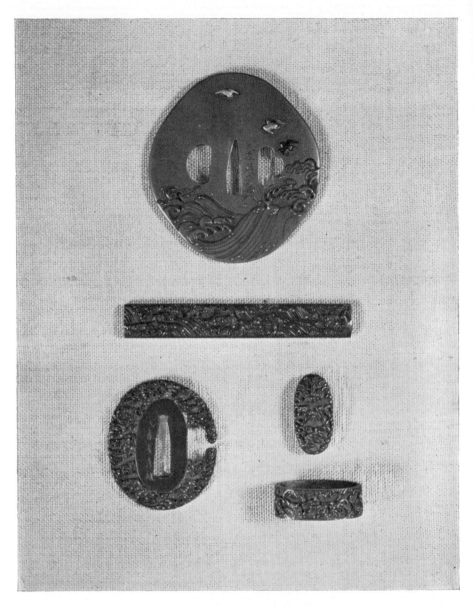

88. THE ŌMORI SCHOOL

(a) *Tsuba* (copper): waves and wave-birds (*chidori*). Signed, *Ōmori Teruhide* [117, 65] with *kakihan*. VAM. M.304–1911 (ex Hawkshaw Coll.).

(b) *Kodzuka* (*shibuichi*): waves. Signed, *Ōmori Teruhide* [117, 65]. VAM, M.534–1911 (ex Hawkshaw Coll.)..

(c) *Hamidashi-tsuba* (*shibuichi*): waves. Signed, *Ōmori Teruhide* [117, 65] with *kakihan*. VAM, M.1439–1931 (ex Hildburgh Coll.).

(d) *Fuchi-kashira* (*shibuichi*): waves. Signed, *Ōmori Teruhide* [117, 65] with *kakihan*. VAM, M.1442–1931 (ex Hildburgh Coll.).

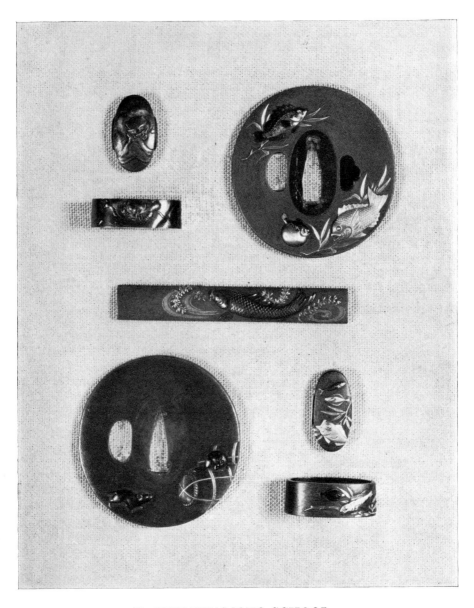

89. THE IWAMOTO SCHOOL

(a) *Fuchi-kashira* (*shibuichi*): tigers. Signed, *Iwamoto Konkwan* [236, 194] with *kakihan*. VAM, M.547,a–1916 (ex Alexander Coll.).

(b) *Tsuba* (*shibuichi*): edible fishes. Signed, *Iwamoto Ryōkwan* [67, 194] with *kakihan*. VAM, M.141–1915 (ex Behrens Coll.).

(c) *Kodzuka* (*shibuichi*): carp and water-weeds. Signed, *Iwamoto Konkwan* [236, 194] with *kakihan*. VAM, M.256–1936 (ex Lee and Ransom Coll.).

(d) *Tsuba* (*shibuichi*): rats and rice-bales. Signed, *Iwamoto Kwanri* [194, 62] with *kakihan* and dated Bunkwa 1 (1804). VAM, M.548–1916 (ex Alexander Coll.).

(e) *Fuchi-kashira* (*shakudō*): edible fishes. Signed, *Iwamoto Ryōkwan* [67, 194] with *kakihan*. VAM, M.88,a–1952.

90. THE TETSUGENDŌ SCHOOL (all iron)

(a) *Tsuba:* a dragon. Signed, *Seiryūken Hidenaga* [188, 187] with seal, *Seiyei.* VAM, M.1549–1931 (ex Hildburgh Coll.).
(b) *Kodzuka:* a dragon. Signed, *Seiryūken Hidenaga* [188, 187] with seal, *Seiyei.* VAM, M.266–1936 (ex Ransom Coll.).
(c) *Tsuba:* two carp. Signed, *Tetsugendō Naofusa* [243, 93]. VAM, M.319–1911 (ex Hawkshaw Coll.).

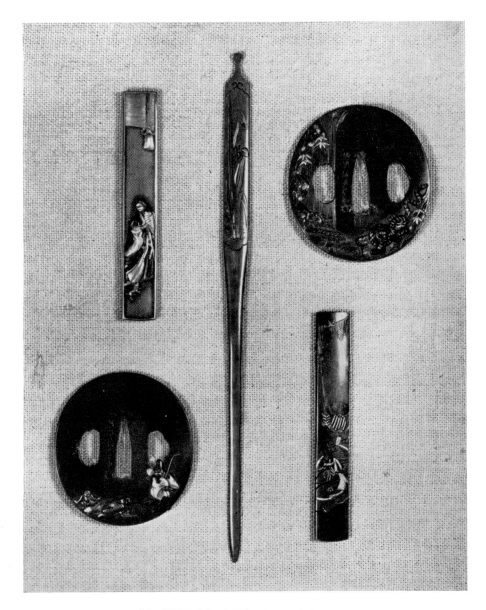

91. THE ICHINOMIYA SCHOOL

(a) *Kodzuka* (silver): court lady and cat. Signed, *Echizen no Daijō Minamoto no Nagatsune* [83, 150] with *kakihan*. VAM, M.267–1936 (ex Ransom Coll.).

(b) *Kōgai* (copper): iris and butterfly. Signed, *Nagatsune* [83, 150] with *kakihan*. VAM, M.1559–1931 (ex Hildburgh Coll.).

(c) *Tsuba* (*shibuichi*): tiger by a cascade. Signed, *Echizen no Daijō Minamoto no Nagatsune* [83, 150] with *kakihan*. VAM, M.579–1916 (ex Alexander Coll.).

(d) *Tsuba* (*shibuichi*): street mummers. Signed, *Echizen no Daijō Nagatsune* [83, 150] with *kakihan*. VAM, M.580–1916 (ex Alexander Coll.).

(e) *Kodzuka* (*shibuichi*): court lady and servant. Signed, *Nagatsune* [83, 150] with *kakihan*. VAM, M.271–1936 (ex Ransom Coll.).

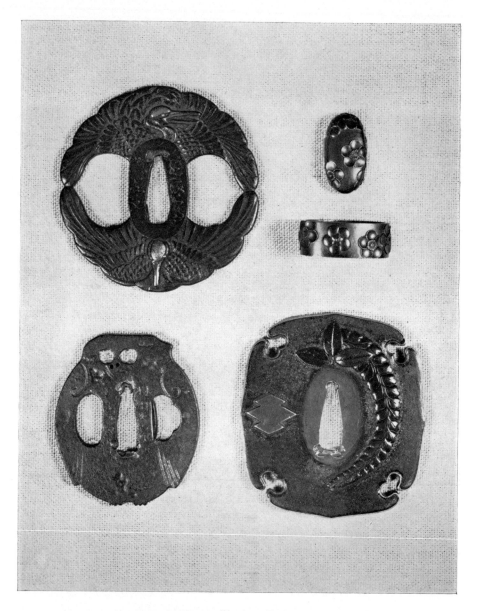

92. THE SHŌNAI SCHOOLS

(a) *Tsuba* (iron): two cranes. Signed, *Yūrakusai Akabumi* [230, 221]. VAM, M.324–1911 (ex Hawkshaw Coll.).

(b) *Fuchi-kashira* (iron): plum-blossoms. Signed, *Akabumi* [230, 221]. VAM, M.405–1911 (ex Hawkshaw Coll.).

(c) *Tsuba* (iron): an owl. Signed, *Akabumi* [230, 221] *of Oidzumi in Dewa province* and dated, Bunsei 7 (1824). VAM, M.292–1920.

(d) *Tsuba* (*sentoku*): heraldic designs. Signed, *Zaisai* [52, 248]. VAM, M.323–1911 (ex Hawkshaw Coll.).

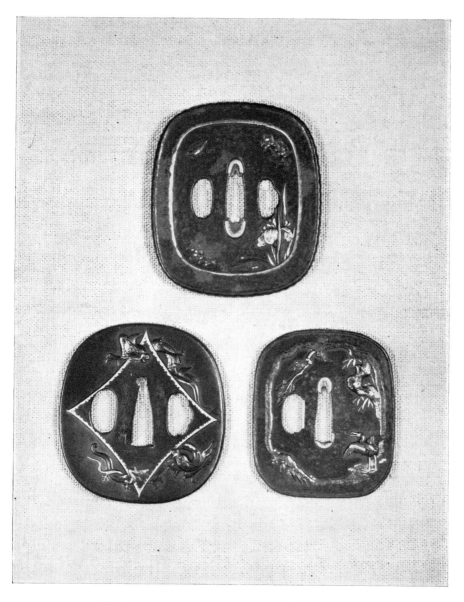

93. THE TANAKA SCHOOL (all iron)

(a) *Tsuba:* iris and cuckoo. Signed, *Masanaga* [79, 187] with *kakihan*. VAM, M.1504–1931 (ex Hildburgh Coll.).

(b) *Tsuba:* 'smooth dragons'. Signed, *Tōzanshi Nagahide* [187, 117] with *kakihan* and dated Manyen 1 (1860). VAM, 334e–1878.

(c) *Tsuba:* crane with pine, bamboo, and plum-blossom. Signed, *Masanaga* [79, 187] with *kakihan* and dated Ansei, Snake year (1857). VAM, M.563–1916 (ex Alexander Coll.).

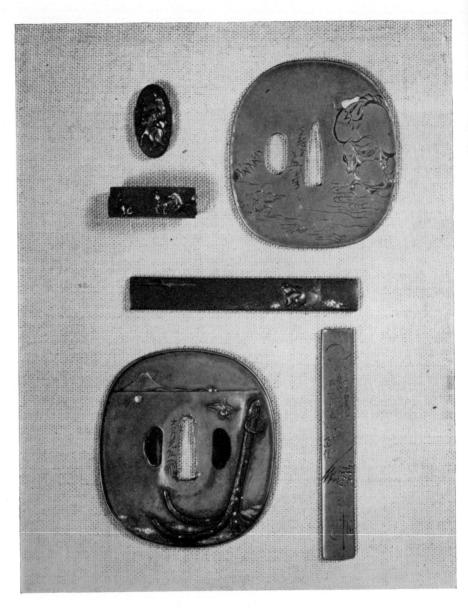

94. THE ŌTSUKI SCHOOL (i)

(a) *Fuchi-kashira* (*shakudō*): horses. Signed, (Ō-)*tsuki Mitsuoki* [55, 202] with seal, *Ryūsai.* VAM, M.624–1911.

(b) *Tsuba* (*sentoku*): Hotei fording a stream. Signed, *engraved by Shiryūdō Mitsuoki* [55, 202]. VAM, M.308–1911 (ex Hawkshaw Coll.).

(c) *Kodzuka* (*shibuichi*): hares and the moon. Signed, *Ōtsuki Mitsuhiro* [55, 29] with *kakihan.* VAM, M.1324–1926 (ex Brooks Coll.).

(d) *Tsuba* (*sentoku*): an old anchor on the shore. Signed, *Ōtsuki Mitsuhiro* [55, 29] with *kakihan,* VAM M.1471–1931 (ex Hildburgh Coll.).

(e) *Kodzuka* (copper): cottage by moonlight, and a poem. Signed, (Ō-)*tsuki Mitsuoki* [55, 202]. VAM, M.534–1916 (ex Alexander Coll.).

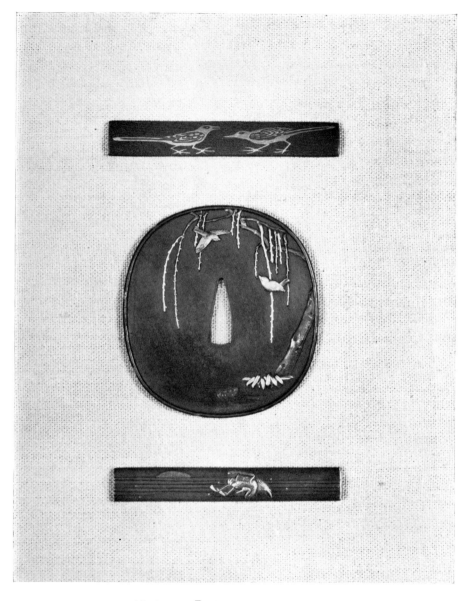

95. THE ŌTSUKI SCHOOL (ii)

(a) *Kodzuka* (copper)*:* two wagtails. Seal of *Hideoki* [65, 202]. VAM, 266/8–1881.

(b) *Tsuba* (iron). sparrows and willow. Signed, *Tokuoki* [270, 202]. VAM, M.1298–1926 (ex Brooks Coll.).

(c) *Kodzuka* (copper)*:* crane and the setting sun. Signed, *made by Tokuoki* [270, 202]. VAM, M.253–1936 (ex Ransom Coll.).

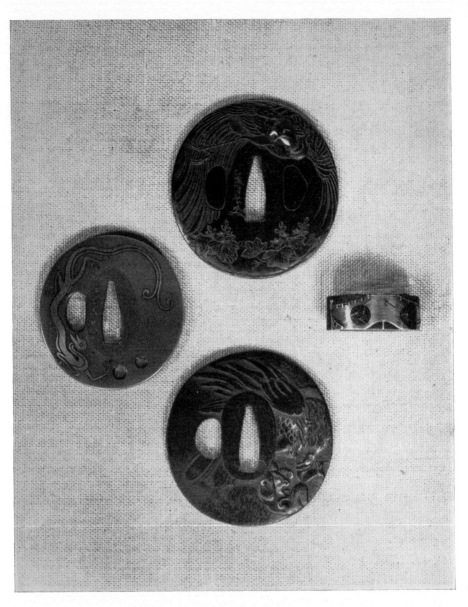

96. GOTŌ SEIJŌ

(a) *Tsuba* (iron): phoenix and paulownia. Signed, *Gotō Seijō* [144, 132] with *kakihan*. VAM, M.352–1916 (ex Alexander Coll.).

(b) *Tsuba* (copper): a 'smooth dragon'. Signed, *Gotō Seijō* [144, 132] with *kakihan*. VAM, M.219–1911 (ex Hawkshaw Coll.).

(c) *Fuchi* (iron): a tent-curtain. Signed, *Gotō Seijō* [144, 132] with *kakihan*. VAM, M.1043–1931 (ex Hildburgh Coll.).

(d) *Tsuba* (iron): eagle and monkey. Signed, *made by Gotō Seijō* [144, 132]. VAM, 336i–1878.

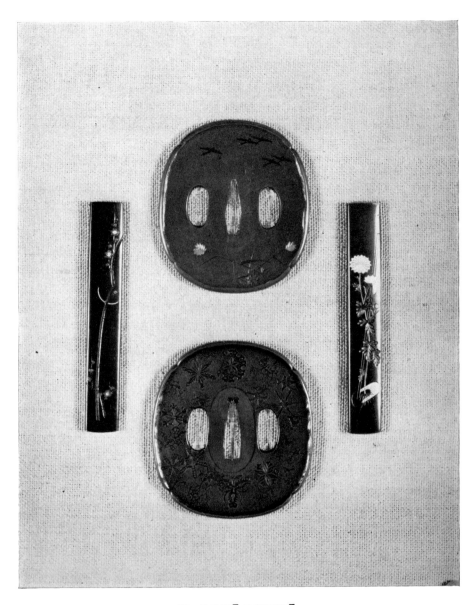

97. GOTŌ ICHIJŌ

(a) *Tsuba* (copper): wild geese and reeds. Signed, *Gotō Kōjō* [55, 132], son of *Ichijō* with *kakihan*. VAM, M.223–1911 (ex Hawkshaw Coll.).

(b) *Kodzuka* (*shakudō*): plum-blossom and the moon. Signed, *Gotō Hokkyō Ichijō* [1, 132] with *kakihan*. VAM. M.522–1911 (ex Church Coll.).

(c) *Kodzuka* (*shibuichi*): hoe and chrysanthemum-plant. Signed, *Gekkindō Yūsai* [249, 272] with *kakihan* 'after a design by *Hokkyō Ichijō*'. VAM, M.85–1936 (ex Ransom Coll.).

(d) *Tsuba* (copper): snow-crystals. VAM, M.515–1911 (ex Church Coll.).

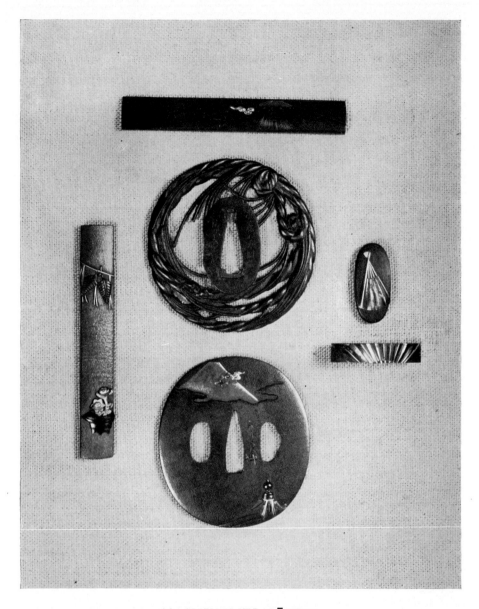

98. SHUMMEI HŌGEN

(a) *Kodzuka (shakudō):* Mount Fuji. Signed, *Shummei* [113, 80] *Hōgen* with *kakihan* and dated Bunsei 14 (*sic:* 1831). VAM, M.211–1936 (ex Ransom Coll.).

(b) *Tsuba* (iron): straw rope (*shimenawa*) and rats. Signed, *Hōgen Shummei* [113, 80] *after a design by Itō Masakata* and dated Bunsei, Cock year (1825). VAM, M.288–1911 (ex Hawkshaw Coll.).

(c) *Kodzuka* (copper): a flower arrangement. Signed, *Shummei Hōgen* [113, 80] with *kakihan*. VAM, M.185–1910.

(d) *Fuchi-kashira (shibuichi):* fans. Signed, *Shummei* [113, 80] *Hōgen* with *kakihan* and dated Tempō, 40th year of the cycle (1843). VAM, M.57,a–1957.

(e) *Tsuba (shakudō):* Mount Fuji and a bridge-post hung with New Year decorations. Signed, *Shummei* [113, 80] *Hōgen* with *kakihan*. VAM, M.287–1911 (ex Hawkshaw Coll.).

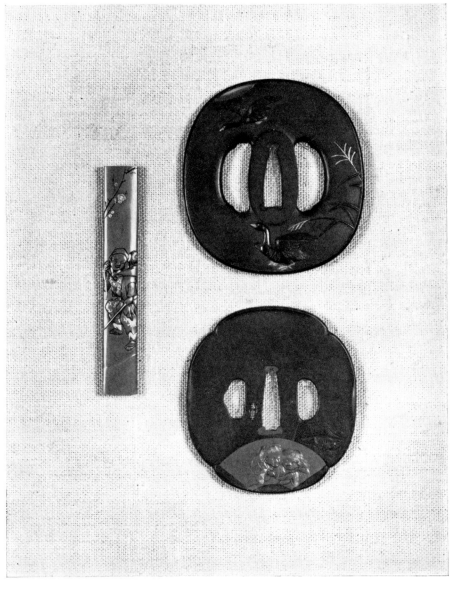

99. KANŌ NATSUO

(a) *Kodzuka* (copper): a monkey-showman. Signed, *carved by Natsuo* [253, 159]. VAM, M.1480–1931 (ex Hildburgh Coll.).

(b) *Tsuba* (iron): wild geese and the moon. Signed, *carved by Natsuo* [253, 159] and dated for 1894. VAM, M.311–1911 (ex Hawkshaw Coll.).

(c) *Tsuba* (iron): Kanzan and Jittoku. Signed, *Natsuo* [253, 159] with seal, *Koshō*. VAM, M.312–1911 (ex Hawkshaw Coll.).

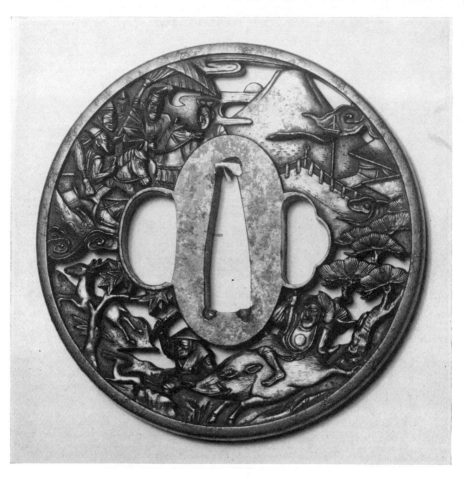

100. DETAILS OF TECHNIQUE (i)

Tsuba, chiselled iron. Yoritomo's hunting party under Mount Fuji; Tadatsune killing the monstrous boar. Signed, *Kinai* [105, 219] *of Echizen.* VAM, M.113–1911 (ex Hawkshaw Coll.).

101. DETAILS OF TECHNIQUE (ii)

Tsuba, chiselled iron. Chrysanthemums. Signed, *Kinai* [105, 219] *of Echizen*, *'an old gentleman of seventy-three'*. VAM, M.43–1957.

102. DETAILS OF TECHNIQUE (iii)

Detail of *tsuba*, chiselled iron with incrustation of brass. A sea-eagle above
the waves. Signed, *Masayuki* [79, 266] '*using a design by Toshinaga.*'
VAM, M.427–1916 (ex Alexander Coll.).

103. DETAILS OF TECHNIQUE (iv)

Tsuba, iron, chiselled, with incrustation of gold, silver and *shakudō*. Frog in a lotus-pond. Signed, *Natsuo*, with *kakihan*. VAM, M.541–1916 (ex Alexander Coll.).

104. DETAILS OF TECHNIQUE (v)

Detail of *tsuba*, bronze, with *katakiri* engraving. Tiger and bamboo. Signed *Sōmin* [87, 244]. VAM, M.1255–1931 (ex Hildburgh Coll.).

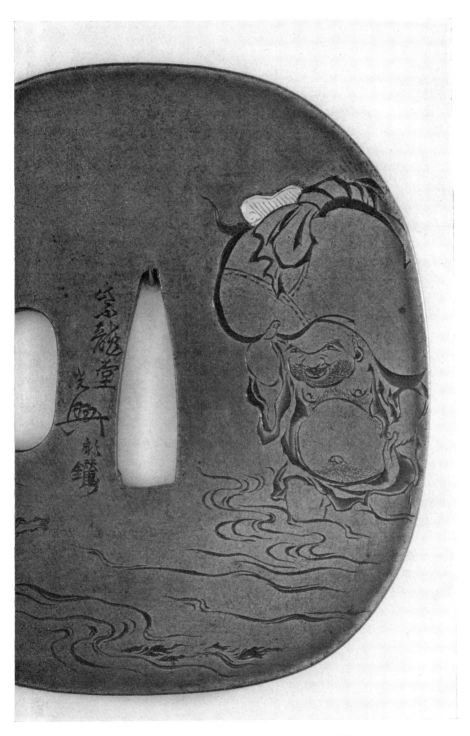

105. DETAILS OF TECHNIQUE (vi)

Detail of *tsuba, sentoku,* with *katakiri* engraving and inlay of gold and *shakudō*. Hotei, one of the Gods of Good Luck, fording a stream, carrying his bag. Signed, *Engraved and worked by Shiryūdō Mitsuoki* [55, 202]. VAM, M.308–1911 (ex Hawkshaw Coll.).

106. DETAILS OF TECHNIQUE (vii)

Tsuba, shakudō nanako with incrustation of gold, silver and *shakudō*. Fishes and water-weeds. Signed, *Iwamoto Ryōkwan,* with *kakihan.* VAM, M.141–1915 (ex Behrens Coll.).

107. DETAILS OF TECHNIQUE (viii)

Detail of *tsuba*, *sentoku* with incrustation of copper, gold, and silver. A wolf on the battle-field. Signed *Ōoka Masataka* with *kakihan*. VAM, M.456–1916 (ex Alexander Coll.).

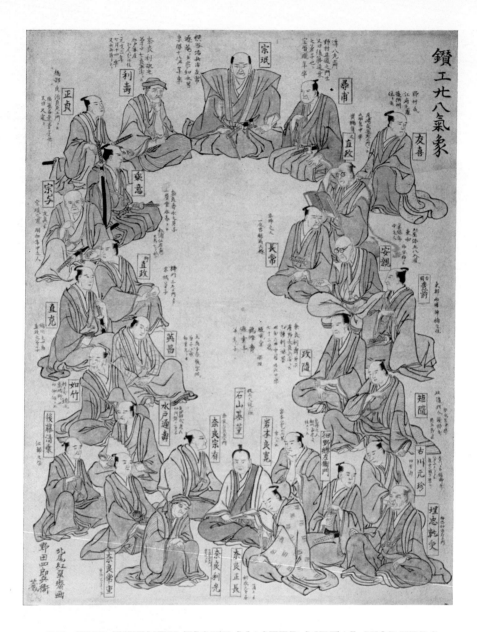

108. THE TWENTY-EIGHT MASTER METAL-WORKERS
Coloured drawing signed, *drawn by Kitao Kōsuisai* (Shigemasa) (about 1790).
W. W. Winkworth Collection. See p. 83.